ANIMAL

ANIMAL

Bad Things Happen When Good Men Do Nothing

PAUL JONES

Matador
9 Priory Business Park,
Wistow Road, Kibworth Beauchamp,
Leicestershire. LE8 0RX
Tel: (+44) 116 279 2299
Fax: (+44) 116 279 2277
Email: books@troubador.co.uk
Web: www.troubador.co.uk/matador

ISBN 978 1780882 796

British Library Cataloguing in Publication Data.
A catalogue record for this book is available from the British Library.

Typeset by Troubador Publishing Ltd, Leicester, UK

For Pat, Katie, Thomas and little one

AUTHOR'S NOTE

Although I have used a very popular seaside resort for the location of this book, the story is a work of fiction, and is not based upon any person or persons, or any actual events. The theme of vigilantes and the anti-social issues depicted in the novel only exist within these pages.

PREFACE

Reaching for the door handle, Dobson was grabbed from behind in a choke hold and shoved head-first into the front of the car.

'What the hell?' he gasped.

The car sped off up the road and turned left at the junction where it suddenly stopped.

There in wait stood the banged up estate and Dobson was swiftly bundled out of one car and into the front of another. The three occupants with him were all clad in beanie hats and sunglasses to conceal their identities then they took off with their hostage. The car, they left abandoned at the side of the road. There was no sign of his mates.

Still held in a tight choke hold, Dobson struggled and gagged. 'Who the hell are you? What do you want?'

A head butt full in the face knocked the batteries out of his voice box. A second butt caused him to fight out in panic. The strangle hold was tightened and a series of short punches beat him into submission.

Dobson tried to shield himself with pleading hands. 'OK, OK, what have I done?'

The punishment ceased for a second and a pair of sunglasses snarled in his face. 'What have you done? What have you done? So you like beating up old men, do yer?'

A spark of discernment registered in Dobson's eyes, although the rest of his face was reddening-up like chopped meat.

'No! No! I was drunk, I didn't mean to.' He choked against the hold.

The attack on him resumed, each new blow coming with a disciplinary reminder. 'Feel good does it? Feel good does it? Now you know how Fred felt and all the other innocent people you've battered over the years. All seem worth it now, does it?'

To Dobson, everything was just a blur of white light and thudding pain, it must have been the longest few minutes of his young life. Finally, the car pulled up down a quiet road on the outskirts of the town. The front door was thrown open, and Dobson was shoved out semi-consciously. As he rolled on the pavement the car skidded off with the door flipping shut again. Dobson lay sprawled on his back, bloodied, battered and finally punished for all the atrocities he had ever committed.

Justice had been served. The vigilantes had claimed their first victim.

CHAPTER 1

It was just after nine pm as Will Thomas stepped down on to the platform at Llandudno train station. Will was forty-one-years-old, stood a shade under six foot and had raven-black short hair that never seemed to grow over a certain length, like a front lawn in the winter time. He was well built, but not too brawny, more like a retired boxer who had kept himself in shape. He had dark brooding eyes and some minor scar tissue around his brow. But what really set him apart was the large black crab he had tattooed at the back of his neck, its jointed pincers gripping each side of his neck and lower jaw.

The keen late-November breeze cut into him and drew out the soporific warmth of the long train journey. Heavy backpack in tow, he steadily made his way with the other passengers towards the main entrance gates. Once through, he stopped for a moment to reflect on his first time back in his home town for nearly twelve years. Feelings of nostalgia caused a mild smirk. The Chinese chippy across the road was still there, although whether or not it was still occupied by the same owners remained to be seen. However, the Indian restaurant a couple of doors away, had now become another Chinese called East. Will sniffed to himself and headed towards a block of flats on Lloyd's street.

So far everything else remained the same, except for one or two shops that had changed trades. The old Albert pub was still there, so was the Cross-keys, and, ahh, he welcomed the sight – a one-stop store that used to be a grocery shop, and it was only yards away from his destination. Get something to eat after the long train ride, he sniffed to himself.

Geoff Harrison called time on his karate class, his voice hollowed out by the cream walls of the dance hall. It was a regular Monday evening with his usual eight students, six men and two women, ranging in grades from green belt up to brown. Geoff was a 4th Dan black belt who had trained in Shokokai karate for twenty years and during that time had been running his children and adult classes in the basement dance hall of the Risbo hotel at the top end of town.

Geoff was a youthful looking forty-year-old who had a shaved head, with a small mole on the cranium. He was a reasonably handsome man, slim, leaning towards muscular, and a cheeky smile that could charm the apples off the trees. He lived in a semi-detached bungalow with Jan, his wife of sixteen years. They didn't have any children and were quite happy living as DINKYS (double income no kiddies).

During the day he worked in the local Asda store as a D. O. (dispensing optician) a position that required 3 years of his life in university.

Geoff's students all lined up and bowed their heads in respect for their sensei; Geoff returned the bow, and ended the class. Everybody returned to their sports bags strewn around the edges of the dance hall. Geoff and a few of the male students returned to their training bags and began disrobing.

Phil Walker, one of his 3rd Kyu brown belt students, was a tall, sinewy 39 year-old with a permanent frown befitting his job as a police officer. He had short greying hair and rich chestnut coloured eyes. Phil had known Geoff since childhood.

'Had another one at the weekend,' he said turning to Geoff

'What's that?' asked Geoff.

'Chap on his way home from the Washington pub, couple of hoodies asked him for a ciggie, he didn't have one so they battered the poor sod, the five of them. Left him unconscious.' He said towelling the sweat off his brow and neck.

Geoff shared his disgust with Tom Perry, one of his 1st Kyu brown-belt students. Tom was a short 32 year-old body builder and bouncer who had lashings of styling gel to tame his curly fair hair. His most striking feature was his piercing blue eyes which were close set under his balcony of a forehead, making them blaze like feral creatures peering out from the rocks.

'I know it's getting bad out there,' Tom said. 'The street violence is really getting out of hand.' He turned to Phil, the copper, 'can't you lot do anything about it?'

'What can we do? Even if we catch the bastards, courts aren't gonna waste their time with it. They'll probably get off with a caution and that's it.'

Geoff began spraying some deodorant over his bare toned torso. 'It's becoming an awkward situation. Even if you can defend yourself, the chances are they'll probably end up suing you. You can't win.'

Phil sniffed thoughtfully. 'Well if it ever comes to that, defending yourself that is, just make sure you say you acted in self-defence because you genuinely feared for your safety. But you didn't hear that from me.'

The two blonde students, quite pretty girls in their late twenties shouted over to Geoff and the others, 'See you next week,' as they made their exit.

'Yeah, see you, Carol, Sandra,' Geoff called over.

Phil continued. 'I have to admit the only thing our governors seem to be interested in at the moment are the bloody traffic offences, because they know they'll definitely get their convictions. It is a bit disheartening though, I'm feeling it myself. I mean my grandfather was a policeman, a real old fashioned bobby with a truncheon and he whacked a few heads in his time, I can tell you. He'd be turning in his grave today if he saw how this scum get away with what is happening. Or, if he was a cop himself today, I'm sure he would have quit in disgust.'

3

'I don't blame him." Tom sneered. 'I mean what with these happy-slappings on the mobile phones as well. These kids in school filming each other kicking the crap out of some poor kid. What's wrong with them? Just all standing there watching it, enjoying it. Tell you what, if I had a kid who was doing that on his mobile I'd crucify him. Or if he was a victim, I'd murder the bastards that did it, kids or not. *Pain*! That's the only thing they know.'

Geoff turned to them as he zipped up his grey tracksuit top. 'Everyday now you switch on the news, or open a newspaper and there's another stabbing, mugging, beating. Something's got to be done about it.'

Tom snorted. 'Yeah, start up your own vigilante group and clean up the mess out there."

For a moment, his words seemed to stun everyone. Whether he was joking or not, or testing the waters, didn't really matter. It was as if everybody had been thinking the very same thing, but didn't dare mention it. Phil reached down for his brown backpack and said uncomfortably. 'I didn't hear that.'

'Yeah, Tom,' Geoff lightened the mood. 'We'll send you out in your Batman suit to round them up.'

Everyone chuckled to themselves and stood ready to leave.

*

Outside with his purchased goods, Will crossed the road, and headed towards the three-storey building converted into rented flats, where he was intending to stay. Standing outside for a moment, he wondered how he would cope in his new living quarters.

'Give us a cigarette, mate.'

Will turned to find three adolescents standing before him, and another on a mountain bike.

'Pardon?' Will asked.

'Give us a fag.' A blob of a lad with an explosion of

acne on his face spoke up. Like a machine switching on, a mental visor came over Will's senses.

'I don't smoke,' he replied, making a particular note of the lads standing by and how they were positioned.

'Well, borrow us a couple of quid then, and I can go and buy me some, can't I?'

Will shifted his position, but disguised it with a reply. 'Now why on earth should I give you any money? Why do you deserve such generosity?'

The lad paused, confused for a second then uttered nonchalantly. 'Because I do.'

Will smirked to himself, his little mind games had worked. His question was designed to assess exactly what artillery this group of youths had. Basically, what Will was saying to him was, what if I don't give you any money, what are you going to do about it? And, had these cheeky lads really intended to intimidate him into handing over anything, the reply would surely have been an aggressive one. Evidently, they were just a bunch of harmless rascals trying it on.

But not wanting to appear too harsh on them, he offered them a bag of cheese and onion crisps instead. The lad shrugged and snatched the bag away from him without so much as a thank you. And as they left, he was already munching into them. Will watched them for a second then turned back to the flat.

'Will,' someone shouted from across the street.

Will swung around, and found a man in a grey track-suit standing outside the shop. Will couldn't quite place who it was, then it came back to him, Geoff? Geoff scuttled across the road to meet him. Will knew Geoff back in their early twenties, when they both trained together in martial arts. This training partnership lasted for about six years, until Will began to pursue other more extreme forms of combat, and they drifted apart.

Geoff held out his hand. Will shook it firmly. 'Good to see you again, Geoff. Doing a bit of late night shopping?'

'Yeah, just going to pick up some stuff after my class.'

'Still training then?'

'Got my own club now.' Geoff said proudly. 'Been going for ten years.'

Will nodded, impressed. 'So what grade are you now?'

'Fourth Dan… taking my fifth next year.'

Will shook his head amazed. 'Doing well. I'm happy for you.'

'Cheers,'

Will sighed uncomfortably, not knowing how Geoff would react about what he had to confess. 'I've been in prison for the last three years.'

'Shit, honestly. I never knew that. What happened?'

Will hesitated. 'It's a long story, I'll tell it to you another time?'

'Yeah, no problem. Shit, if I'd have known, I'd have at least come to visit you.'

Will smiled in appreciation. 'I know.'

'Listen, Will, I'm gonna go, the wife will think I'm having an affair. Can I give you my mobile number?' He said getting his phone out ready to add Will's number on to his list.

Will forced an apologetic grin. 'I don't have one.'

'Oh… OK, is this where you're staying then?'

Will threw a glance at the tenement flats and nodded.

'OK, we've got to get together and catch up on the last ten years or so. How about I pop over sometime in the week?'

'Absolutely.' Will replied.

'Or if you want to come over to the club on training nights, Monday and Thursday 6.30 to 9pm in the basement of the Risbo?'

'Yeah, I may do that. Great!'

Geoff tapped him on the shoulder. 'Nice to see you again, Will.'

'You too.'

He watched his old mate jog back over the road and

disappear into the shop, then turned back to the flats and climbed the stone steps to the entrance. He pressed the illuminated doorbell and waited. Soon an image formed behind the crinkle glass PVC door, and he heard a muffled cough. The door cracked open, and a grey-bearded man with glasses glared at him almost disdainfully.

'Hello, my name is Will Thomas. You have a flat reserved for me?'

The man finished off something he was eating. 'Ah... yes come in.'

Will removed his backpack and entered. Immediately, he caught an odour, most probably just the scent of someone else's home, a smell he would soon get used to. There was a short hallway with stairs leading to the next floor, and midway down the hall the man shook his keys out and dug one into the lock of one of the rooms. He shoved it open with his knee and entered. Will followed him in. Inside the one-roomed flat there was a furnished kitchen, bedroom, and the living room. There was even a 21" TV.

The landlord, who looked a bit like Jim Royale from the TV, began his usual introductory spiel. 'OK, the kitchen, the cooker is gas, fairly straight-forward.' He flicked the switches and turns. 'The tap – watch the hot water – almost turns to lava in a second. Urm, your bed, settee, TV. Bathroom, shower on the second floor. Washing machine downstairs in the basement. OK?' He held up two keys on a key ring. 'One for the door to your room, the other for the main door outside. Your first month's rent is paid, OK?'

Will nodded and took the keys.

'By the way, my name is John, the wife's is Mary – she'll introduce herself to you when she sees you. Any problems, press the doorbell down the hall on your right.'

'Cheers.' Will said. He waited for the door to clunk shut, then laid down his backpack, and drifted over to the window. Outside he could see the one-stop store he'd just visited, and straight down Madoc street where he'd walked up earlier. Something – a racket outside – caught his attention. It sounded like animals in a zoo at feeding time. It was only a group of adolescents coming out of the one-stop. Will drew the curtains shut.

*

Driving back home, Tom stopped to pick up his mate Charlie on the way so they could to go back to his flat for a couple of beers and watch a dvd. Charlie was one of Tom's bouncer mates, he was a six-foot three slab of meat with a slight resemblance to the boxer Joe Calzaghe. But what really tickled Tom about him was that everything Charlie said or described was usually accompanied by the phrases, "wos his name, blah blah and boom boom."

Charlie was already familiar with Geoff and the others at the Karate club as he often turned up at the end of the session to meet up with Tom.

'Got an idea,' Tom turned to his mate as he accelerated away.

'What's that then?'

'What if we started our own vigilante group?'

Charlie gave him a funny look. 'What do you mean?'

Tom sniffed the air cannily. 'What if we could provide some sort of service to people who have been victimised by thugs. What if we stepped in to protect people who couldn't help themselves. You know, people who are too afraid to go to the police. Or people who have just lost faith in them to even try.'

Charlie blew at such an audacious scheme. 'It's a bit wos his name, risky don't you think?'

'Yeah, but it could also be very profitable as well. Just think of it, getting paid for beating up all those criminals.'

'What about your mate Geoff? Do you really think he would go for something like that?'

Tom flicked him a look of irritation, 'forget Geoff, he'd never go for it. Christ, I'd never tell him I was going to start something like that, he'd probably ban me from the club. I tried mentioning it as a joke tonight just to test the waters but I don't think it went down very well.'

'So, who have you got in mind to perform this kind of service?'

'Well, you, me and perhaps Nigel on the doors.'

'I dunno Tom, it's a bit dicey.'

'Aw, come on Chaz, you me and Nige have been going on about doing something like this for ages. Well now is our big chance.'

'What, so we're just going to go around smashing everybody up who looks a bit dodgy. Won't take long for the police to feel our collars.'

'Naw, we do it proper, plan it, organise it, disguise ourselves. We'll use our loafs.

But Charlie still looked as if he needed a bit of convincing.

*

Having showered (and after convincing his wife that coming home ten minutes later than usual was due to running into an old pal and not meeting up with some blonde bimbo), Geoff finally settled in front of his flat screen TV.

Jan, Geoff's wife then appeared with two steaming mugs of tea. Jan, was thirty-six years old, slim and petit. She had jet-black shoulder-length hair, and almond-shaped brown eyes, giving her a slight oriental appearance. She was attractive, but not beautiful, the kind of pleasant natural looks that didn't require any make-up. She and Geoff had met in college back in their twenties when they shared classes in sports and nutrition, a course he had chosen before finally opting to study for a dispensing optician. Nowadays she managed her own health spa near the North promenade in town.

Jan leaned over to give Geoff his tea, her silken hair rolling across her high cheekbones.

'Ta,' Geoff replied, without taking his eyes off the TV.

Jan hooked a hank of hair behind her ears and eased up beside him on the settee.

'So who is this Will Thomas you ran into earlier?'

'Oh... Will. Known him for years. We used to train in the youth centre back in the early days. Bit of a left wing karateka though.'

'Left wing what do you mean?' asked Jan

'Well, he was good at karate, don't get me wrong, but he was a strong pioneer for real hardcore self-defence. He always seemed a bit disillusioned with traditional karate, and thought their outdated techniques didn't really conform to actual street fighting. He always thought there was a better or more efficient way of maximising your power for every strike. As it stood, he thought traditional karate was extremely limited and lacking real power, and in an actual street encounter wouldn't prove very effective.'

'So what did you think about his views?' Jan asked, cupping her mug in her hands.

'At the time, I respected his views, and I think up to a point he may have been right. But I suppose its all down to what you want to get out of the art. When we began in the nineties, street crime was nowhere as bad as it is today. And most people including myself, did it for the sport, the love of the art, and to keep fit. And OK, it was still useful against the average idiot on the street. But today we're dealing with a more savage breed of yob. They'll stab you, stamp on you without mercy, and because they know how lax our justice system is, they have no fear of the consequences of their crimes.'

'So Will's training philosophy would be more suited to the yobs of today as opposed to the generation when you started?'

'Exactly. Will was so anti-crime I suggested he should've joined the police force or the army. Anyone who broke the law, or had no respect for others, was considered an enemy. I used to take the piss out of him, but he would say you'll see one day and I guess he was right,' Geoff huffed wryly.

'But didn't you mention before that he'd just come out of prison?'

'Yeah, but he didn't tell me why he'd been in prison. But knowing Will, it'd probably be for beating someone up he would never take any prisoners.' Geoff raised his brow with caution. 'And a mean bastard he could be as well. He could turn from a saint to a beast in an instant.'

Jan raised her mug to her lips. 'Not sure I'd want to have someone like that as a friend.'

'Oh, no, don't get me wrong. He's one of the nicest people you could meet. A good mate who won't let you down. He just believes that if you do bad, you get punished. And the more serious the crime, the harsher the punishment.'

Jan kept her opinions to herself, and turned back to the TV to listen to a widow of a man recently beaten to death by a group of youths. Standing in front of TV reporters and camera crews, the woman was campaigning for justice on street yobs and giving her reaction to the latest stabbing.

'We must find a way to restore law and order in this country. We must find a way of ridding our streets of this scum. It's time we made these low-life degenerates of society, who have absolutely no regard for law and order, take responsibility for the crimes they have committed. We need to take a stand now before any more innocent lives are lost. We need to take action now against these merciless animals and make the streets safe again for normal law-abiding citizens.'

CHAPTER 2

Will glanced down at his Seiko watch. It had stopped again. He cursed it and tapped it to try and shock it back to life. Under normal circumstances he would have simply binned the out-dated contraption by now and bought himself a new one. After all watches nowadays were a dozen to the pound, but this one was kind of special to him. It was the one Stacey had bought him when they went on holiday to Tenerife some five years ago. Stacey used to be Will's fiancée , and they had dated for about six years. They had met when Will used to go jogging near his home in Warrington, a home he had bought and paid for back in the nineties, when he prospered somewhat in property developing. Maybe it was fate that they met, as Will was not really the sociable type. Maybe it was fate that whenever their jogging routes would cross, Stacey was the one who would stop for a chat. Strangely, Will always seemed to feel at ease with her, and when it was discovered that they were both from Llandudno, well, it was fate again, it just had to be destiny. Alright, she may have been a bit younger than him, ten years younger to be exact, but what did that matter?

Soon after their little flirtatious jogs, they began seeing each other on a regular basis, and within a year or so, Will had proposed. By this time, however, they still lived apart, as each one respected the other's privacy. Stacey would remain in her up-market apartment, and continue working as a PA in a solicitor's office, and Will stayed at his own pad. It was decided between them that when they married, they would give up their independent lives and live like a conventional couple and hopefully start a family.

In the meantime, Will had bought her a puppy Labrador named Georgie to keep her company, and hopefully guard her house for her when he grew up. Yet sadly, Georgie was killed by a couple of thugs a few months later. And that's when everything started to go wrong. Will shook his head as the memories hit him like train carriages shunting into the back of each other at an emergency stop.

Thinking back to that terrible period in their lives, he recalled Stacey sobbing at him after the Georgie incident.

'Why did you have to do that, Will? Why did you have to take the law into your own hands? Why didn't you think about what you were doing? Why couldn't you have let the police sort it?'

And then when Will was convicted and sentenced to three years in prison, he recalled those chilling words she had said to him. Cold, harsh and final like the cold steel of a butcher's knife slicing through a rump steak.

'No, Will, that's it. We might as well call it a day. How can I possibly put our lives on hold for that amount of time? It's just asking too much of me when we had everything all planned out. How can I possibly trust anyone who can act so recklessly in a crisis. All you thought about was getting even with those thugs. You've thrown everything away in one moment of complete madness. It didn't have to be done like that. Grown mature responsible adults don't act that way. How can I possibly commit myself to someone who can so easily risk his own liberty and our future. What if we'd had a baby, a family. How the hell would I have coped with you away in prison? No, Will, you're not ready to settle down, I don't know if you ever will be.'

Then Will retorted. 'It's OK you saying all that. Those two bastards killed my dog! He was only a pup for God's sake. What kind of monsters would do something like that to a poor defenceless animal? They deserved what I did to them. You can't punish me for that. How the hell can you throw everything away after six years, just because I didn't let the police handle it, like every other supposed law-abiding member of the public? Just because things haven't gone according to your plans? Listen, Stacey, life isn't always as straightforward as that. Sometimes things happen in this life, things that are beyond anyone's control. Sometimes you are put in these situations and you have to do what you think is right, not just for yourself, but for everyone. It's those type of decisions that determine the kind of people we are. I'm not proud of what I did, but, yes, if I was put in the same situation again I would do exactly the same thing. Not because I don't give a damn about you or our future. Of course I do. I would never risk that for anything. But this is the way God made me, and if I'd have let them get away with what they did then it's me who has to live with it. You can't always live your life by someone else's rules. Sometimes you've got to say sod it, that's not right, this is what needs to be done, even if it breaks the bloody law!'

'Yes, well, you did break the law, didn't you, Will, and now I'm the innocent one who has to pay the penalty. I just can't start all over again after all that time.'

*

And that was that; she broke off the engagement and Will went to prison. After which, he received no phone calls from her, no letters, no nothing, she completely cut him off. Will even tried ringing her from prison, but she wouldn't even speak to him. That was hard, Will recalled, his bitterness tempered a little with self-pity. How the hell could she just cut me off like that? As for the house he had to leave behind, fortunately a friend offered to look after it for him in exchange for accommodation, and a very minimal rent.

So why was Will back here now thinking about his ex-fiancée? The plan was very simple, he wanted to try to win her back. After all the time he spent in prison, all the anger, the let-downs, somehow he still had a tiny pilot light of hope inside that told him she was worth giving it one more shot.

To him, there was unfinished business to sort out; he couldn't continue with his life, his new found freedom, without knowing for sure that his relationship with Stacey was truly dead and buried. His plan was to give himself two months to try and win her back, and if he hadn't succeeded in that time, then he would give up. But what a long shot it was. He hadn't heard from her in three years. For all he knew, she could be involved with someone else, she may even be married with a family. What if she's not even living in North Wales?

The only thing he did know was that when he was convicted, Stacey had planned to get a job transfer back to North Wales, and move back into her parent's hotel while she sorted herself out. So that was his starting point. But once again, that was three years ago, and the more he thought about his daunting task, the more he doubted his chances. One half of him was saying he was completely wasting his time, the other half said what have you got to lose? If it all went pear-shaped, at least he could say he tried.

Right! He sucked in a short breath, setting his plan into action. I'll go to her parent's hotel tonight, and we'll start there.

*

Jan, Geoff's wife, had the week off from her work (unfortunately Geoff couldn't get the same dates off) and she decided to treat herself to at least one or two days of pure indulgence. That meant a good afternoon's trawl through the clothes shops. She headed towards the new retail shopping centre on Mostyn Broadway.

I'll spend a couple of hours in Debenhams, and British Home Stores, she thought, maybe have a coffee in Costas, then nip over to Asda to pester Geoff, and do a bit of a shop there before home.

A couple of brain-straining hours later, Jan was on her way back to her car parked somewhere in the centre of the car park. In her mind she was bustling over whether or not she should have bought that leather handbag she saw for £44.99. The reason she hadn't was because at the moment she and Geoff were supposed to be saving up for a new bathroom suite. Yet as she sank into her vehicle, now sandwiched between two people-carriers, she let out a yearning sigh. Surely one little handbag isn't going to break the bank, she said out loud. Call it a holiday treat. And Geoff will probably treat himself when he's off at the end of the month. She chewed her lip, and wrestled with her conscience. I know, if it's still there tomorrow, then it's destiny I'm meant to have it. Still mulling over it, she swung the seatbelt over her shoulder and started up, ready to shoot over to Asda. Carefully, she began easing out of the parking space, checking both sides, and her rear view mirror, text-book style, when a loud blare of a car's horn stung her with fright. She slammed on her brakes, and turned to find a blood-red, customised car with music pumping out of its half-open tinted windows. Where the hell did that come from? She frowned – wasn't there a second ago. But being polite, she mouthed an apology, and a wave, and slipped back into first gear ready to move forward and let the car pass. Suddenly, she saw the door of the car swing open, and a lanky adolescent in a grey sweater stormed over. Jan's stomach rippled with concern, as she opened her electric window.

'Sorry, I didn't see you I'm afra ...'

The lad pushed his bony face through her window. 'You want to look where you're going, you stupid bitch!' his raised tone drew looks from passers-by.

Jan immediately went on the defensive from this thick-headed Neanderthal.

'Excuse me, I did try to apologise, and you did just appear from nowhere.'

The lad's face screwed into a snarl. 'Oh, so you're trying to say it was my was my fault, are yer?'

Jan's finger was poised over the auto-door lock button. 'No, that's not what I meant, I'm just saying I did look where I was going, but I still didn't see you.' She couldn't help staring at his stupid fringe that looked glued to his forehead with hair gel.

'Well, you obviously weren't looking properly, were you?'

Jan resisted the urge to argue and antagonise him. 'Look, OK, I apologise again. There was no collision, no damage, let's just forget it shall we?' She gulped.

By now two security men in high visibility jackets had appeared at the entrance of the Debenhams and were looking over inquisitively. The lad spotted them and like a school bully seeing his headmaster watching, his anger abated.

'Yeah, you're lucky you didn't hit me,' he spat, and stormed off.

Jan breathed a sigh of relief, her hands shaking on the steering wheel. She felt like crying, but told herself not to be silly. She glanced in her rear-view mirror once more, and saw that the car was gone, thank God.

All thoughts about nipping over to Asda had now evaporated. Geoff was bound to pick up on her agitated state, and if she told him what had happened, he'd only want to drop everything and go out looking for the yob. No, she decided she would head straight home and have a good strong cup of coffee. Maybe she would tell Geoff another time.

*

Will glanced at his watch, and lifted it to his ear, it had stopped again. He cursed it, and couldn't be bothered to reset it again until he got back to his flat later. Anyway, it was somewhere near eight-fifteen to eight-thirty, and he stood about a third of the way up the North promenade. Down towards the opposite end, near the entrance to the pier's head, was Stacey's parent's hotel. Will crossed the road to the prom walkway and threw a look down the sweep of the shore lined with a necklace of bright sodium street lighting that stretched all the way to the little Orme . The biting November breeze caused him to wince and he thrust his hands deep into his duffel jacket pockets to keep them warm. Passing one of the prom shelters, he could hear shouting and jeering coming from the other side of the glass divider, but he paid it little attention. Nearing Stacey's hotel, Will reached the fifty-foot cenotaph tower used for war remembrance services. He crossed the road to a row of hotels that curved back towards the pier entrance. Finally, Will stood the base of the concrete steps leading up to the front door of Stacey's hotel. Will craned his neck in the hope of catching a glimpse of Stacey in one of the lounge windows. It was empty, but inside it did look invitingly warm.

Will climbed the steps and stood hand poised over the doorbell. Taking a second, he pulled himself together, and rang it. There was no answer. He rang it again, taking note of the no vacancy sign in the lounge window. Through the misted glass door and cosy peach light inside, there was movement. Will braced himself, and the door opened ajar. A short man in his early sixties, with a hang-dog face, straightened up in recognition.

'Oh, hullo, Will.'

'Hello, Gary. How's tricks?'

Gary was Stacey's father, and the relationship he had had with Will while he was dating his daughter had been pretty good. Back then, Gary liked him and always felt that Will would have looked after his daughter. It was just a pity that Will got himself in trouble with the law. Gary was definitely old-school, and although sometimes he could be a crusty old sod, he was still generous to a fault. Everybody makes mistakes, and all that.

'Just got out, have yer?'

Will nodded.

'How did it go?'

Will made a face. 'Just glad it's done really ... you know?'

Gary nodded back. 'Want to come in?'

'Is she here?'

'Not at the moment.'

'She *is* living here though, isn't she?'

'Yes, she's still here, Will, but she's out with friends tonight.'

That's a start, Will said to himself. 'No, thanks then, I won't come in, this is just a quick visit.' He paused, before asking nervously, 'So what do you think, Gary? Is there any chance she'll talk to me?'

Gary leant his head against the door frame, and blew ponderously. 'Dunno, Will. To me and Jo, it seems like she's put it all behind her now.'

Will's hopes sank. 'Really?'

'Yeah, she doesn't even talk about it anymore.'

Will held his breath. 'Is she seeing someone?'

'She was, up until about a couple of months ago, a guy from her college. She finished her other job and started a course in business management. But as for that chap, I don't think it was serious, and it's over now.'

That's encouraging, Will thought. 'So what time is she likely to get home then?'

'About ten, ten thirty, I guess.'

'OK, then, I'll call back another time. What night would be best to call again?'

'Friday, she's usually at home.'

Will nodded. 'I'll try again then, that's if you and Jo don't mind?'

'Not at all, Will. It'd be a good to clear the air once and for all.'

Will wasn't sure what he meant by that, but didn't let on. 'Can you let her know I'll pop over about the same time on Friday then?'

'Sure. No problem.'

Will thanked him and they said their goodbyes. Gary waited for him to descend a couple of the stone steps before closing the door.

Back on the prom again, Will began to doubt his chances of even getting to speak to Stacey, let alone anything else. Well, he thought to himself, if she's in when I call on Friday, then at least she's willing to talk. If she's not in, then I'll know where I stand. But what if she won't talk to me? Do I go back to Warrington and say I tried, or stay and give her a bit longer to adjust, before having one last throw of the dice? Will drew his hands tight in his duffel jacket, and felt he was standing at a crossroads not knowing which way to turn.

Up ahead were a group of youths on mountain bikes were circling the noisy prom shelter he had passed earlier. As he walked by they began to jeer and heckle him. Not taking any notice of them, Will continued on. Then a foot or so in front of him, an empty lager bottle clinked on the tarmac. It didn't smash it just rolled in a wide arc. Without even breaking his stride, Will simply fished it up and continued on, ready to dispose of it in the nearest litter bin. However, had the bottle have hit, touched, grazed, even tickled his foot, then that would have been a different story. And whoever had chucked the bottle – grown-ups, teenagers, kids it didn't make any difference. By the time Will had finished with them, they would rue the night they chose to play chicken with a juggernaut.

CHAPTER 3

Seeing the confident smirk flash on Tom's face, Geoff thought cocky sod. Tom had just parried a weak left, right combination from his opponent Phil (the police officer). It was sparring night at the Shukokai karate club and Geoff circling the two combatants was acting as the referee and point adjudicator. The rest of the class, all having had their chance to fight, stood back in a line and watched avidly as the two most experienced students squared off against each other. Tom, the body builder and bouncer, wasn't so much the technical fighter, and relied more on his brute strength. He liked to bully his opponents into defeat. Phil, on the other hand was much lighter in stature, and quick with his rapid-fire combinations. However, his main problem was that whenever he faced a bigger opponent, he tended to become a bit intimidated, and fought most of his fight defensively on the back foot. Geoff had always known this about him and was forever badgering him about it. But more importantly, his opponent, Tom, was also aware of it. And with that extra edge, Tom had that predatory glint in his eyes as he prepared to move in for the kill. As usual, Phil started to back pedal and Geoff eyed him impatiently.

'Come on, Phil, don't choke on me.' Geoff bristled, but Phil just couldn't pull the trigger.

Out of desperation, he threw a half-hearted front kick, and Tom bulldozed in with left and right punches almost knocking Phil over with the weight of his body. This wasn't full contact sparring, but a tap-contact, just enough to know that if it was a real-life confrontation you would get hit.

Geoff shouted for them to stop, and Tom halted his attack, sniffing valiantly as he returned to the centre of the floor.

Phil shook his head at himself, and lumbered back to face Tom. Still seething with himself, he tugged hard at the tails of his brown belt. Geoff raised his arm in Tom's favour signalling another point, and a five to one win.

'OK, that'll do for tonight.' Geoff called an end to the session, and everyone formed into a line and bowed to their sensei. Geoff returned the bow, and the class dispersed with weary and accomplished sighs.

'Bloody hell!' Phil hissed as he followed Geoff back to their training bags.

'Confidence!' Geoff lectured him. 'You've gotta have faith in yourself. Believe in yourself.'

'I know, I know. Why the hell can't I do it?'

'Only you know the answer to that one I'm afraid, mate.' Geoff shrugged helplessly. 'That's the only thing holding you back from getting your black belt, you know?'

Phil didn't answer him, he just stood there grumpily towelling himself down.

Tom breezed in, and nudged his fellow student in the arm playfully.

Got you again, didn't I?'

But Phil tried his best to ignore him.

Geoff began disrobing. 'Perhaps you should go and do a bit of door work with Tom here to try and develop your nerve a bit.'

'No thanks, I deal with enough morons out there in my own job thanks very much.'

'You've just gotta learn to switch off and become an animal,' Tom said, enjoying his hard- man image.

It wasn't that Tom was a real bully, he just loved the hard-as-nails, burly-doorman reputation. For the best part of him, he was a disciplined student of the martial arts, but when things didn't go his way on the sparring floor, his immediate reaction was to lose his temper. Sometimes when he and Geoff would spar together, Tom couldn't help trying it on a tad, nothing serious. But when Geoff started picking him off with his short, sharp combinations, he would get frustrated and start trying to push Geoff about. That's when Geoff had to go up a gear to put him back in his place, which usually involved sweeping his feet out from under him.

'Maybe Geoff's right about coming on the door with me.' Tom settled down again. 'I mean in my game nowadays you're guaranteed a bit of physical at least once a week."

'Really?' Geoff asked.

'Oh yeah, these days people start a fight over next to nothing. Believe me. The other weekend this chap had a tear up with this guy outside Wetherspoons, and because he knew the guy's family were inside as well, he went back in and attacked them too. Even the poor Granny got a smack.'

Geoff and Phil looked at each other repulsed.

'And when we were dragging him out, all his mates who had been watching were cheering him because of what he'd done.'

'Just what is the matter with these sick cretins?' Phil scowled.

'I hope you gave him a good sharp slap,' Geoff added.

'Oh, yes!' Tom lit up. 'Me and Charlie accidentally fell on him a few times. But that's just it, you see, all these violent yobs love to put the hurt on people, but when they get a taste of their own medicine, they don't like it at all. Bloody cowards, they make me sick.'

'Squealed like a stuck pig, did he?' Phil snorted.

Tom gave his impersonation of the pathetic yob. 'That's out of order that is. You've got no right to do that to me.' Then back to his own voice in reply. 'No, but it's OK for you to do that to other people though, isn't it? You stupid git!' Tom slung his towel down into his training bag. 'I'll tell you, it's getting worse out there, you know, you can see it every week.'

Geoff and Phil listened as they changed back into their tracksuits.

'People just don't give a shit about anything these days. Charlie, Nigel and I were talking about it at the weekend. I mean the three of us have been bouncing on and off now for the past five years, and during that time, you can see a steady decline in society. OK, people out on the piss are always gonna get into a ruckus at some point, but these days you can see it in people walking around, they're like time bombs waiting to detonate. The way things are today, the social climate, the recession, the corrupt government. OK, I'm not making excuses for some of these idiots, but in a way you can understand why there is so much violence.'

'Yeah, I agree,' Phil chipped in. "All of us are feeling the pinch of the credit crunch, but it doesn't mean we're gonna go out and thump someone. You still have to maintain law and order, you can't go and take it out on some innocent chap walking his dog down the street.'

'Yes, I know that.' Tom retorted. 'There will always be the mindless gits out there who have no regard for anyone, and those are the ones who need sorting out. But this recession is turning normal decent law-abiding citizens into animals as well.'

'All our Dr Jekylls are turning into Mr Hydes,' Geoff commented, zipping up his training bag.

Tom continued. 'But getting back to what I was saying, there are so many arrogant people out there now, the three of us I would love to go around cleaning up this town. Punishing all these bastards who have no respect for anything. Teach them respect, instil discipline back into society.'

'Yeah, but what about the rest of the country, Wyatt Earp?' Phil joked.

'Yeah, OK, you can't very well take on the whole country. I know that. But figuratively speaking, you can't just check one bulb, you've gotta check them all.'

Geoff listened with interest.

'Anyhow, sod the rest of the country!' Tom growled. 'Let each town or city look after their own, and we'll look after our own.'

'Yeah well, speaking of looking after one's own, I'm out on the piss myself this weekend, so I may be relying on you to look after me.' Phil said.

'Oh, yes, got the weekend off have we?' Geoff asked. 'So what's the occasion?'

'Oh, the missus's mate's birthday, a few of us are going out for a bit of a pub crawl, that's all.'

'Yeah, we'll keep a look out for you. For a small price,' Tom joked zipping up his bag.

Geoff gave Phil the brow. 'Yeah, well, just be careful. As a copper, I don't need reminding you of the perils of late-night drinking.'

Phil picked up his backpack. 'Don't worry, I'll take care.'

*

Friday night, Will was making his eagerly anticipated return to Stacey's hotel. Talk about nervous, it felt like he was about to give birth to a baby elephant. After all, this was the moment of truth for him. For the last three years he had waited for this opportunity, and, in that time, he had gone through at least a hundred different scenarios of what might happen. Some turned out well, but most of them did not. Yet tonight, the atmosphere, the setting, seemed more welcoming, dark but not quite so chilly, and no hooligans festering in any of the prom shelters. Not at the present anyway.

Will tapped his duffel jacket pocket to make sure the new mobile phone he had bought that day was still in there. It was only a twenty quid pay-as-you-go Nokia. And the only reason he had bought the damn thing was that if things didn't go quite as planned and Stacey wasn't yet ready for a face to face, then at least she would be able to ring him. Maybe he was being a bit pessimistic, but at least he was preparing himself for the worst. Anything other than that could only be looked upon as a bonus.

Will checked his watch. Amazingly it was keeping the right time – he knew this because he had set it against his mobile earlier. Yeah, working now, aren't you, he bristled, now you know you've got some competition.

It was eight pm, and once again he pressed the door-bell to the Birch Tree Hotel. For a moment, it felt like he was in a kind of vacuum. Nothing seemed able to penetrate that tiny space in the universe that he occupied. This was all completely new ground for him, and whatever may happen in the next few moments he had no control over whatsoever.

Nobody appeared to be answering. 'Come on! Come on!' He fidgeted anxiously. Was this a good or bad sign? She definitely knew he was coming. Was she punishing him by making him wait? Was she too nervous to answer the door? Did she still hate him?

At last, movement behind the frosted glass door; a shape, a short lumbering gait. Doesn't look like Stacey, he thought. The door opened. It was Gary.

Will studied his face for any clue, any hint of encouragement, but his expression was a blank piece of paper.

'She's not in, Will. I'm sorry!'

Will's body sagged. 'Did she know I was coming?'

'Yeah, I told her,' Gary replied, shifting uncomfortably from one foot to the other.

'Doesn't she even want to talk?'

'She's not ready to see you, Will. It was a bit of a shock when I told her you'd been, and the thought of you coming again so soon was a bit too much for her to handle.'

Will went out on a limb and sighed. 'I'll try one more time! Tell her we really need to talk. We can't just leave it at that. I just need to know. I need to hear it from her lips. She owes me that at least.'

'I know.'

'Did she say anything else?'

Gary gave him an empty shake of the head.

Will reached into his pocket, and pulled out a piece of paper. 'Can you give her this then? It's my mobile number and the address where I'm staying.'

He handed it over to Gary who gave it a brief look before folding it over. 'Course I will,' he replied.

'I'll be staying here for another couple of weeks or so. Just got a few things to do, catch up with some old mates and that. Then I'll be heading back to Warrington. Just to make it easier for her, if I haven't heard from her in that time, she won't ever have to worry about me turning up here again."

Gary nodded that he understood, then Will offered his hand as if this might be the last time he would see him. Gary shook it, and watched Will walk away once again.

*

About a mile further up the north promenade, in a middle-class residential area stood the Washington public house. Inside the pub customers could either dine upstairs on the second floor, or enjoy a drink and a dance at the bar downstairs. Some nights, they even had Karaoke.

Phil, the off-duty police officer, lay a tray of drinks down on a table near the window and a quiet cheer rang out from his group. There were six in all, Phil and his wife, and two other couples, all of about the same age ... fairly respectable folk, you might say.

'I was just saying, Phil?' Carol, Phil's wife, shouted down his neck. She was a hefty woman in her thirties, who looked a bit like one of those seaside postcard fatties.

'What's that? He asked, straining his ears in the surrounding racket.

'It's not quite as bad where we are at the moment, probably because everyone knows you're a copper. But Susan and Danny were saying that the anti-social behaviour is getting much worse where they live in the junction.'

'Yeah,' Phil nodded to them. 'We've had quite a number of complaints from that area."

Susan, a woman who strangely resembled a penguin with a slight arch to her features and a bit of a hook nose, chimed in, 'these days you're getting kids nine or ten years old throwing bottles at moving cars – absolutely disgusting behaviour.' She gasped, then husband Danny, joined in.

'And the parents are no better! If you happen to find out where the little sods live, and complain to their parents, all you get back is a mouthful of abuse. They make you feel as if you're the criminal for accusing their precious child.'

In a hurry to get her words out, Carol almost choked on her vodka and tonic.

'Is it any wonder all these kids grow up into yobs with parents like that? They just won't accept responsibility for their own kids. It's always someone else's fault. They should damn well make these parents accountable. If they won't discipline their kids, then fine them.

Phil tried to keep out of this debate. As a police officer, he knew the latest crime statistics only too well, and he was also aware what little could be done to combat it, especially with juvenile crimes.

An hour or so later, all six of them decided to make one last port of call, the Linx hotel. It was only a five minute walk, so they opted to get there on foot. Outside, Phil started to feel the effects from the six pints of ale he had consumed during the evening, and shook his head to try and dissolve the fuzziness. The route they chose was to turn off the prom, past the Broadway night club, straight on across the roundabout, and follow the road up to their destination. It wouldn't take them very long, and the keen evening air would probably clear their heads somewhat.

Gaggling like geese, the ladies lead the way, and the men followed behind. Passing the nightclub, they scuttled across the road opposite the roundabout. Phil was gabbing to Danny about some leggy young woman he'd seen earlier in the Washington, when his mobile chirped in his trouser pocket. He stopped to see who the caller was, and saw Tom's name. Phil told the others to walk on and he would catch them up.

'Who is it?' Carol enquired.

'It's OK, it's only Tom the bouncer.' He waved her on, and they left him to it.

As it happened, Tom was just calling to find out if they planned on going up town to the Wetherspoons? Because if they did, he wanted to warn him to be on the lookout as there were a lot of troublemakers out and about tonight. Phil told him not to worry as they were going home after the Linx hotel stop anyway. Phil ended the call with a laboured sigh, as a group of revellers from the nightclub breezed past him. He slipped his mobile back in his pocket and broke into a light jog to catch up to the others who were already down the other end of the road and out of sight. Overtaking the youths in front, he accidentally brushed the shoulder of one of the lads and quickly uttered a humble apology.

'Yer clumsy git,' he got back in reply.

Under normal circumstances, Phil would have simply brushed it off with a contemptuous shake of the head. Being a police officer, and regularly dealing with the general public, he was used to a bit of verbal every now and again. But maybe it was because of the alcohol, or the fact that at the moment, he was an aggrieved member of the public who didn't deserve to be spoken to like that. He stopped to face the three lads in their early twenties, who were with two girls dressed up like hookers.

'Pardon?'

'You 'erd.'

'What's the problem? It was an accident. I only brushed

past and I said I was sorry, didn't I, for Christ's sakes.' Phil turned away incensed by the yob's arrogance. Ding, the ringing sound, and a brilliant white light. It took a second to realise he'd been hit. Phil spun around on unsteady legs, and saw the white shirt of one of the yobs, and smelt some exotic aftershave. His senses began to clear somewhat, and he began to protest, but when he did, his head rocked back with another blow. His back hit the tarmac, and his body started to get a right pummelling with kicks and punches. Phil instinctively tried to shield his head with his arms. His only remaining thoughts were that it felt like he was in a car tumbling over and over down a steep hill.

All three lads, and even one of the girls had a go at booting and stamping on Phil's twitching body like they were trying to put out a fire. The sheer force of these blows shifted Phil's body about six inches at a time. They kicked him everywhere, and when one of them hoofed him in the back, it gave out a hollow thud like the sound of snare drum.

One of the lads even took a step back as if he was lining up to take a free kick at a football. He aimed for Phil's head, but the brunt of the kick was taken on the arms, although the impact still flipped Phil's head up like a lid. Phil gave out a muffled 'Humph'.

'Oi!' someone shouted.

The gang stopped as they saw three bouncers from the nightclub racing across the roundabout towards them. In panic, they left their prey, and fled down a side road. One of the bouncers stopped to tend to Phil, while the other two followed in pursuit of the yobs. There was no chance of catching the lads, but the bouncers soon caught up with the girls, who they quickly restrained and led kicking and screaming back to the scene of their crime.

Carol, Phil's wife, and her friends were just about to cross the road to the Linx when they heard something of the commotion.

'Where the hell is Phil?' She frowned suspiciously, then she asked Danny and Rob to go back and check on him.

30

Minutes later, Carol and her friends were alerted to the full horror of what had happened. And after the paramedics had arrived to treat Phil, who was only semi-conscious, it was the turn of the police, who then gathered all the relevant statements. Of course when the two girls gave their versions, they both accused Phil of starting the fight, and to protect the identities of their boyfriends, they claimed they had only met them for the first time that evening.

Fortunately, one of the bouncers standing at this post on the doors of the nightclub had witnessed the white-shirted youth strike Phil first, and described how the rest of them proceeded to stick the boot in on Phil. This immediately refuted the girl's false testimonies. After hearing this, Carol, Phil's wife, tried to swing for one of the women for what she did to her husband and had to be restrained herself.

After everything had calmed down, Carol accompanied her husband to the hospital in the ambulance, and by the time they had reached A and E Phil was completely compos mentis. Unfortunately, that didn't prevent him from puking buckets all over the interior of the ambulance. Thankfully though, the injuries he sustained weren't serious, and he was just treated for minor cuts and some facial swelling, but for the rest of the night he would be nursing a thunderous headache. Lucky for him the bouncers intervened, or it could have been much worse.

*

Next morning, Geoff was pottering about in his garage trying to hunt down a tin of old emulsion to touch up his living room door. In between stubbing his toe on the lawnmower and knocking over some boxes, the theme tune to *Mission Impossible* chirped in his trouser pocket. Geoff took out his mobile and saw Tom's name. He made an odd face and answered it. 'Hello, Tom. To what do I owe this pleasure?'

Tom's voice seemed somewhat highly pitched. 'Have you heard from Phil yet?'

'No, I haven't. Why?'

'He got a bit of a kicking last night.'

Geoff's stomach churned. 'No! What happened?'

'Apparently he was on his way to the Linx when these bastards started on him.'

'Is he alright?'

'Yeah, spoke to him this morning. He's just got a bit of a shiner and a swollen jaw. It could have been much worse though.'

'Why's that?'

'A few of my bouncer mates, witnessed it from the Broadway, and they rushed over to help cause he was getting a right pasting. Even the girls were getting stuck in.'

Geoff's head shook with anger and contempt. 'What the hell did Phil do to deserve that?'

'All he did was accidentally brush past one the lads and that was it. Bastards!'

'What is the matter with these people?' Geoff growled.

'Well, the bouncers who went after them managed to catch the two girls, but the lads got away.'

'So what about the police, were they called?'

'Oh, yeah, police and ambulance, but when the two girls were questioned they tried to protect the lads, didn't they.'

'Oh, yeah, I bet, so the police can't do anything about it, I suppose?'

'Police? No, probably not, but I know someone who can.'

'What do you mean?'

'My mate, Charlie the bouncer, knows who these three lads are they pop into the Boulevards every Friday without fail. They're well known for putting people in hospital. They even batter women as well. Really nasty pieces of work.'

Geoff sensed what was coming next, and the cocktail of fear, anger and adrenalin began to simmer in his stomach.

'It's got to be done, Geoff, an eye for an eye. Do unto others as they do unto you. The time has come to strike back and clean up. What do you think? Are you in?'

At first Geoff was numbed by the fear of a fight. That sudden rush of pure undiluted adrenalin that courses through the body, powering it ready for battle, or revving it up to do just the opposite – run for your life. Most psychologists call it the fight-or-flight syndrome.

'Me, you, and Charlie and Nigel. Next Friday. Wait outside the Boulevards in a car. Are you in?'

Despite the fact that this breached the code of ethics held sacred to a martial artist, Geoff knew this was something he couldn't refuse. No way could he let the side down, or more importantly Phil, his friend and student. If he was to refuse this task, how could he ever expect any of his students to have any faith or respect for a sensei who wouldn't fight for the right?

'Geoff, are you in?' Tom repeated, and the reply simply rolled out of Geoff's mouth as if he didn't have any choice.

'I'm in!'

CHAPTER 4

That afternoon, Geoff drove the couple of miles over to Phil's home in the junction. Phil lived in Marl drive, a street that trickled down the side of the Vadre hillside and into the bowl of the junction.

Phil's wife Carol, still looking a bit mournful, ushered Geoff into the living room where Phil lay resting on the sofa chilling in front of the TV, Carol then left them alone. Seeing Geoff standing in the doorway, Phil straightened himself up on the couch.

'No... no relax.' Geoff tried to wave him back down, but Phil had already made the effort.

Looking at him, Geoff was relieved to see that Phil didn't quite look like the elephant man he had half expected to find. The side of Phil's jaw beside his ear had bulbed out a bit, and Geoff immediately thought of the famous jutted out jaw of the Godfather, played by Marlon Brando. Plus the side of his eye above his brow had doubled in size.

'Rocky Balboa,' Geoff quipped as he eased himself on to the edge of the easy chair. Phil gave him a pitifully crocked smile.

'How are you feeling, mate?' Geoff asked.

'Oh, the face lift didn't go quite as I'd expected.' He snorted, and Geoff shared the joke before taking on a serious note.

'Tom filled me in about what happened.'

Phil nodded, as if he didn't really want to be reminded.

'It's definitely a war zone out there now isn't it?' Geoff remarked. 'They're literally out of control now like animals.'

Phil just sat there looking a bit sorry for himself, then Geoff paused before asking. 'How many pints did you actually have?'

Phil huffed wryly. 'Well I'd had about six or seven pints so it was safe to say I was a little bit pissed.'

'Well you couldn't have done anything to protect yourself in that state.'

But Phil didn't appear convinced. 'But could I have done? Had I been stone-cold sober, could I have handled the situation? Would it have been any different?'

Knowing that Phil's greatest weakness was his self-confidence, Geoff certainly didn't want this unfortunate incident to drain him even more. 'Of course you would have handled it a lot better! Don't forget alcohol affects your speed, your reactions, your judgement, and your co-ordination. After consuming that many pints it would have been like trying to fight underwater. You'd have had no chance. None of us would, not even Tom.

Phil just sat there sulkily.

'Phil, I've seen you in the dojo when you've got your head screwed on properly. When you've got the juice and your confidence is firing on all cylinders. You're a bloody handful! Even Tom's admitted it, and he works on the door, and he has much more street experience than any of us. So don't worry about it. You are quite capable of handling any average idiot out there no problem, believe me. The only thing holding you back is your own self belief.'

'Yeah, but something like this doesn't help, does it?'

'No, it doesn't! But neither does downing seven pints of lager help either.'

Phil shook his head. 'Shit, what would have happened if the bouncers hadn't have come when they did? When would those bastards have stopped kicking me? These days you don't just get a beating, they really don't care now if they kill you or not. I'm a policeman, and I know what it's like following up a case like that. A load of unnecessary paperwork, thousands of pounds of taxpayer's money on a court case you have no guarantee of winning and for what? A paltry few months in a luxury prison at the most. Failing that a suspended sentence, or just some crappy community service.' Phil looked reproachfully at Geoff. 'It's just not enough, something needs to done.'

'Something is being done,' Geoff replied.

'I know. Tom told me what you all are planning to do.'

'Well, you're not going to arrest us, are you?' Geoff joked.

Phil gave another crooked smile before getting back to business. 'Something's got to done about these feral bastards, Geoff. Even I've had enough now. Officially I would say to you, no don't do it, leave it to the police to handle. Unofficially, I would say knock their blasted heads off.'

*

On his way back to Llandudno, Geoff decided he would pay his old friend Will Thomas a visit. Knowing that Will had a lot more experience in street fighting than he did, he thought it might be a good idea to see if he had any advice to impart on the situation. Besides Geoff had already promised to drop in on his old training partner, so he viewed it as a way of killing two birds with one stone.

Geoff stood at the front door to the tenement flats where he first spoke to Will over a week ago, and muttered under his breath. 'What do I do... just walk in or ring one of these buttons and ask for assistance?'

'Geoff?' Someone called him, and he spun around to find Will standing at the bottom of the steps holding a carrier bag. Geoff looked a bit sheepish, as if he'd just been caught spying. 'I was just wondering how to get in.'

Will climbed up the steps towards him. 'You see all the buttons on the side there, the one beside flat 1, that's me. Just press that next time.'

They shook hands again. 'How are you, mate?' Geoff asked.

'Good. Good. Come in,' Will told him, and ushered Geoff through to his flat. Inside Will told him to have a seat, while he unloaded his shopping. Geoff duly obliged, briefly looking over the place.

'So how's things, Geoff? Karate club going OK?' he asked quickly, shoving items of shopping away.

'Yeah, good. Good,' Geoff replied a bit vaguely.

'Tea, coffee,' Will offered.

Geoff tapped his car keys in his hand as if he was on the verge of shooting out the door.

'Yeah, go for it!'

'Come on, Geoff, spit it out lad.' Will mimicked a cranky old school teacher from his past. 'That's the same agitated Geoff ready to defend his beloved art against the outspoken radicals who dare to question its age-old values and traditions. How many times did we lock antlers over all that?'

'No. No, it's not any of that. I need some advice.'

'Not on women, I hope. I'm going through enough problems of my own thanks very much.'

Geoff cleared his throat. 'Retribution! We're going to give some people a pasting.'

Will's coffee-stirring slowed. 'Retribution? Geoff Harrison. Am I hearing right?'

'Oh yes!' Geoff replied dead serious.

'What's all that about then?' Will handed Geoff his coffee, and sat on the table seat facing him.

Geoff filled his lungs. 'A mate of mine, a student at the club, Phil the copper got a bit of a kicking at the weekend. These three morons including their girlfriends started on him just because he accidentally brushed past one of them. Luckily the bouncers from the Boulevards intervened otherwise they'd have just kept beating him up.'

Will listened while he supped on his coffee.

'Police can't do anything about it they don't even know who these gits are. But we know where we can get hold of them, and we're going to pay them a visit next Friday. So what do you think?'

'Revenge is a dish best served cold,' Will lectured. 'They also say that those who plan revenge should dig two graves instead of one.'

'So what does that mean?'

'All I'm saying, me old mate is that once you start a plan of action like that you have to see the job through. There are no half measures in that game.'

'What, like losing your bottle, or changing your mind, you mean?'

Will placed his mug on the table top in front of him. 'Kind of yeah! What I'm trying to say is that you have to be completely sure of yourself to start getting into this payback thing. It's not like they portray it in the movies. Someone does you and you do them, and then the hero goes off and shags the girl. That's not the end of it believe me. You've got to stay switched on all the time. All the time! I'm not trying to put you off or anything. The problem with these situations is that most people think, shit. They've battered my mate, so we'll batter them, sorted.' Will shook his head with caution. 'Then their mates want to get into the equation. They want revenge and it goes on and on until in the end you have to defeat the whole bloody army. That's what you've got to be prepared for. If you honestly, truly, believe in the justification of revenge and its consequences, and you can handle all that, then do it. But always sleep with one eye open. One the other hand if you don't want to take any risks, and can't handle the possibility of comebacks from your actions, then I would suggest you find out who the attackers are and let the police handle it.'

Geoff mused for a moment, then shook his head defiantly. 'Even if I wanted to back down now, it's too late. I've already given my word. Imagine what the others would think if I told them to let the police sort it out instead. They would think I've bottled it, and would probably have no faith in me ever again.'

'Well, that's the problem. A lot of people get themselves into these dilemmas all because of male bravado. Not that I'm saying this has happened in your case. I know from experience that you have plenty of bottle. But that's how a lot of these situations actually happen. People don't really possess the experience to realise what they're getting into until it's too late. Take for instance two people having an argument over which is the better football team. At this stage they have no intention of having a fight. One of them raises his voice to try and get the upper hand in the dispute, so the other one raises his voice. One starts to shout, and the other shouts back. Then he pushes, and the other pushes back, and the fighting begins. But I guarantee you that while they're going at it, they'll both be wondering why the hell they're fighting over a stupid football team.'

'So where does the justification come into it then?' Geoff asked.

'First of all remove the ego. Then calm your anger. And keep hold of your fear. Never let someone else push you into doing something against you will. They may be up for it, but you might not. Or they may not be up for it, and they just want you to do their dirty work for them. That's the ego.

Anger clouds your judgement. You do, and say things you may regret, and once it's done it's too late to take it back. Fear... Fear is the friend of champions. Fear keeps you alert. Fear gives you strength. Fear gives you the will to survive.'

'Sounds like you have more experience than I thought.'

'I do. And I've also made the mistakes that go with them. It's not always easy to be able to practise what you preach. I'm human just like the next person.'

'So where did all this experience come from then?'

Will stalled. 'It's a long story, Geoff. Too long to get

through in one afternoon. We'll save that for another day. So you still up for it then?'

Geoff took a thoughtful sip of his coffee, then confirmed his decision.

'It's got to be done, Will. There comes a point when someone has to make a stand. These bastards out there have no respect for anything, police can't do anything, courts hand out pitiful sentences. It'd be easy to just turn the other cheek, run away and hide. But who the hell wants to live like that? I haven't trained all those years just so some vicious hooligan can start pushing me or any of my friends around.'

Will looked on with a satisfied little smirk.

'And yes, I know all those years ago you were right about how all this was going to happen. But someone's got to punish these bastards. If the police can't protect us, the courts can't protect us, we have to start protecting ourselves.'

Geoff's spiel was stopped by his mobile ringing in his tracksuit pocket. He flipped it out and saw that his wife was calling. He answered it.

'Yes Jan, I'm in Will's flat, yes I know. I won't be long. Bye.' Geoff blew as if he'd been on the phone to her for hours. 'Promised her we'd go to B and Q and have a look at those bloody bathroom suites. Suppose I better make a move.' He stood up and placed his mug on the table.

'Oh by the way, give us your mobile number, I've got a new phone now?' Will told him.

Quickly, they swapped numbers, then, Will saw him to the front door.

'Listen, Geoff, be careful, mate. Try and hide your identity as best as you can, and watch for weapons.'

Geoff turned at the front door. 'We will.'

'Pop over when it's done. You've got my number now. Any trouble give us a ring.' They shook hands, and Will watched him leave before shutting the door.

Going back inside, Will looked down at the caller

display window on his mobile as if, he, too was expecting a call.

*

The three of them, Geoff, Tom, and Charlie all sat in Tom's navy blue estate parked on Mostyn Broadway, some fifty yards away from the town's main nightclub. It was Friday night, 10pm.

To cover himself for the evening, Geoff had told his wife Jan that he was having a few drinks with the lads. So even if he was unfortunate enough to get marked up tonight he could always say he got it trying to break up a fight in the pub.

Geoff felt the adrenalin surge through his intestines, and for a split second he wished he was back at home on a regular Friday night with nothing else on his mind to worry about. Normally, by this time he would languishing in front of the TV with a bottle of *Stellas*, and wondering whether or not he would get a shag with the missus.

Geoff took in a huge breath, the body's natural preparation to feed the muscles oxygen ready for battle. The last time Geoff had actually got into a physical with anyone was about five years ago in one of the local chip shops. Two, salty-looking chaps had accused him of jumping the queue even though Geoff had ordered his meal long before they arrived. All it took was a left-right combo, an empi (elbow strike) and one more straight right and it was over. There was no time for any adrenal build up, it just kicked off and Geoff sprung into action. However, afterwards driving back home he was shaking like a leaf mainly due to the post-confrontational shock.

This time was much different. Geoff had had nearly a whole week to build himself up for this confrontation. And this type of preparation was probably the most destructive. The fear of confrontation itself, a slow-drip of adrenalin that over a long period of time, is capable of draining you physically as well as mentally.

Geoff sucked in air through his nostrils to try and calm himself down.

Tom's phone chirped in his jacket pocket and he answered it.

'Yeah, right, OK, cheers.' he said, then ended the call.

He turned to Geoff and Charlie. 'They're on their way up to the Boulevards, they're going through town now.' He raised his brow to warn them. 'There's five of them.'

Geoff glanced at his two companions wondering if that last bit of info might pose a problem for them.

Tom sneered and looked straight ahead. 'Obviously they're travelling with some back up just in case.'

Geoff felt a stinging urge to give Will a call to come and give them a hand, but stopped himself. Even though Will had graciously offered his services, it just didn't seem the right thing to do. No. Getting Will to fight their battles for them would look weak. No. If it was going to be done at all, it had to be done by the three of them.

'What do you think?' Tom turned to Geoff in the back.

Geoff fought hard against the urge to say sod it, let's go home, there's too many of them. But this was the defining moment for all of them. This was make or break time, fight or flight, the hero or the coward scenario.

Then Geoff said without even realising the consequences. 'If we're gonna do it, let's just do it!'

'Right then.' Tom gunned the accelerator.

'Boom, boom.' Charlie added.

With an added adrenalin top-up, Tom almost screeched the car off and around the roundabout towards the prom. 'We'll park down Adelphi Street, and get them before they reach the swimming pool.'

Geoff's heart thundered in his chest. 'Hope there aren't any CCTV cameras about?'

They turned the car down towards the swimming pool, and shot up a dimly lit Adelphi street. Getting themselves ready for the ambush, they all pulled on their beanie hats to try and conceal their identities, and then dived out of the car. Tom raced over to the boot, flung the door open, and grabbed a teak baseball bat.

Geoff gave him a that's not part of the plan look.

'There's five of them isn't there, we only want three, so this is the deterrent for the other two.' Tom explained.

Charlie alerted them 'They're coming up to the wos it's name, coach park.'

Tom slammed the door shut and led the way down a short side-street that cut into Mostyn Broadway, where they would intercept them.

Tom and Charlie gazed down the road to check on the gang's progress.

Geoff breathed in and out slowly, he felt nauseous.

'Shit, where's that other tosser?' Tom snarled. 'Only two of them are there.'

Geoff leaned over. 'Where are the ones we need?'

'The one with the white shirt hanging out, and the tall one waving his arms about.'

Geoff nodded making a mental note.

Tom issued last minute instructions. 'Wait till they're almost in line with us and then rush them. Here, Charlie, you have the bat, keep the others away.'

Charlie took it off him. They stayed midway down the side-street out of sight, and waited until the gabble of voices were almost dead ahead, then Tom broke into a run followed by the other two. Startled by their appearance, the five youths stopped dead in their tracks and wondered what the hell was going on. Tom went straight for Lanky arm waver, and Geoff squared up to White Shirt. Tom's head smashed into Lanky's face with a squelchy thud. Geoff front kicked White Shirt just above the groin, and fired non-stop left rights at him. Charlie swung the bat towards the other three.

'Get back! This is business, any of you interfere and you'll be next.'

Out of pure shock the three lads obeyed, but for how

long their conscience would allow before one or all got brave, that was the question.

White Shirt was down on one knee, overpowered by Geoff's quick-fire left and right shots. He tried in vain to grab at Geoff's legs, but Geoff began pummelling him with thumping knee strikes to the head.

Lanky was still on his feet trying to grapple with Tom, but Tom banged away at his body, sickening blows that almost made him double-up. Tom quickly switched to swinging left and right hooks to the face. You could hear the slaps a mile away. White shirt was now on his back trying to use his legs to fend off Geoff's attack.

'OK, leave off. I've had enough,' he cried.

Geoff booted his legs a couple of times. 'You ever touch any of my friends again and I'll come back and finish the job properly. You got that?' he snarled.

'OK, OK!' White Shirt held up his hands in defeat, his nose mashed and bloodied.

Meanwhile, Lanky couldn't take any more punishment from Tom, and succumbed to one more left hook before dropping to his knees. But Tom didn't stop there, he remembered how these vicious yobs had apparently tried to kick Phil's head off. In a fit of pure rage, he kicked and kicked as if he was trying to break through a heavy door. In desperation, Lanky curled up into a protective ball.

Suddenly, his three mates looked like they were about to charge in. 'Leave him! Leave him, he's had enough!'

'Sod you!' Charlie spat just missing the head of one with his bat to keep them at bay.

'How do you like it, eh?' Tom soccer-kicked Lanky up and down his crouched body making him squeal like a little sissy.

Geoff was just about to tell Tom that that was enough when the beating stopped. In disgust, Tom gobbed down at Lanky, and stormed off.

Geoff backed away from White Shirt who was still lying on his back, and Charlie moved away from the three lads, still brandishing his bat should any of them find a set of balls. 'Tell that other bastard he can run, but he can't hide. Boom, boom!' Then off he jogged to catch up to the other two. Behind him the three lads dashed to the aid of their beaten comrades.

Back at the car, all three dived inside, and whipped off their beanie hats. Charlie threw the baseball bat in the back seat with Geoff. Meanwhile, Tom fired up his motor, and reversed back towards the swimming pool ready to shoot off on to the prom. Now they began to relax a little.

'Jesus Christ!' Geoff sighed flopping in the back seat trying to steady his quivering body.

Charlie ruffled out his flattened hair. 'Mission accomplished. Boom boom.'

'Bastard!' Tom seethed, still some anger left in him.

'What?' Geoff asked.

'Still missed that other tosser though didn't we?'

Charlie gazed awkwardly out the window. 'He'll be expecting it now as well, won't he?'

'Shit, we'll just have to let him stew for a while,' Geoff groaned. 'At least we'll have the pleasure in knowing he'll have to be looking over his shoulder from now on. Anticipation of death is worse than death itself and all that.'

Geoff lay back again, and wiped the cold sweat off his brow. His mind replayed every second of every blow he had delivered in the ambush. The fact that he wasn't repulsed by his actions surprised him.

Thinking back on the whole ambush Geoff didn't regret anything they had done. After all, those cowards had beaten the hell out of Phil without any provocation. Not a one-on-one fair square-off, but four or five, including those drunken girls, against just one. At least they had afforded the two lads that gladiatorial chance of a fair fight. Geoff was satisfied justice had been served, they got what was coming to them, and so would the remaining thug when they finally got hold of him.

However, the night shift for these three avengers was not over yet. Travelling up Measdu Road, something hit the hood of Tom's car with a loud clang.

'What the hell?' Tom cried pulling opposite the old Bodnant, Annex Clinic.

All of them dived out to investigate. Tom examined his roof and found only a minor scratch.

'Over there.' Charlie pointed to a lager bottle lying in the middle of the road.

Obviously someone had thrown it, but from where? On one side of the road was an empty school field, on the other stood the backs of a housing estate facing the main road. Perhaps it was someone from one of the gardens.

They all jogged down to the panel fences lining the back gardens. Tom picked one yard and Geoff and Charlie chose others. Almost on command they all leapt on to the panel fences hoping to catch the culprits hiding on the other side. But it was Tom who struck lucky when he spotted three ten year olds, two boys and a girl, scuttling off like cockroaches.

Tom swung over in hot pursuit. 'Got em.'

But by the time Geoff and Charlie had caught him up, Tom had all three kids rounded up at the back patio window. Just as it looked as if he was going to give them all a backhander for their cheek, the patio door rumbled open. Someone wearing a red football tee shirt with a football-sized belly to match blocked out the light.

'Hell's going on?' The man's eyes darted between the three strangers standing on his lawn.

'One of these little toe-rags just lobbed a bottle at my car!' Tom explained giving the brats a now-you're-going-to-get it look.

'So what that got to do with you chasing them in my garden?' The man nodded his head arrogantly.

Tom eyed him with disgust. 'You what?'

'Get off my property now, or I'll get all three of you for trespassing.'

Tom grabbed the fat man by the throat with such force that the man tripped back over the patio step. Tom used the momentum to tip him over and pin him on his back, his hand never leaving the man's flabby throat.

'No, leave him, leave him.' the young girl cried.

'Hey what going on?' his even fatter wife cried, as she waddled through.

'Shut up!' Tom barked at her, then turned back to fat man.

'Listen, you piece of shit, you're lucky I'm not suing you for the damage your brats have done to my car.'

The fat man didn't say anything, he wouldn't dare, the fear shone clearly in his bolting eyes, and his heavy breathing.

'I'm sick of scummy parents like you who probably live on benefits and breed like rats. It's always someone else's fault with you lazy deadbeats isn't it?'

Geoff and Charlie swapped uneasy glances.

'Sort yourselves out,' Tom growled thrusting his hand against the fat man's throat. 'And sort those brats out too. Don't make me come back and have to do it for you. And don't think about phoning the police, or I will be visiting you again. Got it?'

The fat man tried to nod through Tom's tight grip. Tom released him and stood up. He turned and nodded to Geoff and Charlie lets go. Behind them the fat man tried to climb back to his feet with the aid of his children and his cursing wife. He looked like a beach turtle turned upside down.

Back in the car as they drove off, Charlie began to snigger.

'Certainly didn't expect all that.'

Geoff glanced out of the rear window. 'Hope they don't take down your car registration number.'

'So what if they do, I'll sue them for the damage to my car. Good job it's only my run-around.' He snarled. 'Had he apologised and given the kids a good bollocking I would have left it at that. But when he tried to have a go at me,

47

and not his brats for what they had done to my car I thought you ignorant git. So I kicked off.'

'One more down, another twenty thousand or so to go before we clear up this town. Boom, boom.'

'Boom bloody boom,' Geoff concluded, looking forward to a couple of well-earned lagers waiting for him back home.

CHAPTER 5

Will stopped by the Presbyterian church on Gloddaeth Street, and began walking the rest of the way down the street back to his flat, he was knackered. It was the first real jog he'd had since coming out of nick. Boiling hot, he pulled off his beanie hat, heart drumming in his chest, his throat raw from exertion, and his legs wobbling as if they had no bones in them.

It was Saturday morning, the sky was leaden grey, it was cold and uninviting, and it looked like it was going to be one of those dark gloomy days that never seem to wake up.

Will took out his phone, and looked for any text messages on the caller display window. This time it wasn't Stacey he was thinking about, but his mate Geoff. Will wanted to know how everything went last night, and thought he should have heard something by now. As he reached the Tribells chip shop on the corner, he searched for Geoff's number so he could call him to find out, then paused. Perhaps ten o'clock on a Saturday morning, was too early to ring? Most people usually like to have a lie in. But burning curiosity overpowered any consideration, and he decided he would take the chance. He punched in the number and pressed the phone to his ear and that's when he saw her.

Stacey was standing in the doorway outside his flat. For a second Will almost forgot about the call and quickly hit the quit button on his mobile. She was wearing a purple fleece jacket that covered the behind of her jeans. Her hair was raven-black, and was cut into an old-fashioned bob. Her eyes, her eyes were of the darkest brown, just as he'd remembered. And whenever she got angry they would glisten like chocolate minstrels. The first time he ever saw her he thought she wasn't classically pretty, but plain-looking leaning towards attractive, a bit like that young sexy teacher in school all the lads had a crush on.

As Will strolled towards her, he was a bit lost for words, and judging by the look on her face, he couldn't tell whether she was pleased to see him or not. It was the same type of look she used to give him after they had had an argument. Cold and defensive, as if he had a lot of explaining to do before she even considered speaking to him again.

Will stood at the base of the steps, and uttered the first thing that came into his head. 'I had almost given up on you.'

Stacey's expression remained the same. 'So how have you been?'

'Great!' Will replied, climbing the steps towards her. 'I've had a really wonderful three and a half years in prison, thanks.'

Stacey appeared annoyed by his sarcasm.

Will stood before her, and she glared up at him with those delicious brown eyes. 'Wanna come in?' he asked, digging into his tracksuit bottoms for the key, and Stacey nodded.

Inside the flat, Will tossed his keys on the kitchen work-top, and began filling up the kettle. 'Fancy a brew?'

'Yeah, why not,' she replied, looking around as if she was trying to figure out why he would want to stay in a hovel like this.

'Have a seat,' he told her.

'Bit of a come down, isn't it, Will?'

Will threw her a quick look. 'You probably won't understand, but I don't want to get too comfortable too quick.'

Stacey sighed impatiently as if she wanted to get down to the nitty-gritty. 'Listen, Will, I came over because I thought it was best to explain things face to face. I felt I owed you that.'

Will listened while he waited for the kettle to boil.

'My mind still hasn't changed from what I said three years ago. That's why I completely cut all communications with you. I wanted a clean break.'

'You certainly made that clear, that's for sure.' Will finished off making the teas and walked over. He handed Stacey hers.

Stacey cupped her mug while Will sat in the window seat facing her.

'The problem with you Will is that you're a ticking time bomb, and I really don't want to be around you when you go off.'

'Christ Stacey, I'm not that bloody bad.'

'Yes, you are, Will. I always knew you had a temper, but what I saw on that day was a complete stranger, a maniac, someone completely out of control. I saw the devil in you.'

Will listened as he supped up his tea. He wanted to defend himself and call her melodramatic but at the same time he also wanted her to have her say, and get it off her chest.

'I know you also had a bit of a past as well. Those once or sometimes twice a month meetings you used to go to, I'm not saying you were seeing someone else on the sly, but I know those secret meetings were more than just a lad's night out. And lets be honest, I never badgered you about it, did I? OK, you explained that these outings were a regular occurrence long before I came along, fair enough! But when you're planning to share your life with someone and start a family things have to change, you have to change and make sacrifices. And call it women's intuition or whatever I just knew that whatever secrets, dark sides or dubious meetings you were involved in, it had something to do with the way you acted that day. I could feel it, and that was the final straw for me. Yet still to this day you still can't come clean about everything. You're still hiding something.'

Will gave her a worn look. 'Stacey, all that is in the past now. What happened on that day was nothing to do with the way I am or what I used to get up with. That day with the dog and the thugs was just a bad day for everyone, and that's it.'

Stacey snorted bitterly. 'You call spending three years in prison away from your fiancée just the result of a bad day?'

'Of course not! But those meetings you keep going on about were just a group of very close friends simply looking out for each other. I already told you that.'

'Come on, Will, all those marks that would suddenly appear on your face and body?'

'You make it sound like I was involved in some sort of a mass orgy or something,' Will huffed.

'Well, go on then, Will, tell me everything? Tell me all about your so called mates? Tell me all about why all of a sudden you would have to go out in the middle of the night, and not come back until the early morning.'

Will dropped his head guiltily. 'I can't!'

Stacey shrugged with frustration. 'Well, there it is. And you expect me to just accept that and keep quiet?'

Will said nothing.

'Just how on earth can you expect to build a relationship with an attitude like that?'

'Stacey all that is in the past now. I'm not a part of it anymore. And back then I would have proved that to you if you'd have given me more time.'

'And what about what you went to prison for, would that have still happened?'

'Maybe, maybe not, I just don't know. That day I reacted like any other man. It's just a natural alpha-male instinct to want to maim or kill to protect the things that mean the most to you. You can't domesticate it by dressing it up in fancy civilised rules. But that aside, I've also had some counselling for some of that excess anger, I'm trying so hard to start afresh. All I ask is a chance to prove it?'

Stacey swung her head ponderously. 'It's too late, Will. You've left it too late, and I've moved on.' She stood up, ready to leave. 'I suggest you do the same.'

Once again Will could feel her slipping through his fingers.

'Stacey, I came back for you. I came back because I can now give you the kind of life we had planned before I went inside. Are you really ready to throw all that away again? We're both not getting any younger you know.'

That last statement seemed to burn her somewhat. 'No, we maybe not, but at least I'm getting wiser.'

'I didn't mean it like that.' Will backtracked, but the damage was already done.

Stacey silenced him with the palm of her hand. 'Will I don't think you could truly commit yourself to anyone. All you want is someone to come home to, someone to look after the house and the kids while you go out and do your thing . And that's not the kind of life for me.'

Will shook his head. 'You're so wrong about that, Stacey, and I can prove it to you.'

Stacey looked at him like she was listening to an alcoholic with a beer in his hand saying he had quit.

Will stood up in frustration. 'How can I prove it to you?'

'I don't think you can Will. Let's just leave it at that shall we?' She gave him a flat, sad smile and turned to leave.

Will watched her, powerless to do anything, powerless to say anything that would make any difference. The door clunked behind her, and Will slumped back in his chair, anger welling up inside him. His fists clenched into balls of molten rage, knuckles and fingers turning ivory white. The bones in his hands popped under the strain, and all the scars and scratches glowed like beacons as a reminder of a past filled with terrible violence. The watch on his wrist, the one that Stacey had bought him suddenly became the trigger of all that broiling frustration. He whipped it off and drew his hand back ready to smash it against the wall. But then he froze, the blazing fires in his eyes beginning to die. He could not let go of that cursed watch.

*

That afternoon an emergency meeting had been called at Phil's home in the junction. The celebration of last night's revenge ambush was about to be cold showered by what Tom and Charlie had found out.

'What do you mean we're now marked men?' Geoff frowned concerned.

Tom explained. 'The three lads we went after are all members of the Colwyn Bay gang called the Wilkinsons, and they're notorious for carrying blades.'

'Wilkinson swords.' Geoff joked.

'Are you sure?' Phil asked, his face now showing the bruising from the recent attack.

'One of our bouncer mates at Wetherspoons phoned us up this morning to warn us. Apparently the news has spread like wild fire.'

'But did they recognise you lot though?' Phil asked.

Geoff made a face. 'Would have been hard with the beanie hats, and we were more or less straight in and out.'

Tom turned to Geoff. 'Well, even if they did get a good look at us they wouldn't know you from Adam. But there's always a chance they might know Charlie and me from the doors.'

Phil chewed his lip with concern. 'Those Wilkinsons, we know all about them, they're a bit of a handful, and they have a lot of drug connections as well.'

'How many are there in the gang?' Geoff asked.

'As far as I know, they're about fifteen to twenty strong.' Phil replied.

'Yeah, bunch of cowards.' Tom snarled. 'Can't fight

for shit by themselves, they always need their mates as back up.'

'Too right.' Charlie agreed.

'Be careful, lads. I mean it!' Phil warned them.

Geoff began to feel the effects of post adrenal dump, the fear of consequence, and he recalled what Will had said about revenge, and how in the end you may have to defeat the whole army.

'So what's the plan?' Charlie asked.

Geoff swallowed defiantly. 'We made the choice to do what we did, so we have to accept the consequences.'

'I think we should all carry our own weapons at all times.' Tom added.

Phil ignored that last remark.

Geoff continued. 'We should all stay in close contact on our mobiles day and night, and be on hand for back up.'

Phil cut in. 'Ring me anytime, and I'll make sure the police get there as soon as possible. OK? Don't go anywhere alone at night either.'

Tom grimaced sheepishly 'We may have to get some more back up ourselves, you know?'

That thought had already crossed Geoff's mind and he had a short list of possibilities. But the one at the top of his list he wanted to keep secret for the time being.

'We may be able to get Mike on board.' Tom turned to Charlie for confirmation.

'Yeah, he'll definitely come in an emergency.'

'I've got a few possibilities,' Geoff confessed. 'One especially that I can look into, and there's Guy in Colwyn Bay who runs a judo club, known him for years. Back when his brother was beaten into a coma some ten years ago, he wanted to start a kind of vigilante group, so he won't need a lot of convincing. We're going to have to have our own team, not just anyone. They have to be people we can trust, people who are willing to act at short notice, and people who are up to the mark. This is going to have to be a special team.'

55

Tom and Charlie nodded, impressed. This was right up their street.

'Once every fortnight, or whatever we can manage, we all train together at a certain location away from where we normally train. Nobody discusses these sessions with anyone, everybody should attend, no shirking. OK? All this may seem a bit of an over reaction, but I don't want to wait for one of us to get maimed or worse before we do anything about it. Forewarned is forearmed.'

Tom smirked amused. 'Ever done a stint in the army, Geoff?'

Geoff loosened up a tad. 'Hopefully, nothing will happen, and all this will blow over, after all they've been paid back for what they did.'

'Except for that other one we didn't get,' Tom grumbled.

Geoff ignored him. 'But even if this does blow over without any comebacks. It's gotten to the stage out there now were we have to have some sort of back-up protection should we need it. Maybe the time to do something about all this crime out there has come to a head. And, no disrespect to Phil, the law isn't much help anymore is it?'

Reluctantly, Phil had to agree.

'And I don't know about any of you, but I think I'll be able to sleep much better at night knowing that if any of us, or our families, face any serious hassle or danger from those animals out there, then retribution is only a phone call away.'

'What about me?' Phil asked feeling a bit left out.

Geoff turned to him. 'You'll be our eyes and ears, you're in a position where you can supply us with the necessary info we might need, like addresses etc, if it comes to that.'

Tom gave Charlie a sly nudge.

Phil shifted about in his seat uncomfortably. 'That could be a bit iffy for me, you know?'

Geoff realised this and didn't want to put Phil on the

spot. 'Phil, I would never ask you to risk your job or anything, but any inside info you could get for us could give us the edge we might need. But if it's too risky, then fair enough, we'll understand, OK?'

In response, Phil told Geoff that he couldn't make any promises.

'So is everybody alright with this? Does anyone have a problem committing to a pact like this?'

Tom spoke up. 'So is this going to be our own sort of vigilante group?'

'No, I don't want to think of it like that. It's not our job to clean up the whole town. We're not the *A Team*. All we're trying to do is provide a kind of minding service for ourselves, family and friends that's all. Something like a ready tube of Bisodol in our pockets should we ever get an attack of heartburn.'

Phil rolled his eyes at Geoff's wit, while Tom's and Charlie's imaginations were already beginning to run wild.

CHAPTER 6

Later that day, Geoff pressed the doorbell to Will's flat. While he waited, he gazed around at the street's mid-afternoon, hustle and bustle. When Will finally answered the door, he looked pleased to see that Geoff was safe and sound.

'Geoff, come on through,' he said and Geoff followed him in.

As they entered his flat, Will turned impatiently.

'So how did it go the other night? Sorry, I was going to phone you but something came up.'

Geoff noticed a packed rucksack on the couch and paused before replying. 'It went OK, we got our revenge, but we missed getting the third lad, he wasn't there.'

Will walked through to the kitchen, which appeared spotlessly clean, as if he'd had a bit of a tidy-up. 'Glad to see you got through it without any complications,' he remarked, then became somewhat preoccupied with trying to find something. Again, Geoff glanced at the bulging rucksack.

'You planning to go somewhere?'

Will stopped his searching. 'Yeah, f'raid so, things didn't work out with Stacey. I thought after all this time she would perhaps be ready to wipe the slate clean, but no such chance. Thought it was worth trying one last time.' Will tried to look busy again as if he was trying to hide his obvious disappointment.

Geoff scowled to himself. All this didn't quite fit in with what he came to ask him and now certainly wasn't the best time to mention it. Instead he did what a true mate was supposed to do, he lent him his ear.

'Wanna talk about it?'

Will sighed heavily. 'What's to say really. I gave it a go, it didn't work out, so I might as well head off back to Warrington.'

'Will, make us a cuppa,' Geoff said settling himself down on the couch next to the rucksack ready to hear the whole story.

A mug of tea later, Will had more or less told Geoff the entire history of his relationship with Stacey, minus the bits about the reasons behind his late night get-aways, and why he ended up in prison.

Geoff tried to be as diplomatic as possible. 'Listen, Will, women are very funny creatures, especially about things like trust and responsibility, and shit like that. If they suspect you are up to no good, believe me they will move heaven and earth to suss you out.'

Sitting at the window table, Will's eyes flicked up and then back down again.

Geoff winked slyly at him. 'So what were you up to then? Was it a bit of skirt on the side or what?'

Will sat up in defence. 'No! Nothing like that at all!'

'Well, what then? Can't you even tell me? Is it that bad?'

Will thought about it, then stood up and turned uncomfortably towards the window. 'Swear to me that what I'm going to tell you now, will never leave this room?'

Geoff nodded his head, 'Of course I swear!'

Will settled as if he was relieved at actually having the chance to get it off his chest. 'I used to be a member of an organisation whose sole purpose was to tackle serious organised crime and the supply and distribution of drugs.'

Geoff looked bewildered. 'No shit! So how did you get involved in all that?'

'I first started out as a mixed martial arts fighter, I had about seven or eight bouts and was doing very well, I'd gotten a bit of a name for myself, a bit of a reputation.

Then through an associate of mine, I got the chance to join this kind of anti-crime outfit committed to tackling serious crime. Remember how you used to joke that I should have joined the police force? Well that's about the closest that I got to it. But this outfit was sort of like The Serious and Organised Crime Agency. We used to help track down and apprehend career criminals, notorious gang leaders, and the easy-graft criminals...

'Easy-graft criminals?' Geoff asked.

'Yeah, that's how a lot of them start out. The gang leaders send someone by Easy Jet to Amsterdam and Spain to deliver messages. Not bad work, they just get paid to sit on a plane. Did you know that Amsterdam is the world's drugs supermarket where most drugs in the UK come from?

In the late eighties a group of scousers set up there, and ever since then they have a stronger presence there than any other UK gangs. Drugs come back into Liverpool then get divided up. It costs a criminal £24,000 for a kilo of pure cocaine in Amsterdam. Slip it back into Britain and they can double their money.'

'So what happens then once the drugs have got back into Britain?'

'Someone cuts it down mixes it with various stuff, then it goes to the next guy who cuts it, then the next guy and so on. By the time a punter buys a gram on the street for £40 or £50 they're lucky if it's 40 percent cocaine.

An area like Liverpool might be run by about twenty lads, they have punters who come to their patch to buy drugs, and they'll do anything to defend that.'

Geoff was having trouble absorbing it all. 'So how did you get trained up for all that then?'

'Well we didn't handle the operations and setting up side of the raids, we were the just hired muscle to look after the agents who went in. We were the back-up. Some of these drug gang members are as hard as nails, especially when they're on the weed themselves. They're like non-stop machines, and they'll come at you with anything.'

'So did you have any training in that sort of thing?'

'Yeah, we had a basic training in the weapons you're allowed to use, and you're given protective wear, but at the end of the day, it was our own fighting skills that were needed.'

'So how many of you were there?'

'In all there was about twelve of us used for various operations. But after a couple of my mates got killed in separate raids, I starting looking for the back door – it was getting too risky. And then I met Stacey and that confirmed it for me that I had to get out. Thing is in a job like that you make a lot of enemies, and I couldn't risk my life as well as Stacey's, I mean if any of those Merseyside gangs found out who I was, they would go after her first.'

Geoff could see his point. 'So how did you end up in prison then?'

'Oh that was nothing to do with the organisation. That was purely my own doing. All that happened because of a completely separate incident. Besides, going to prison actually freed me from the organisation.'

'So Stacey had no idea about this organisation?'

'Christ no! I couldn't risk telling her about it for her own good.'

'So what did you actually do to be put in prison in the first place?'

Will's mouth opened to tell him, but the text beep on Geoff's mobile stopped him. Geoff snarled and took out his phone to see what the message was. It turned out to be Guy, one of their old friends who ran a Judo club in Colwyn Bay. After suggesting his name as a possible candidate for the team Geoff had sent him a message to get in touch ASAP. The text replied... will ring you tonight about 7.30. Ideally, Geoff had wanted to wait until he'd spoken to Will about it first. Yet now with Will threatening to leave town, it looked like that conversation wasn't going to happen.

'Who is it?'

Geoff decided to lie so he could keep everything under wraps for know.

'Oh it's just Jan wondering where the hell I am, that's all.'

'I won't keep you if you have to go.'

'That's OK, she can wait for me for a change,' Geoff replied and got back to the business of talking about Stacey. 'Listen, Will, the way I see it is if you're going to have any chance at all you must tell her everything you've just told me. Come clean. Stay and give it one more try.'

Will gave him a drained look.

'No, honestly. What have you got to lose? It's got to be worth a try, hasn't it?'

Will didn't appear so optimistic. 'To be honest, Geoff, even if I told her about all this, I don't think she'd believe me now. I know how she thinks, she'd say, well you've had three long years to dream up that one.'

'But what have you got to lose? I mean you're all packed up ready to shoot off back to Warrington. You've already accepted that it's now over. How much worse can it be?'

Will stood up and rubbed his face in frustration. 'You don't understand. Even if I did tell her everything, and she did believe me, she wouldn't leave it there. She would have to know exactly what jobs I did, how far did I go, and to what kind of people did I do it to. And if I held back she'd accuse me of being dishonest again.'

'Well, why can't you tell her?' Geoff asked.

Will slumped back down in his chair. 'Geoff I've seen some pretty nasty shit in my time. And I've done some pretty nasty things in and away from the organisation. Things I'm not particularly proud of. Things I couldn't even tell you about. I could never tell her everything. In the end it nearly destroyed me. I've even had some counselling myself. But things are different now. That's not me anymore, Geoff. And that's why I can't tell Stacey about it, because she'd end up dredging it all back up and judging me in a completely different light. She already thinks I'm a monster and if I had to tell her of some of the jobs I had to do. She wouldn't want to come anywhere near me.'

Geoff felt inclined to ask out of morbid curiosity, but decided not to. Not now, perhaps not ever, maybe some things were best left unsaid.

*

Driving back home, Geoff breathed in deep through his nostrils, his mind was muddled with everything, especially with what Will had just told him – an operative for some kind of Serious Crime Squad. Christ it made him sound like a secret agent. Geoff's head tottered at the idea, and he wondered what other dark secrets Will might be harbouring about his past? Plus what was the terrible thing he did to get sent down to prison? And how could it be so bad that it still haunts Stacey to this day?

Geoff needed some fresh air so he pressed down the electric windows. The icy November air breezed in and felt refreshing against his face. He thought about Will again and prayed that there was some way of making him stay just a while longer. Not just for the fact that Will's knowledge and experience alone would be perfect for the team; but also because he would miss him as a mate.

CHAPTER 7

Inside the chemical storage warehouse down Builder's Street West, they all met up for their first session. There were seven of them in attendance; Geoff, Phil, Tom and Charlie, plus the new additions to the team; Mike, Guy and Brad. All of them donned casual sport's wear, T- shirts and hooded tracksuits.

Mike, the bouncer mate of Tom and Charlie, was a shaven-headed Jamaican only five foot eight, but looked like a concrete shed with a head on it.

Guy, an old friend of Geoff and Will, was also somewhat vertically challenged, and stood a mere five foot seven, but unlike Mike he had a 4th dan black belt in judo. To look at Guy one would probably imagine a mild-mannered David Banner type before he turns angry and bulges into the Incredible Hulk.

Except when Guy got angry he didn't turn green and bulk up to 400 pounds, he just tied someone's balls to their feet quicker than one could say Brian Jacks.

Guy, with an untidy bowl of mousey-grey hair, stood to attention hands behind his back as if he was in an army inspection, and peered analytically through his fifty pence glasses.

Last but not least, we had Guy's protégé – Brad. Brad himself was a dead ringer for a young Charles Bronson, he stood a shade under six foot, sinewy muscled, and slightly bandy legged. The credentials he brought to the team were a judo brown belt and five years experience of Ninjitsu, another martial art he had been a student of for five years. He was also very proficient with weaponry.

After the brief introductions were made, Geoff stood

before them in the wide open space surrounded by pallets and racks of chemical containers and cleaning agents. To Geoff it felt like the start of one of his usual karate classes.

'OK, lads, we all know who we are now, so lets get down to why we are all here, shall we?' He took a breath, and paced about to focus himself. 'First of all I think you are all aware of what happened to Phil when he was out with friends on a recent night out.'

All heads turned to Phil whose facial bruising had begun to fade since the merciless attack. Phil grinned bashfully.

'And I know you are also aware of our revenge attack on two of the three thugs who were responsible for the assault. The thugs themselves happened to be members of a Colwyn Bay gang called the Wilkinsons, and because of that, we now seem to have started a bit of a war with them. That's the first reason we're all standing here. We need a back-up team.

The other reason concerns the nature of protection. Now I don't need to remind you about the alarming crime statistics out there. And I don't need to remind you about the fact that the police have basically lost control of the streets. With this in mind, who can we now rely on to protect us and our loved ones? What assurances do we have of justice being served when someone tries to mug us out on the street, or burgle our houses when we sleep? What is going to happen if one of those bastards rapes our wives or stabs one of our friends?' Geoff took a moment to calm himself.

The rest of them stood arms folded, and legs akimbo like an army squad being briefed by their commanding officer. Geoff continued.

'So what do we do about it?' He gave anyone the chance to reply, but no one answered.

'Well, we surely can't fix the whole of broken Britain. We surely can't win the war on street crime all by ourselves. And we surely can't be there to protect everyone. But we can be there to protect ourselves, our families, and our friends. Charity indeed begins at home.'

'So this is definitely not a vigilante group then?' Tom asked.

Geoff turned to him. 'No, that's not what I'm asking for. The problems with vigilante groups are once you start, where do you stop? Let's say for instance you target a group of youths causing trouble on a street corner and sort them out. Next you start looking for anyone wearing a hoodie, or anyone who even looks a bit dodgy and start harassing them just in case they start any trouble.

'Finally, you end up wanting to execute some kids just for kicking a football outside your bloody house. No, I certainly don't want us to end up like that.'

Guy the judo expert raised his finger. 'What if someone comes to us for our help?'

'Well, really, we don't want to start advertising our services? If word gets around who we are and what we're trying to do, the police are going to start trying to track us. And if our enemies get wind of who we are then we're in trouble. But let's just say in exceptional circumstances, for instance someone we know is getting hassled by a group of bullies, or a friend of a friend's wife is getting knocked about by her husband, then of course who wouldn't help?'

Phil, raised his hand 'So how is all this going to work? What's the plan?'

Geoff scratched his bald head. 'This is how it's going to work. Once a fortnight, we all meet here and train together. We must all be ready to respond to any emergency night or day. Obviously, I don't expect everyone to be able to respond to every call-out every time. But there are seven of us here so I expect at least half of us to make the effort when needed.' Geoff held up his mobile phone. 'In an emergency, a text should be sent to every member. HELP. And then the address!'

'Why can't we have a bat phone?' Tom jested and everyone smiled.

Geoff gave things time to settle again. 'The reward for this honourable commitment will be the protection of the

66

team 24-7 for ourselves, our families, and any of our friends. Any questions?'

Guy raised his finger once more. 'So I gather this is all definitely hush-hush, but are we expected to keep this from our wives and girlfriends as well?'

Geoff filled his jowls thoughtfully. 'Yes, I've already chewed on this one myself and I think as long as they're not all blabber-mouths, it'd be best just to tell our spouses and girlfriends. In all honesty, I really don't want anybody to know about this, but I also don't want anyone to have to sacrifice their relationships because of it either. Not that any of you would do that for something like this. But I know how paranoid some partners can get, and I think you will all agree it wouldn't be worth all the added stress and tension trying to hide this from them day and night.'

Mike the muscle-bound doorman raised his hand. 'So what if someone we know does need help, what do we do?'

'Discuss it with the team first. Don't any one of you take it upon yourselves to do anything without back-up. Even if your wife has just been raped, we will sort it as a team.'

Tom and Charlie exchanged questionable glances.

'So is everyone in agreement with all this then? If anyone here thinks they cannot commit to the team, they are quite welcome to leave right now?'

All eyes shifted back and forth to see if anyone was going to move, but nobody did.

'Don't worry, there will be no bad feelings or criticism on those who might want to leave, the rest of us will fully understand.'

Everybody stood their ground. Satisfied, Geoff bent down to pick up a pair of Thai focus pads. He clapped them together with a loud thwack that echoed around the small warehouse. 'OK, let's get to work...'

*

It was splashed across the front page of the North Wales Weekly news.

"RESIDENTS OF LLANDUDNO COUNCIL ESTATE TERRORISED BY YOBS."

The notorious estate itself was situated near the Llandudno General Hospital, and was also known as Beirut to the unfortunate occupants who lived there.

Inside the issue, one resident gave her harrowing diary of her life on the hell estate, but wished to remain anonymous for fear of any reprisals, from the young thugs.

'Two years I have been living on this cursed estate, and in the last twelve months or so, it has become like Beirut. Kids as young as eight are still out wandering at eleven o' clock at night. They shout, swear, and throw stones while their parents are either out or at home too drunk to care about what's going on.

'But it's the older ones who are worse, the fifteen-sixteen-year-olds who actually intimidate the elder residents for money, and if they don't get it, they break windows, or worse. A couple of weeks ago, one elderly woman had to be rushed to hospital with a heart attack because she was so distressed by the harassment. And even as the ambulance arrived, the yobs began pelting it with empty lager bottles. They will stop at nothing!

'Some of them even throw excrement at neighbours front doors. One of them, apparently their ringleader, gives the order, and they do whatever he says. (the names of these youths have been given to the police). Over the last twelve months dozens of complaints have been made to the police, but nothing has been done. We have written to the council, yet all we get back is a letter saying they are looking into it, and that's it!

'Meanwhile, we all have to live in this hell day after day. Some of the residents have been re-housed or have

found alternative accommodation themselves. But for the rest of us who can't afford to move out, we have to wait in line to be transferred, and that could take years. Isn't there anything that can be done to help us? We can't go on living like this.'

A text message beeped on someone's mobile phone, and a meaty hand with scratches across the knuckles, picked it up.

A navy Escort van pulled up at the top of hospital road on the west side of the infamous Beirut estate. The whole town had just been saturated from a light shower which made everything glitter like jewels under the orange sodium streetlights. The time on the van's dashboard read 8.21pm. Two of the occupants wearing beanie hats, exited the van and spread out. One went back down towards the corner shop, the other walked through the estate itself. The third member remained in the van.

Two teenagers pulled wheelies on their mountain bikes, while another hooded teen stood leaning with his hands in his pockets, down one of the estate's alleys. Soon the hoodie was joined by two more teenagers, and without any fear of being exposed, they exchanged small packages. Completely unperturbed by this little business transaction, the bikers continued showing off performing their bunny-hops.

All sorted, the youths dispersed in opposite directions. Hoodie continued through the estate hands still in his pockets, but now clutching his prized possession. Behind him, the two bikers picked up the trail of their leader.

A few doors ahead of them, a medium-built man in his fifties opened his door to let in his cat. Hoodie turned his head towards the man about to close his door. 'Hoi you... wasn't you was it?'

The man widened his door. 'Pardon?'

'Wasn't you who went blabbing to the papers, was it?'

The man shook his head vigorously. 'No, of course not.'

'Better not be, cos if it was, I'll butcher your cat, and post it back through the letterbox in bits.' Hoodie glowered at him before swaggering off.

The man said nothing. He just stood there as the bikers following behind gave him a maniacal smile, and mimicked the sound of his cat to torture him.

Hoodie and his two lap dogs on wheels reached the end of the estate about to cross the road on to the rugby field when a navy van skidded up in front of him. Hoodie and his biker companions jumped back irritated at the idea of something getting in the way. But irritation quickly turned into surprise as Hoodie's arms were seized from behind by two men in beanie hats.

'Hey what the...?' he squealed.

A third man whipped out of the van to open up the double doors.

'Get off me?' Hoodie struggled as he was frogmarched toward the van.

The two bikers were so stunned by what was happening, they didn't know what the hell to do. In panic, Hoodie tried to wrench himself free, but a thumping blow to his abdomen soon put pay to that. Swiftly, he was bundled into the back of the waiting van, and finally his two impotent accomplices managed to find a set of balls.

'Hey, let him go!' they bleated.

One of the men turned before jumping into the van and said. 'Piss off or we'll take you two as well.'

The doors were slammed shut and within a second, the van, with the number plate removed, was off down the street. The bikers themselves fumbled with their mobile phones to try and call whoever they thought might be able to help.

Inside the van, an extra large woolly hat was secured over Hoodie's face, and he was held down to the floor. His bray-like cries of protest were duly ignored.

A couple of streets ahead, a switch of cars was made, and the navy van was cunningly stored away in a nearby garage.

On the North side of the Orme at a place called Pigeon's Cove, three shadows set about their task down on the steep rocks, over looking the rushing sea. Hoodie's hands and ankles were tied with rock-climbing rope, and slowly he was being lowered head first, down over the jagged rocks towards the freezing black sea thirty feet below. Being so scared out of his tiny young adolescent mind, he was unable to utter anything more than a pathetic whimpering. And if he tried to grab a hold of anything to stop the decent, his tortures had told him, they would let go of the rope completely.

Lower and lower went Hoodie down over the craggy rocks. The cold, rough limestone grated his head and face, and the sound of the heavy rumbling water drew closer and closer.

'How does it feel?' one of the men shouted down.

Hoodie's life began to pass before him. 'Please. Please you can have the drugs for nothing. I'll never deal with them again I promise.'

'Sod the drugs, mate. You ain't getting them back anyway.'

Down below, the black rolling sea was now only six feet or so away from his face. It was like being sacrificed to a gigantic slumbering serpent. The smell of algae and seaweed began to burn its way into the young man's brain.

'OK, OK, what do you want?' he cried.

The descent stopped for a moment, silence, then... 'the people on your estate, the ones you have terrorised and in some cases almost driven to suicide because of the hell you have put them through, all want you dead.'

Hoodie grimaced as icy sea-spray lashed at his face, and he could taste pure salt on his lips. 'I've never killed anyone, why do they want me dead?'

'Because they can't go on living like that anymore. They won't go on living like that anymore. Most of them have now reached the point that it's either you or them. Now the way we look at it is which is the best solution?

Should we let all these innocent hard working people end up broken or commit suicide all because of you? Or do we rub out some irritating little parasite like you who not many people would miss anyhow? In fact we think getting rid of you would probably improve the quality of life all around.'

Hoodie squealed. 'You won't get away with killing me. My friends are witnesses.'

'Oh yeah? Judging by the way they just stood there before, I think they'd be more concerned about keeping schtum to save their own little yellow skins. Don't you?'

'You still won't get away with it.'

'I think we will! You see when everyone on your estate hears about what has happened to you, and it comes down to witness statements, I don't think any of them will be doing you any favours. Do you?'

Slowly the descent continued, and panic seized young Hoodie by the throat.

'Shit!' He quivered, trying desperately to think of something that may save him. 'Wait, wait!' He cried out.

He stopped again.

'OK, you win, I'll do anything you want, I'll even move away if you tell me to.'

Beneath him the monstrous sea was licking its lips in anticipation for this tasty little morsel. Yet the anticipation was all it was going to get for now, as Hoodie began to rise back up. He breathed a sigh of utter relief as the tug on his ankles grew stronger and stronger, and the inky black waters drifted further and further away. Finally, he made it back up to the top, and was lifted on to his back on the chilly rock edge. Looming over him were three dark silhouettes. Hoodie held his breath with apprehension, wondering what they were going to do next. One of the men squatted down beside him.

'Listen, we know who you are, Kevin Webber, and we also know where you live. Tonight, this was just a warning. If we hear even a murmur of trouble from you or any of your mates anywhere, we're coming back and we'll drop you in with just your legs tied. And if we have to come back a third time, we'll drop you in with your arms and legs tied, and you'll be blindfolded too. Now do we understand one another?'

Kevin nodded vigorously. 'Yeah, yeah, sure.'

'Good boy,' he was told, and his limbs were duly untied. The man stood back up with the others.

'Don't forget, we'll be watching you and your mates from now on. If there's anything in the papers about this you'll be going for a swim. Oh, and that doesn't necessarily mean that we'll be bringing you back here either. It could be anywhere.'

Kevin nodded in reply.

The three men turned away and began their steep climb back up Pigeon's Cove, Kevin sat up to watch them.

One of the men stopped. 'By the way ... town is on your left.'

*

Back in Tom's 'L' shaped kitchen all three of them Tom, Charlie and Nigel stood, hair flattened by their balaclavas, gazing down in awe at the transparent parcel lying on the worktop as if it was the baby Jesus. Nigel, was the third member of their secret vigilante group, a six-foot-four, good-looking former rugby player and also fellow doorman. Their first planned mission to start clearing-up their town of the worst thugs had proved to be a success.

'So what are we going to do with the drugs then?' Charlie sighed.

'Well,' Tom paused, 'we can flush it down the toilet, or we can sell it off and make a killing.'

'Yeah, but, do we really want to get involved in that kind of business?' Nigel asked.

Tom licked his lips at the prospect. 'There's about twenty grand lying on the table here.

Twenty grand.'

'But is it worth the risk?' Charlie gave a thin smile. 'I mean, whoever owns these drugs, especially if they're worth what you say, they're gonna find us in the end for that amount of money, aren't they?'

'How are they going to know? We were in disguise, remember.' Tom almost chastised him for being a bit timid. 'Besides, once we've sold it off who's going to know?'

'OK, then, who are we going to sell it to?' Charlie again.

Still gazing down at his wondrous bundle, Tom uttered shrewdly, 'Snoopy will know. That walking cokehead knows everybody.'

CHAPTER 8

Early evening, Geoff lumbered into the kitchen where his wife Jan was busy making a salad sandwich for supper. With his back to the sink, he fidgeted awkwardly while working up the courage to tell his wife about his involvements with the team. Jan threw him a glance and chewed on a slice of cucumber. 'Alright, hun?'

Geoff smiled blandly. 'Yeah, just need a bit of a chat about something, that's all.'

'Why, what's up?' she asked, wiping her hands on the tea towel ready to slice up the next vegetable for her sandwich.

'Well, you know how dangerous things are becoming out there on the streets at the moment?

'Yeah.' Jan listened while she sliced some onion ringlets.

'A handful of us chaps have got together to form a sort of neighbourhood watch team. You know? So we can protect our loved ones and any of our friends.'

Jan looked up solemnly from the bread board. 'So how exactly is that supposed to work then?'

Geoff folded his arms uneasily. 'Basically if any of our family or friends are getting any hassle from anyone out there, yobs, thugs or whatever. We're there to help them out.'

Jan turned to face him. 'Help them out – you mean beat them up?' she said with a note of reproach.

'Listen, Jan, who else have we got to protect us out there now, the police? Dixon of Dock Green? You've seen the news, you've read the papers. Everyday now there's a new mugging, stabbing, beating. Those degenerates out there need teaching a lesson. There's no discipline anymore, no deterrent, someone has got to make a stand.'

'Yeah and what happens if you get caught, Geoff? You'll be the one going to prison not them.'

'I think we'd all prefer to be judged by twelve than carried by six, if you know what I mean?'

Jan didn't seem impressed by his sarcasm and continued making her supper in a bit of a huff. 'And what happens if the thugs find out who you are and they come looking for you? Or even worse they get me?'

'Believe me, Jan, it'd never come to anything like that. I would never put you in any kind of danger. I'm doing it to protect you. Besides, it's not as if we're going out on the streets at night looking for trouble. Anyway, you heard what they did to Phil, and all he did to deserve all that was brush by some little shit with an attitude problem. And the police still haven't done anything about it.'

'Yeah, and what does Phil think about all this then? Being a policeman I bet he doesn't agree with it does he?'

'He's eh... part of the team.'

Jan turned aghast. "What? He's in on it too? I don't believe it.'

'It's true, luv. Phil's just as disillusioned with the justice system as the rest of us. Even he says the heads of the Metropolitan Police are now run by bloody politically-correct-hand-wringers who are now more concerned about the criminal's human rights than they are about the victim's. And that's coming from a bloody policeman. What kind of message is that sending out to all those law-breakers? They'll all be rubbing their hands with glee, thinking they're all untouchable, and they'll be right.'

'Geoff it's still too risky. These thugs out there now have guns – how the hell are you supposed to defend anyone against them?'

'Jan, we can't just stand by and do nothing. Besides guns are mainly used in burglaries, they're much harder to conceal than knives.'

'Yeah, for now maybe, but what happens when things get so bad that guns on the street become the norm like

America? How will the team handle that?'

'Jan, we're not trying to take on the world, all we're trying to do is stand up for ourselves, try to make our community a safe place for ourselves, our families and our friends. What's wrong with that?'

'I bet all this is that bloody Will's idea, isn't it? This had never occurred to you lot before he came along.'

'Will's got nothing to do with this, luv. He doesn't even know about it yet, in fact I was going to ask him if he would like to join us, but I haven't got around to asking him. So don't try and blame him.'

'Well what about all the wives and girlfriends, what do they say about it?'

Geoff shrugged. 'Don't know yet, but judging by your reaction I'll be interested to find out. But apart from wives and girlfriends, nobody else must know. Anonymity is essential if it is to work at all.'

Jan turned around with a doleful look. 'Geoff, do you really have to do this?'

'Yes, Jan, I'm afraid we do,' he said walking over to her and taking her in his arms. There's an old saying that goes... the Devil triumphs when good men do nothing. And it's time a few of us good men stood up and did something.'

*

At dusk on the west shore prom, Will's early evening run came to end. Almost spent, he leant on his knees for support, and tried to catch his breath. Getting his fitness back to what it used to be wasn't easy. Sliding off his beanie hat, he stood up and sat on the sea wall to enjoy the rest of the winter sunset.

At this time of day, it was such a beautiful and serene place to be. Will was convinced that the winter dusks here could easily rival any of the famous Caribbean or Mediterranean sunsets. The whole western horizon was gorged in a romantic lemon and rouge. The glorious splendour splashed over the tips and the flanks of the Penmaenmawr mountains, making them stand out like giant red icebergs. For a moment, Will felt relieved of the everyday stress and tensions of the real world, and he quite lost himself in this heavenly glow.

Fifty yards away, Geoff drove up and parked beside the beach. He locked his car, and wandered over.

'Thought I'd find you here.'

'Lovely, isn't it?' Will replied, without even turning.

'You never could resist a good sunset,' Geoff said, hopping up on the wall beside him with a grunt. 'Just been to your flat and thought I might try here next, and lo and behold.'

'Well, I mean, how can you not like a beautiful sky like that, It's like losing yourself in an exquisite painting.'

Not being quite as much the connoisseur, Geoff had to spoil the atmosphere by getting serious. 'So are you going to stay on to tell Stacey everything about your past?'

Will's eyes dropped from the horizon, as if a hypnotist had snapped his fingers and woke him up from the spell. 'I'm thinking about it.'

'Listen Will, half a dozen of us chaps have decided to put together a team of fighters.'

Will turned his ear towards Geoff.

'The main reason for this is to have a back up crew ready in case we get any trouble from this Colwyn Bay gang that are supposedly after us. And the other reason we're getting together is because, well, we're all so sick of this depraved society we now live in. We just want to try and make a difference to our community as a kind of neighbourhood watch.'

Geoff waited impatiently for Will's reaction.

Will sighed heavily, 'I suppose in these desperate times you need desperate measures. But can you handle the consequences, the pressures you'll be putting yourselves under? And can you handle all the risks and the dangers that come with it?'

'Yes, I think we're all aware of what we're up against, but the safety of our family and friends far out-weigh all those risks.'

'And what about your team, Geoff? In a crisis can you really count on them as much as they will count on you?'

Geoff nodded with conviction. 'Definitely!'

'I really hope so, Geoff, because for a commitment of that magnitude you have to be one hundred percent sure of yourself before you even consider your mates. Trust me, it's not so much the thought of going into battle that gets you, it's the threat of the consequences, the outcome, the revenge attacks, the comebacks. And it's for that reason, most people lose their bottle before they even get on to the battlefield. Remember that.'

Geoff nodded as if he was agreeing to some kind of warrior's code.

Will began to fiddle with his Seiko watch. 'So have you told your wife about all this then?'

'Yeah, I thought I'd take advantage of your mistakes. Of course she's not happy about it, but deep down I think she can see the sense in it.'

'Perhaps if things had been as bad five years or so ago, Stacey might have been in a position to understand my situation.'

'She still might,' Geoff replied, watching him tinkering with the dial of his watch.

'Well, Geoff, if there's any advice I can give you, don't hesitate to ask. Just remember, always be on your guard now. Always stay switched on. Never take anything for granted, always be prepared for the worst case scenario.'

Geoff grinned awkwardly. 'Actually, Will, the other reason I've mentioned all this is because I was wondering if you were interested in joining us. The team?'

Will gave him a wry look. 'Me? I really don't think so, Geoff. I've been there, bought the T- shirt blah, blah. I think I've done my time as a soldier of the peace. Besides, it's taken me nearly four years to tear myself away from all that, and I don't really want to dive straight back in again, do I? Anyhow, what about Stacey? It wouldn't actually enhance my chances with her after confessing all about my past, and then telling her, by the way I'm thinking of joining the local vigilante group.'

Geoff appeared disheartened then suddenly chirped-up. 'Hey, what about you giving us the benefit of your experience then? Maybe you can coach us in certain aspects of our training. What about that?'

'Dunno about that, Geoff. I mean I can't expect you all to pick up in a couple of sessions what took me years to learn.'

'Anything is better than nothing, Will. A crumb is a banquet to a starving person.'

Will struggled to find a suitable reply.

'Just taking a few sessions isn't going to hurt, is it? I mean, God forbid if anything should happen, you wouldn't want to feel guilty if any of us got hurt because of our lack of experience?'

Will gave him a look, but Geoff winked at him.

'No, seriously, anything you could teach us, anything at all would be much appreciated, and you did say not to hesitate asking you for help.'

'Yeah, but I didn't actually mean training you.'

'You know, Guy's agreed to be a part of the team. He's gonna be teaching us some judo.'

Will's head spun around. 'Guy's involved as well?'

'Yeah. Didn't have to ask a second time, he was straight in there. And as well as judo, we also have Karate, a bit of boxing and maybe some Ninjitsu to throw in the mix. And if we had the benefit of your experience too, that would wrap it up very nicely.'

Will gazed back at the horizon.

'So what do you say, Will, just supervise a few sessions, meet the guys?'

Will sighed. 'I'll think about it, OK?'

Geoff seemed happy with that. He leaped off the sea

wall, and tapped his keys with a sense of accomplishment. 'Come on, I'll give you a lift home.'

CHAPTER 9

The front doors to the Llandudno magistrate's court swished open. A smartly dressed young man, hands in his pockets and chewing gum wandered out on to the pavement. He spotted two of his mates standing over by the railings, and swaggered off to meet them. As he approached them, they waited anxiously to find out how it all went inside the court. The young man gave them a cheeky little wink as if to say sorted, and, relieved, they all dived into a waiting sky-blue car and boomed off down Conway road.

Behind them, close on their trail, was another car, a banged-up Toyota estate, with three occupants sitting inside.

The young man from the court was James Dobson, a nineteen year old thug with a history of convictions ranging from robbery to G.B.H. His most recent court appearance was a charge of assault and battery upon a seventy-five-year-old man.

One night, a couple of months ago, James and his mates, were staggering down a street, all blind drunk, when one of them suddenly possessed the brainy idea to hurl one of their empty lager bottles at someone's front door.

Up until that point, the elderly occupant inside, one Fred Ward, a widower of two years was getting ready to retire to bed. Earlier that evening, Fred was warmed by the long distance phone call from his daughter in New Zealand telling him she was pregnant again. Afterwards, Fred sat in his living room chuffed at the thought of his beloved Laura becoming a mum once again. And how he wished his dearly departed wife Joan had been alive to share the wonderful news with him. Yet deep down he suspected that up there in heaven, or wherever you might end up, she probably knew. However, the thought of Joan on this emotional occasion brought a lump to his throat, and he had to swallow it to pull himself together.

The last couple of years had been very difficult for him, and trying to adjust to being a single person again after living with someone for so long was tough. Especially at night, that was when old Fred would miss his wife the most. Fred's whole body heaved with one mighty sigh, and he jabbed the remote control button to turn off the TV. It was time to turn in. Hauling his old, creaky body out of the armchair, he grunted at the stab of pain from his waking sciatica. That was when he heard the sound of smashing glass at his front door.

Forgetting his crumbling joints, he hobbled to the front door, and snatched it open. Shards of green glass lay scattered on his doorstep, and he just caught sight of the four youths including James Dobson marching off with accomplished cheers.

'Oi!' Fred shouted, storming up his driveway to confront the moronic yobs.

All four of them turned.

'Which one of you just smashed a bloody bottle outside my house?'

Dobson's face contorted into an ugly scowl. 'Yer what? You accusing me of smashing bottles?'

Fred noticed that the other three were still holding theirs. 'So where's yours then?' he asked.

Dobson raised his arms innocently. 'I didn't have one.'

His mates thought this was incredibly funny and choked on their drunken sniggers.

'No, you haven't got one because you just threw it at my bloody front door, didn't you?' Fred insisted.

Dobson became irate again. 'No I didn't, you silly old git. Where's yer proof?'

Fred pointed to the glass at his illuminated doorway. 'There's my bloody proof, mate.'

Seeing that the joke had run its course, one of Dobson's mates tried unsuccessfully to drag him away. But Dobson seethed. 'Naw sod it! I'm not standing for that shit from this old fart.'

Fred could sense trouble now, and not wanting to endanger himself, he thought it best to leave it at that and call the police instead. Dobson, roused by his drunken ego, started towards Fred. Immediately, his mates tried to haul him back, but this only encouraged him even more. Warily, Fred took a step back, his heart beating a bit too fast for a man his age.

Dobson shoved him in the chest. 'What's your problem?'

Fred stumbled back, his weary legs trembling with fear, but still the proud old soldier stood his ground. 'Don't you bloody push me, you little...'

Crack. Fred was blinded by a flash of light and his head was rocked back.

Dobson had head butted him. Yet, it took two or three more blows before poor Fred hit the tarmac flat on his back. The only thing he was aware of now was the star-spangled night sky above, then a large size eleven sole stamped on his face, and the back of his head cracked against the gritty tarmac. For Fred, everything suddenly went calm and serene as if the world had switched into slow-motion. Slowly, sounds and images began to form behind his concussed stupor, and the world began to speed up back to normal.

But when his senses returned, it wasn't the sight of his assailant who was standing over him, but three concerned neighbours, two middle-aged men and a woman with a hand clasped over her mouth in horror. Fortunately, the presence of Fred's neighbours had caused the youths to flee from the scene. One of the men tenderly lifted his head to cushion it with a jacket.

'It's OK, Fred, the paramedics are on their way.'

Lying prostrate on the cold tarmac badly injured, Fred began to sob. But he wasn't crying in pain or for himself, it was for the wife who he missed, his daughter who he couldn't be with and for the sorry depths to which this society had plummeted.

Thankfully, Fred soon recovered from his injuries, and was able to identify his attacker from a list of computer mug shots at the local police station. James Dobson was subsequently charged with assault and battery, but in court, despite his criminal record, all he received was a fine and community service.

Feeling extremely let down by the penal system, Fred had since become a recluse in his own home and now constantly lives in fear of any revenge attacks.

James Dobson sat in the back of the car gloating on his good fortune at the court's verdict, and that evening, he planned a monster binge-drinking session to celebrate. Approaching the corner newsagents at the far end of Craig-Y-Don, he ordered his mate to pull up so he could nip in for a packet of fags.

Moments later, fags in hand, he strutted out of the store back to the waiting motor. As he reached the door handle, Dobson was grabbed from behind in a choke hold and shoved head-first into the front of the car.

'What the hell?' he gasped.

The car sped off up the road, and turned left at the junction where it suddenly stopped.

There in wait stood the banged up estate, and Dobson was swiftly bundled out of one car and into the front of the other. The three occupants with him, the secret vigilantes, were all clad in beanie hats and sunglasses to conceal their identities, then they took off with their hostage. The car, they left abandoned at the side of the road. There was no sign of his mates.

Still held in a tight choke hold, Dobson struggled and gagged. 'Who the hell are you? What do you want?'

A head butt full in the face knocked the batteries out of his voice box. A second butt caused him to fight out in panic. The strangle hold was tightened and a series of short punches beat him into submission.

Dobson tried to shield himself with pleading hands. 'OK, OK, what have I done?'

The punishment ceased for a second, and a pair of sunglasses snarled in his face. 'What have you done? What have you done? So you like beating up old men, do yer?'

A spark of discernment registered in Dobson's eyes, although the rest of his face was reddening up like chopped meat.

'No! No! I was drunk, I didn't mean to.' He choked against the strangle hold.

The attack on him resumed, each new blow coming with a disciplinary reminder. "Feel good does it? Feel good does it? Now you know how Fred felt and all the other innocent people you've battered over the years. All seem worth it now, does it?'

To Dobson, everything was just a blur of white light and thudding pain, it must have been the longest few minutes of his young life.

Finally, the estate pulled up down a quiet road on the outskirts of Craig-Y-Don. The front door was thrown open, and Dobson was shoved out semi-consciously. As he rolled on the pavement the car skidded off with the door flipping shut again.

Dobson lay sprawled on his back, bloodied, battered and finally punished for all the atrocities he had ever committed.

Justice had been served.

*

Later that evening, Will was sitting at his kitchen table, reading back the letter he had just written on lined note paper.

Dear Stacey,

This is probably the only line of communication left open for me now, and will probably be the last time you will hear from me. I am at last beginning to accept that there is very little hope of a future for the two of us. After our last meeting you made that perfectly clear. But before I finally disappear out of your life forever, I feel that I need to come clean about certain things that I have kept from you during the last few years of our relationship. Hopefully after everything has been said you will understand.

All I ask is that you grant me one last visit at my flat 8 o' clock next Friday night. Should you not want to come, you need not reply, and we will simply leave everything where it is and bring final closure to our long standing relationship.

Will.

Will sighed to himself, the importance of what he'd just written weighing heavily on his mind. This was his last chance, one more try. If it didn't work out he would be buying the next train ticket back to Warrington.

Thinking back, through long deliberations with himself when he was in prison and during his training runs when he got out, Will had already entertained the possibility that he may not get back with Stacey. And amid those dark, solitary moments thinking how he might piece his life back together, he began exploring the idea of perhaps opening up his own gym and health spa in Warrington. To him it made perfect sense. He had always been interested in keeping fit, and he knew that in this day and age many other people were taking it up. So what could be better than to start up his own fitness centre. And with the substantial amount of cash he had accrued over the years from his secret work with the organisation, plus his lucrative dabbling in property developing, he would have a very healthy outlay for such a business venture.

Will nodded, satisfied, then awoke from his little pipe dreams. He folded up his letter ready to send in an envelope. Checking the time on his Seiko watch and tapping it to make sure it was still working, he wondered if he should either post it, or deliver it by hand. His conscience told him it would be better to deliver it by hand, that way Stacey would get the letter much quicker, and she might do him the favour of putting him out of his misery much sooner.

Ten minutes or so later, Will silently slid the brown envelope through the metal letterbox at Stacey's hotel. Afraid it might snap shut and give him away, he held open the flap with his finger. Tonight, he didn't even want to be seen let alone be heard. Just deliver the damn letter and leave everything else in the hands of fate. Job done, he leapt back down the flight of steps, and was off like a whippet. To anyone watching it must have looked like he had just delivered a letter bomb.

*

The hollow thuds echoed around the interior of the chemical warehouse, and the odour of body sweat and detergent was thick in the air. It was the second training session for the team, and all were in attendance. Some were working on the focus pads, some were grappling on the rubber scrimmage mats, and the rest were lightly sparring. They even had a heavy duty punching bag hanging from a rope attached to the concrete and steel rafters.

In one corner of the warehouse, Geoff had a giant four foot curved striking pad strapped over his shoulders, and was trying to put a bit of zip into Phil's punches.

'Phil, equal weight on both legs, and turn that hip with the punch, shoulders relaxed.'

Phil snapped out another straight right, whack.

Geoff grimaced, unsatisfied. 'Still not feeling it. It's still just an arm punch.'

Phil blew annoyed with himself. Geoff waved for him to stop, and glanced over at Tom who was practising his jab on the heavy punch bag. Geoff shouted over to get his attention. Tom turned his head and left the bag swinging from one of his punches as he trundled over.

'Show Phil how to put that beast into your punches.'

Tom wiped his nose with the back of his mitt, and laid one into the striking pad. Geoff felt the impact, but as hard as it was, he thought it could have been better. Nodding to himself, he made the decision then and there that they definitely needed to polish up on some technique training.

Yet to be fair this was only their first proper session together, and was viewed only as a feeling-out-getting-to-know everybody workout. Over the next couple of months, Geoff had planned each gathering to concentrate on one specific style at a time. For instance, one week they would isolate the technique of kicking, then another week, punching, grappling, Judo, fighting at close range and long range etc. Geoff even hoped to cover areas such as strategic offence and defence, and just as importantly, weapon attack and defence.

'OK, guys.' Geoff called time on the workout.

Everybody stopped what they were doing, and moved to the centre of the floor. Geoff told them all to take a seat on the rubber mats, and all six bodies flopped down with tired grunts and groans. Geoff towelled his sweaty body down.

'OK, just one more thing before we go, has anyone heard anything more about this Wilkinson gang?'

Charlie spoke up. 'Last week a couple of bouncers spotted two cars parked further up from the wos his name, Boulevards. They only stayed for a few minutes and off they went.'

Geoff chewed his lip as he considered whether it was important or not.

'What about the third one who we didn't get that night, has he shown his face back at the Boulevards yet?'

Tom shook his head. 'Nope, probably knows what he'll get.'

'OK, we still have to stay on standby for now. And if anybody hears anything don't forget to let the team know as soon as possible. And you three – meaning Tom, Mike, and Charlie – 'be especially careful when you finish your shifts just in case they do know who you are. If you need us, send the message, and we'll be there ASAP.'

Tom raised his hand. 'Oh, by the way, Charlie and I might miss the next session because we have to pop down to Liverpool for a bouncer's course.'

Geoff shrugged 'is that it then?'

Guy sheepishly raised his finger.

Geoff gave him the nod.

'You did say under certain circumstances, the team might be available to help vulnerable people unable to fend for themselves.'

'Yes?' Geoff replied.

'Well there's a middle-aged couple a few doors down from me, the McMurphys who are struggling a bit just like everyone in the recession at the moment. Well they went to a loanshark to borrow a few grand, but the greedy bastard put a ridiculous interest rate on the loan, and now he's demanding something like three or four-times the amount in return.'

Everybody looked in amazement, and Tom bristled. 'Why the hell did they agree to something like that in the first place?'

'They were probably desperate, they have their reasons, I suppose. But now this chap and his meatheads are going around to their house trying to intimidate them, threatening to break bones if they don't cough up quick'

'So why don't they just go to the police?' Geoff suggested.

'Because they've been warned that their house will be burned down with them in it, if any there is any police involvement.'

Phil, the off-duty police officer couldn't contain himself any longer. 'Tell them to go to the police straight away, and tell them everything including the threats. Make sure they get it all down in a diary, especially all the visits by this arsehole, the times and dates. He doesn't want them to go to the police because he knows he's breaking the law. I bet this guy is running a consumer credit business without a licence. And if he is he can be done under the Proceeds of Crime act. Or even by the illegal money lending unit.'

Geoff asked. 'So how do you actually know about all this, did you just get talking to him about it in the street or something?'

'My wife Joyce works with the woman.'

'Then tell them to do what Phil has suggested, and if that doesn't work we'll see what we can do.'

Guy nodded obediently.

*

Tom's car was parked down some quiet backstreet on the outskirts of Liverpool. They were sandwiched between the back of a clothes outlet store and an old storage warehouse. Sitting in the car with him, and just as nervous was Charlie in the front and Nigel in the back. Charlie glanced at his watch impatiently. 'They did say, wots his name, three o'clock didn't they? It's gone a quarter past now.'

'They'll be here, don't worry.' Tom replied suddenly spotting a young man exiting the clothes store wearing a black woollen jacket and carrying a blue backpack.

All three of them eyed the man as he approached their car and stop outside Tom's window. Tom quickly wound it down. The man ducked his head inside, he was about early twenties with an untidy mop of brown hair and looked as if he'd been rolled around a sticky barber's floor on his head.

'Alright, mate?' He greeted them in a broad scouse accent, then pulled out a pair of jeans from his coat. 'Couldn't get the levis, but these will do.' He said dropping them on Tom's lap.

'No problem.' Tom replied unfolding the jeans and patting them down until he found a bulge in one of the back pockets. He slipped out a brown envelope and checked that the thick wad of money was inside. Satisfied, Tom reached under the car seat and yanked out a pair of sports trainers and handed them over. Without wasting a moment the lad pushed his hand down the toe-ends of the trainers until he found the soft parcel. Content, he tapped the roof and left. All of them let out a sigh of relief.

'Jobs a good un.' Nigel chirped from the back.

'Yeah, that's if the people who we stole it from never find us.' Charlie fretted.

'Don't worry, it's out of our hands now and we're up fifteen grand.' Tom smiled pleased with himself and started up the car.

Five minutes later, the scouse lad walked through the basement of a multi-storey car park. As he passed a black BMW he tossed the trainers through the open passenger window. In the front seat, a man in his early forties, wearing sunglasses and chewing gum, grinned showing a shiny gold tooth.

CHAPTER 10

The old boxing gym was filled with the sounds of grunts and groans and the smell of dust and sweat was thick in the air. A young man wearing a heavy parka jacket walked over to his associates who were standing watching someone training on the heavy-duty punchbag. The bald man digging vicious body hooks into the punchbag was known as 'Razor'. He was an illegal bare-knuckle fighter, who had won two death matches to date and had another lined up for New Year's Eve. The chap in the parka stood beside the three men watching Razor and waited respectfully for his chance to speak. One of the spectators, a shaved-headed man in his early-forties who had a single gold tooth turned to the men beside him.

'So, what's the story with Morrison?'

'Word is, he hasn't been out that long and they don't think he'll be ready in time Boss.'

Boss, was short for Boss Man and he was the leader of one of the most dangerous drug gangs in Liverpool. He was also an illegal boxing promoter. Boss Man snarled showing his gold molar. 'He better be ready. It's gonna cost me a fortune if we have to call this fight off, unless we can get a replacement and there's fat chance of that now.'

The man with the parka saw his chance. 'Boss, I have some news.'

Boss Man gave him a look that said it better be good news.

'The merchandise we sold to those chaps in North Wales, it is the one that went missing.'

Boss Man, flitted a glance to his companions, a look that confirmed what they had suspected.

'So, they steal our gear and then sell it back to us, cheeky bastards. Check out who our contacts are down that way, we need to find those dead men walking.'

The parka man nodded obediently and slunk off. Boss Man then turned back to Razor on the punchbag and growled at him, 'come one Raze kill that bloody bag.'

Razor, his white T shirt soaked in sweat and looking like a second skin on his flabby body gave him a toothless grin and detonated another big right into the bag with deep humph.

*

Still wearing her dressing gown, Donna McMurphy eased herself on to her couch with a coffee and a fag to watch her favourite TV programme, ITV's *This Morning*. Today was her only day off, all the house work chores had been done, and her husband Norman, who had been made redundant six months ago, was out looking for work.

Donna was forty-six years old, not much to look at now, but in her youth she had been a bit of a looker. Unfortunately, being a heavy smoker all her life, the nicotine had starved her once creamy-smooth skin of its precious oxygen, and had now left it lined and pasty. Her eyes, too, were once bright and sparkling like polished gem stones, but now looked more like eggs in a pickled jar.

Tragically, there didn't seem to be anything in Donna's life at the moment worthy of bringing any luminescence back into those baby blues of hers. The recession was hitting everyone hard, repossessions were reaching an all time high, the cost of living was becoming near impossible. Then you had council tax, and water rates hikes, privatised fuel bills, just basically out-and-out doom and gloom.

However, in Donna's case, the recession seemed to be the least of her problems at the moment. Not so long ago, she had found out that her husband Norman had been hiding a terrible secret from her, he was a compulsive gambler. And during one mammoth betting spree, he had squandered away most of their life savings. In a panic, he had foolishly borrowed cash from a dodgy loan shark to replace the money he had lost, so his wife would never know. But what he didn't expect was the crazy interest rate the lender had put on the loan, and now he was expected to pay back about three times the amount.

Having dug himself so deep in debt, he found himself backed into a corner and couldn't get out. So, Norman had to come clean to his wife, and all hell broke loose. Yet, now, they were unable to meet the exorbitant repayments of the loan. And as a result, their lender was beginning to lean on them quite severely, even resorting to intimidation and blackmail. Donna and her husband were now completely lost and at the end of their tether.

Back in her living room, she took a sup of her sweet coffee, the warmth and the taste momentarily relieving her of the burden of her problems.

The front door bell rang making her pause in mid-sip. The gripping dread stirred in her chest like a serpent waking from its sleep. Surely to God, not him, not now? She fretted. What if I pretended to be out, would he go away? No, probably not she thought. Knowing him he would more than likely wait on the doorstep all day for his money.

She closed her eyes, and took some deep breaths to work up the courage to answer the door. Finally, she climbed off the settee and trudged off as if she was going to the gallows.

When she answered it, she almost cried with relief at the welcoming sight of an attractive young lady standing there. The woman was about early twenties, wearing a chequered coat and jeans, and smiling while she chewed gum. To Donna she looked like Cheryl Cole from the pop group *Girls' Aloud*.

'Hello, would you be Mrs Donna McMurphy?'
'Yes, that's right.'

'My name is Karen White I represent a small group of people who may be in a position to help you with your problem.'

Donna leant curiously against the door's edge. 'Problem?' she questioned.

'Yes, I understand you are being harassed and terrorised by a certain debt collector who you owe money to?'

Donna became concerned. 'Who are you? What...'

'Please don't be alarmed. I'm here to help you.' Karen explained. 'Like I've said, I belong to a group whose main objective is to try and help vulnerable people like yourself who are being hounded and exploited by the criminals of society.'

Donna looked a bit nonplussed.

Karen continued. 'Now I know you're probably thinking that it's none of my business, and how do I know about your predicament, but the fact remains that you don't have anyone else to turn to, do you?'

Donna felt uncomfortable with this. 'I really don't think...'

Karen politely raised her hand to hush her. 'I'm not going to go into the whys and wherefores, all I'm going to say is that if you want this particular loan shark off your back we will do it for you. Obviously for a reasonable fee, of course, but I guarantee that in the long run you'll be saving a lot of money. There's no contract, no extortionate payments, just a one-off fee based on the task that needs to be performed.'

Donna shifted awkwardly from one foot to the other. There was definitely something shifty and sinister about all this, yet on the other hand the thought of having that despicable lender off their backs for good was a very alluring prospect indeed.

'I really need to think about this, and discuss it with my husband. I mean I don't want us to get into any more trouble than we are already. Isn't what you're saying actually illegal?'

Karen smiled shrewdly. 'It's like you've just said, you're

already deep in the you-know-what, so how much worse can it get?'

'I understand that, but there are legal ramifications to what you're saying.'

Karen stopped her again.' Mrs McMurphy, look around you, look at the state society has become because of the so called justice system you and everyone else depends upon. If you honestly think that the law will sort all this out for you, and can protect you from those kind of people, then you don't need us, and we'll be quite happy to wish you good luck.' Karen pinched the lapels of her coat like she was making out to leave.

Donna fidgeted with frustration, she was crying out for the help that was being offered, but still she couldn't find a voice to accept it.

'Listen?' Karen reached into her pocket, and handed her a slip of paper.

'Here's our number! If you change your mind give us a call. Thanks for your time.' She smiled and clacked off in her River Island high heeled shoes.

Donna looked down at the mobile number and leant her head against the frame of the door. She thought long and hard about what the lady had said, and the words law and justice system echoed loudly in her mind.

Would it be worth going to the police after all? What if they were unable to do anything to help her? What if the loan shark got wind of her going the police? Would he seriously carry out the threat of burning down her house? Of course, then it would become a police matter, but by that time it would be too late anyhow. What if this woman, Karen White and her associates were her only chance? Maybe, maybe not?

Indeed, time was running out and Donna was becoming more and more desperate for answers. Thwarted, she closed he eyes and scrunched up the piece of paper wondering what the hell to do.

CHAPTER 11

It was front page news in most of the local newspapers:

"YOBS TARGET ONE STOP STORE."

During the last month, popular West shore mini-store has been plagued by a wave of crimes committed by youths disguised in hoodies. These crimes include damage to the store, thieving stock, and threatening behaviour towards the staff members. As a result, the owner of the shop, Mr A. Jameson now feels great concern for the future of his store and the safety of his staff workers.

'Oh, it's been absolutely terrible! I don't know what's happening to this community anymore. These bloody youths probably aged between 16-17 years old and cloaked in their hoodies just come in and go straight for the boxes of lagers and blatantly try and walk out with them. They don't even attempt to hide what they're doing. And when you confront them, out come the knives and they threaten to cut you. A member of my staff has already been beaten up by a gang of four who he valiantly tried to stop stealing some fags from behind the counter.

'Because of that incident, some of the staff have refused to work because they are too frightened. The other day, I threw one lad of about 12 years old out of my shop for trying to nick some Snicker bars. That evening, I got a brick through one of my poster windows. Obviously, they're all part of the same gang.

When asked about what measures the police had taken to combat this, Mr Jameson conveyed his frustration.

'What a waste of time that is! It takes them at least an hour or so to arrive at my store, and what good is that? As if the little thugs are going to hang around waiting to be caught. And even when they do arrive, all they can do is take a statement and advise me to keep a diary of the incidents. And... oh...yes, don't try and tackle the youths yourself otherwise you might be liable for assault. I might be the one liable for assault. Can you believe that?

'So they seem to be able to get away with smashing up my store, attacking my staff, stealing my stock, and all they get is reported. Yet if I dare to hurt any of them while they're committing any of these crimes, then it's me who will end up in court, not them!

Just further proof that that today's justice system protects the criminals and penalises the victims.'

When this reporter contacted the Llandudno police station to investigate the matter, they issued a statement as follows...

'We take every reported incident very seriously indeed, and together with the assistance of Mr Jameson we aim to resolve this particular problem as soon as possible.'
Copy end.

As for the police getting around to "resolving this particular problem," Mr Jameson decided that he wasn't going to wait that long, and intended on doing a bit of DIY himself.

Friday early evening, the beginning of what many big-drinkers call the weekend booze-up, Mr Jameson was forced to do the late night shift at his shop himself. And the reason for that was because all his staff had now refused to work the weekends because of all the trouble.

Serving the last customer in the store, Mr Jameson was loading some groceries into a plastic bag for some portly gentleman waiting with a fiver in his hand. As he added up the items on the till, Mr Jameson knew in the back of his mind that once the man had left, he would be alone in his store again. After totalling the cost, Jameson took the money off the man, and handed him his change with a polite "thank you." The man grabbed his bag of shopping and marched out of the store. Yet the second the automatic doors had closed behind him, they swished back open for three teens dressed in black parka jackets with the hoods pulled down to hide their faces.

Mr Jameson switched onto red alert.

'Hoods off lads,' he ordered, but they just ignored him, and headed straight for the alcohol aisle, while the third stayed behind to guard the entrance.

Jameson's heart began to race as he eyed them through the convex security mirror at the end of the aisle. All he could hear was a rattling of bottles, then the two lads emerged each holding a pack of six lagers. Realising they had no intention of paying for them, (even if they could prove they were old enough to buy them) Jameson raced from behind the counter to stop them.

'Hold it right there,' he cried, blocking them off, but the third member keeping watch by the door, pulled out a hunting knife.

Jameson's face grew with alarm, and he backed away. The two holding the lagers strode on out of the store, cackling smugly to themselves into the chilly night air. Standing his ground, the knife youth flashed the blade at Jameson menacingly.

'Yeah, and if you say anything else to the police or the papers, we'll cut you up.'

Jameson's fear turned to astonishment at hearing such a threat coming from a child as young as this. Christ he couldn't have been any older than fourteen.

Backing away still brandishing the knife, the youth turned at the door, and fled with his accomplices.

Jameson was rooted to the spot, self preservation preventing him from going after them and getting stabbed, these days anything was possible. Giving it a minute or two, he worked up the courage to have a peep outside, and as he did, he caught sight of the two boxes of lagers stacked neatly against the poster window. Stumped by this, he scratched his head, and while he still had the chance, he reached down and took them back in, half expecting at any second for the youths to dash around the corner and jump him. When this didn't happen, he stood in the doorway doubly confused, and moaned to himself that there wasn't much point in phoning the police now.

About a mile away, inside the dark interior of the van, the three young offenders from the store, sat wide-eyed like frightened kittens stuffed in a cardboard box. Sitting on guard eyeing them as a potential late supper were two panting Rottweiler dogs. Holding on to their leads was a man in a balaclava, and in the front of the van were two other disguised men. For now their destination was a secret.

'Let us go,' cried the oldest member of the teen gang, a tall hook-nosed kid. 'My dad's gonna kill you when he gets hold of you.'

Beneath the black balaclava, a creepy little voice spoke. 'I really don't think so.'

The middle-oldest of the trio, a chubby-faced brat sounded like he was going to cry.

'What do you want? You better let us go.'

Their captor didn't answer them, but stared coldly back at them. The thought of what he was planning to do to them only adding to their fears.

Eventually, the van came to a stop, the location unknown, but outside it was complete blackness.

The youngest of the trio began to sniffle, the strain of what might happen to them becoming too much too bear. Balaclava flicked on the open door light, and shifted into a more comfortable position.

'Boys I want you to meet Jake and Tyson. Jake and Tyson haven't eaten all day, and believe me they have a very big appetite. At the moment, all their thinking about is meat. Warm meat, cold meat, any meat, and because I love my dogs to bits, I have to make sure they get fed.'

The sniffles of the youngest member grew into hiccups of panic, while the older two bravely clung on for now.

'This recession is killing me, honestly,' Balaclava told them. 'And I'm finding it extremely difficult to find money to buy food for my babies here.' He patted their bony skulls, and they stopped panting to sniff their master's hand.

'You see, boys, this is the only way I can feed my pets.'

'Bollocks,' Hook-nosed kid raged. 'There's no way you're gonna feed us to them.'

'Why not? You're just a couple of nobody's going around stealing and terrorising people, who's going to care?'

'Our parents, and our friends.'

'Really? Well, let's just say that amounts to a dozen or so people that you already know. But what about the rest of the town, who else is going to care about a few naughty kids who were only known for beating up innocent people, stealing, and threatening them with knives? I think most of them would say good riddance. I know I would.'

'Bugger off!' The oldest one called his bluff.

Balaclava turned to his dogs, who up until now had sat there very controlled, very calm, and well behaved. He began making little whistling sounds to them and the two dogs, reacted with guttural snarls and growls. He continued to wind them up until he had got them into a frenzy. They frothed at the mouth and bared their teeth, their eyes blazing like the devils. The three kids tried to flinch from the animals, and back as far away as they could against the rear doors. Balaclava simmered them down again, and showed the kids the lead he was holding.

'Now if I let go of this, there will be no stopping what these two will do.'

'You wouldn't dare,' said Hook-nose.

'Shut up.' Chubby shoved him in the arm.

Balaclava set his dogs at ease. 'Right, the only thing that is going to stop me from leaving you three alone in here with Jake and Tyson is your names and addresses, plus the names and addresses of everyone in your little gang.'

Balaclava tapped the arm of his accomplice sitting in the front who passed him over a mobile phone. He held it up to the youths ready to take their photographs. 'Say cheese, and don't any of you dare to try and hide your faces or I'll get my dogs to rip your arms off, and then we'll start again.'

All three of them sat there like frightened lambs going to the slaughter, and Balaclava clicked the photo button sending out a flash of light.

'By the way, should the info you give me turn out to be false, the police will have these pictures anyhow, so they'll be able to track you down. And, urm, I'm going to keep the hunting knife as a souvenir, besides you're too young to be playing about with knives.' He tapped his jacket pocket where he put the knife securely. 'Last but not least, if we hear of any of you lot letting so much as fart off anywhere near that store I swear to you, you're dog food. We'll get you, even if we have to break into your house at night. So watch out.'

The three kids sat there with billiard ball eyes not even making a whimper.

Balaclava pulled out a small note pad and pen. 'Right then, who's first?'

*

The next morning, winter sunshine filtered through a blanket of clouds as a young lady in high heels and a chequered jacket clacked into the one-stop store. Under her arm she carried an A4 sized envelope, and she waited for Jameson to finish serving an old lady with a terrier in tow. As the old woman passed her on the way out, the young lady gave her a chewing gum smile, and clacked over to Jameson. The package she was carrying was placed on the counter, in front of him.

'The names and addresses you required, plus identification photographs of the culprits,' she said.

Jameson took out a bulky envelope from his own pocket, and handed it over to the young lady. Discreetly, she slipped it inside her coat, and flashed him a grateful smile. 'You shouldn't have any more trouble, but if you do, you have our number.' She nodded and turned to leave.

'Thanks very much,' Jameson said in return, and watched her clack back out of the store.

Once she had gone, he stood there musing until another customer approached the counter. With renewed enthusiasm, Jameson gave him a big, happy smile.

*

Relaxing, in front of his 32 inch screen TV Tom took in an increasingly bored sigh and sank even deeper into the couch. Just as he was about to flip over the channel to relieve himself of the torture of listening to some whinging teenager on the *Jeremy Kyle Show* in walked Karen White, his girlfriend.

'Hi, hun?' She sighed dropping the bulky envelope onto the seat next to him and breezing through to the bedroom.

'He paid-up alright then?' Tom asked, not even bothering to take his eyes off the TV.

Karen's voice sounded muffled coming from the bedroom. 'Yeah, no problem, I told him if he gets anymore hassle from those kids he's to get in touch. He already has our number.'

Satisfied with that, Tom lay his hand flat on the envelope as if he expected it to try and escape from him. Thinking to himself, he began to realise that this secret vigilante service with his accomplices, Charlie and Nigel was proving to be a good little earner. Even more so, now they were going to get extra help from another close friend and colleague. Tom huffed to himself at the irony, never thought in a million years that *he* would want to get involved, Geoff would go bananas if he ever found out. Tom was especially glad that he'd got his girlfriend, Karen in on it too. She had always possessed a no-nonsense, go-getting approach when it came to money. Either that or she was just a gold digger. But, that aside, she was perfect as their debt-collecting representative. Karen then reappeared in her pink-towelled dressing gown and went to plonk herself on the settee next to Tom. Tom quickly yanked away the envelope before she sat on it and watched as she aimed the remote control at the TV.

'What do you think you're doing?'

'Repeat of *Home And Away* is on.'

That was it, Tom grabbed his envelope and leapt to his feet, he knew it was a waste of time arguing with her over the TV. He would have more success at cutting off one of her fingers than he would at changing the channels while one of those dreaded soap-operas were on. As he lumbered off to the bedroom he heard her mutter after him, 'don't forget my split.'

'Bloody gold digger.' He shook his head.

*

It was the beginning of December, the countdown to Christmas had begun, and with the start of this festive month there was the usual expectant tinge of goodwill in the air. Except that is, if you were a police officer on route to a bit of a domestic fifteen minutes before your shift was due to finish. It was 7.46pm and Phil, hissed at his bad luck and began moaning that he probably wouldn't get back home now till at least nine.

Beside him in the patrol car was PC Davies, a 27-year-

105

old woman from South Wales, whose eye-catching features closely resembled the singer *Danni Minogue*. PC Davies yawned. 'Hope we can wrap this one up quickly, and then go home. My bloody feet are killing me.'

Phil took in a lungful of air. 'Just be our luck if it turns into an all-night siege.'

PC Davies rolled her eyes at him, and made a call to the control centre to let them know they were arriving at their destination.

'Seagrove apartments, this is it,' Phil alerted his colleague, and stopped outside. Both officers disembarked and marched up the footpath to the old three-storey house that had been converted into one-bedroom flats.

They stood outside the apartments in their standard police officer kit, which consisted of a stab vest and duty belt containing a radio, speed-cuffs, an ASP extendable baton, and incapacitating CS spray.

Phil tried the main entrance door, it was unlocked so they entered. Inside, the dank odour of decaying wallpaper and decrepit carpets almost made them want to sneeze. In front of them was a dimly lit hall and stairway leading up to the other floors. SMASH! From above, they heard what sounded like a wardrobe crashing to the floor, accompanied by shouting and wailing.

Immediately, the officers leapt into action, and tore up the stairs, adrenalin surging through their bodies. On the second floor, a young couple from one of the rooms stood in the hallway, alarmed and concerned they pointed towards number 8.

'It's been going on for hours now,' the fleshy young woman told them.

Behind the door, they could hear a man yelling at the top of his voice. The officers sensed danger. Phil's heart thumped at the thought of a physical confrontation as he banged on the door with the palm of his hand.

'Sir, Sir, this is police, open the door.'

Either the order hadn't been heard, or was simply

ignored, but the shouting continued.

Again, Phil pounded on the door, and repeated the command. This time the yelling ceased, and a woman could be heard whimpering. Phil glanced at PC Davies and saw apprehension in her eyes, but nevertheless duty called and she took over. He knew that in these type of situations a female voice can be found to have quite a calming effect on a raging maniac.

'Sir, can you please open the door?'

In the room the man growled at his woman. 'You see? You see what you've caused now, you silly cow?'

PC Davies repeated her request, and they could hear the sounds of shuffling, accompanied by the man snarling "don't you dare open that door." There followed the sound of a vicious clout, and the woman shrieked in pain.

Phil took over again, while PC Davies radioed for back up just in case.

'Open the door or we're going to break it down.'

They listened for any response and it sounded like the woman was making another attempt to let them in. Unfortunately for her, this seemed to spark off one more brutal attack. In the room, they could hear the woman yelping like a tortured animal, and it seemed to Phil that she was being pinned to the door. The force of the blows she received rocked the sturdy oak against the lock and frame. And the rhythmic thumping they heard was evidently her head bouncing off the door. The vicious bastard must be booting the shit out of her, Phil thought to himself.

Fearing for the woman's safety he decided that he couldn't wait for back up, he had to do something now. He nodded to PC Davies as a signal to ready herself, and they both felt their teak batons. Phil took a step back, lining himself up to kick down the door. In his mind he could hear Geoff's instructions on how to execute the front kick correctly. Bring your knee up, push your hip through, arch your back.

Phil slammed his foot into the door, which sounded like a cannon being fired. It didn't budge, so he tried again, and this time the lock snapped open.

But with the added weight of the woman slumped behind it, both officers had to heave their way through. Inside the room which reeked of spliff smoke, the ponytail man in a white vest was still beating his girl, oblivious of the two officers. He just managed to get in one last boot to the side of her head which sounded like banging two football boots together. Enraged by this, Phil went straight for a rear choke hold using his baton to apply the pressure. The man evidently under the influence of drugs, roared and struggled like a wild animal. He backed Phil up, and slammed him into the far wall. Phil felt the wind crash out of his body, and his grip weakened. The man seized the baton wedged to his throat and a battle of strengths ensued. However, PC Davies saw her chance and began hacking at the man's legs and knees to try and disable him, but he seemed impervious to the pain.

Desperately, he kicked out at PC Davies trying to make it harder for her to get in her blows. This diversion gave Phil the chance to re-establish his grip on the choke hold and finally the two officers began to overpower the raging lunatic. Gasping for breath, the man dropped down to his knees, Phil continued with the pressure, while PC Davies put down her baton to reach for the speedcuffs. However, by the time her hand got anywhere near them, she was clunked repeatedly with her own baton.

The woman who they were trying to protect had picked up the baton and like a screaming witch, she let fly at PC Davies catching her across the forehead with sickening whacks. PC Davies reeled away and tried as best as she could to defend herself. Concerned for his colleague, Phil had no alternative but to release the man, so he could help her. Seeing his chance, the man thought only of himself and bolted off like whippet. He was out of the door before Phil even had the chance to react. Furiously, Phil grabbed hold of the woman and swung her into a disabling arm lock, forcing her to drop the baton. Incensed by the woman's ingratitude, the two officers now treated her like any other criminal and slammed her down to the ground. Phil, using one knee to secure her, quickly handcuffed her.

'You OK, Mandy?' he called to his fellow officer who dropped on to the easy chair, nursing her battered head.

She nodded back, but the trickle of blood running over her face indicated to Phil that she may need some first aid. After radioing for the paramedics, Phil stood up leaving the woman face down and sobbing into the carpet.

'Mandy, keep an eye on her I'm going have a look for him,' he told her and she nodded an OK.

Darting out on to the landing, he passed the young couple who had stood watching the whole time and hadn't lifted a finger to help. Phil felt like saying to them thanks for your help, but couldn't be bothered. Yet as he ambled down the flight of stairs he heard the man shout down to him "he went straight out of the front door."

You don't say, Phil muttered under his breath as he reached the ground floor and burst through the entrance. He sprinted down the footpath and reached the main road. He stopped, chest heaving in and out, and scanned the entire street, but couldn't see anything.

His breaths started to slow, and he hissed with frustration just as the wailing sounds of back up arrived.

CHAPTER 12

Down at the local gym, Will was finishing off his workout with a couple of rounds of skipping, when he was interrupted by the sound of his phone beeping. Determined to finish off his set, he ignored it until he was finished, then hung the rope back on its nail and sat down on one of the weight training benches. Pulling out his phone he saw the text received symbol, and his first thought was that it might be from Stacey? If so this could be the moment of truth. Before reading the message, he sniffed the air to prepare himself then opened the text message.

REQUEST GRANTED, WILL BE THER @ 8 ON FRI – STACEY.

It was from *her*, and it wasn't a rejection, thank God. Will looked up and managed half a smile. To say he was pleasantly surprised was an understatement. God bless the unpredictability of a woman's mind, he muttered to himself. Inspired by the news, he began texting back without even thinking properly what he wanted to say.

GREAT! HOW ABOUT WE DISCUSS IT OVER A MEAL – MY SHOUT – NO STRINGS?

He sent the message back and waited. Beep, beep, came the reply, and it was a simple OK. Not wanting to push his luck anymore, Will left it at that, wishing that he could end every workout on such a high.

However, on his way back home to his flat, the froth on his bottle began to settle, and he realised that despite the encouraging news, it was still only a foothold on a precipice. There simply wasn't any point in getting carried away with any romantic thoughts of a dream reunion, kiss and make up and all that.

This just wasn't going to happen. In fact the truth, the whole truth may actually send her even further away. Hence, the main reason he had kept it all from her in the first place.

Will pulled down the edges of his beanie hat and told himself to keep up his defences, prepare for the worst, and anything else would be a bonus.

*

Friday night, 7.51pm, Will paced about in his flat like a caged lion. Everything had been set, he had booked a table for two in the Italian restaurant around the corner. He had even made the effort of throwing on something half decent to wear which for him certainly was an accomplishment. Yet to him, the most terrifying aspect of the evening was the fact that this was probably his last chance at Stacey. And the only glimmer of hope he had of maybe pulling this thing off was to try and make Stacey somehow understand about his darkened past, and why he had to do the things he did. And just as importantly the fact that he certainly wasn't the person she had made him out to be.

Will furtively peeped through the side of the window to see if there was any sign of her. Would she walk? Would she taxi? Would she be driving herself? Should he have gone to pick her up himself? It was driving him mad. He checked his watch, it had stopped at 7.52. Will prayed that, that wasn't a bad omen.

Outside his flat, a white taxi pulled up and he saw Stacey lean over to pay the driver. Will's heart bounced up into his throat and he took a few composing breaths as if he was about to begin the ring walk for one of his mixed martial arts fights. On his way to the front door to greet her, he wondered why she had gone to the trouble of getting a taxi when she only lived a stone's throw away.

Will opened the door and was treated to a dolled-up version of Stacey. The smart conservative clothes, the make-up – the works. Seeing her in make-up again reminded him why he had gone to so much trouble in trying to win her back. Somehow a touch of woman paint always seemed to give her a smoother more seductive appearance, but deep in those delicious brown eyes there was also poison, the clear warning sign, look but don't touch. Like lying in a hospital bed and knowing that the only interest the obliging sexy nurse had in you was getting a urine sample to test if you had diabetes.

Will felt flattered that Stacey had made such an effort for him, and to show his gratitude, he could have picked her up in his arms there and then.

However, her steely defensive look soon reminded him of the task at hand, so he tried the friendly approach. 'Alright?'

'Yeah, great, shall we go?' She said clacking her way back down the concrete steps.

High heels, ankle breakers, perhaps that's why she got a taxi for such a short distance, he pondered. The walk up Chapel Street and around the corner to the Italian restaurant was mainly filled with polite conversation. Purposely, they avoided the main topic until later, or when the time was right for discussing all the nitty-gritty.

In the restaurant itself they placed their coats and jackets over the shoulders of the chairs and sat down to look over the menu. While Stacey was musing over hers, Will stole a quick peep at her over the rim of his menu board. To him it was clear she was trying very hard to keep her composure. Soon the young waitress arrived to take their orders, and they both made their choices.

Gratefully, the waitress took back their menus, and asked if they would like a drink while they waited for their meal. Both of them opted for a glass of red wine.

As soon as they were alone again, Will glanced concisely about the room half filled with murmuring folk, then turned back to Stacey who had her eyes firmly trained on him. Will placed his elbows on the table and balled his hands under his chin as if he needed the support to make his confession. Stacey glanced at Will's Seiko watch.

Will spoke in a soft tone so only she could hear him. 'Stacey remember when we first started dating I told you that I was into property developing, and a bit of entrepreneuring?'

Stacey eyed him warily.

Will continued. 'Well that was true, but it wasn't the only thing I was involved in. The work or the job I actually did included a much higher level of commitment, loyalty, and working many unsociable hours.' He shifted forward in his seat. 'I actually did a lot of work for a Serious and Organised Crime Agency.'

Stacey frowned incredulously.

'Its main purpose was to tackle serious organised crime and the supply and distribution of drugs. I was one of the back-up team members who used to mind and protect the agents on raids, very dangerous indeed.'

Stacey snorted. 'So what you're trying to tell me is that you were some sort of secret agent?'

'No, nothing like that, I had nothing to do with investigating and the planning of these raids, we were just the hired muscle.'

'Oh, yeah, and how in the hell did you manage to train for something like that then?'

'It was because of my martial arts skills, my fighting skills. I had built up a bit of a rep as a mixed martial arts fighter, and someone thought those attributes might be better used to help with this agency. OK, we had a basic training in weapons, and procedures, but in the end we were just like their minders, or bodyguards. There were about twelve of us all together, and we were split into two or three groups and used for separate raids.'

Stacey wasn't having any of it and looked on with utter scepticism.

'I mean it wasn't just martial artists like myself, they were ex-minders, ex-boxers, combat and weapon specialists. We had all been carefully selected and trained to go out with the agents, do the job, and get paid....' Will stopped talking as the waitress arrived with their orders which were placed in front of them.

Both Stacey and Will said their thanks, and the waitress left them to it.

Will continued. 'Once a month, sometimes twice but very rarely, we would get the call, and be picked up, and off we'd go.'

Stacey picked quietly at her plate of tagliatelle.

'In all I worked for them for about six years, but when two of my mates were killed, I decided I wanted out. One was killed in a raid, and the other at home, somehow one of the drug gangs found out who he was and where he lived. That's why I couldn't risk telling you. If any those gangs had found out who I was, they might have come for you first. But after my mates died, I wanted to get out, and then you came along, and I knew I had to get out for the both of us. But then that thing happened with Georgie and the thugs, and I went to prison. And that seemed to solve the problem, because it got me out of the agency straight away.'

Stacey looked at him as if he was crazy. 'You don't honestly expect me to believe all that do you?'

'Stacey, it's true.'

'Aw, c'mon, Will.' She raised her voice then remembered where she was. 'It's a bit far fetched isn't it? I mean what kind of mug do you take me for?'

Will hissed back at her. 'Well you wanted to know the truth, didn't you?'

'Yeah the truth, not that load of tosh.'

Will was irked by her cynicism. 'Would you prefer if I made something up for you instead? Would that make you feel better?'

Stacey munched angrily on her pasta. 'That's quite a story, with an imagination like that you should become a writer.'

Will supped on his wine while she got it off her chest.

'You've had a good three years to dream up a whopper like that,' she said, in between mouthfuls of creamy pasta shells. 'If you'd have said to me, look, Stacey, I messed up, I had a few affairs on the side. I got another woman pregnant. I even used to visit brothels and dress up as a woman at the weekends, I could have accepted that. Maybe I wouldn't have forgiven it or even understood it, but at least I could have had the chance to deal with it in my own way.' She stopped eating and calmed herself down. 'Will, I'm not a stupid person, and for you to bring me here with the bare-faced audacity of trying to fool me into falling for such an over-imaginative, self-deluding excuse as that, you must be thinking a hell of a lot less of me than I ever thought.'

With that, she dropped her knife and fork on the plate with a loud clatter, and stood up. Will watched her grab her coat from the back of the chair.

'What are you doing?'

'This meal is over!' She glared down at him, and stormed off, drawing one or two inquisitive looks from the other diners.

Trying not to show his embarrassment, Will quickly followed her. Although, by the time he had sorted the bill out and exited the restaurant, Stacey was already across the road and heading back to her hotel on the prom.

Will shook his head, and jogged off to catch her up. When he reached her, he told her to stop but she ignored him and kept going. Not wanting to make a fool of himself he slowed down to a fast walk until he got in front of her. Then he blocked her path and fumed.

'Now look, Stacey, I'm not going to chase you any more, I've had enough of this. Now you either talk to me right now or I'm off for good. I'm not going to let you walk away from me any more. You've got two choices. We can walk and talk this thing out right now, or you can go straight home and you'll never see me again, I promise you that! Now what's it going to be?' He stood aside giving her the option.

She glared at the open space in front of her, then turned to him, her taut, thunderous expression beginning to weaken.

Five minutes later, they were both sitting on one of the promenade benches by the railing wall. Both of them gazed out towards a horizon that was so dark, there didn't seem to be any line between the sky and the sea.

Will was the first to speak. 'I don't know, Stacey, it looks very much to me like you wanted me to say I'd been seeing other women as if that gave you the excuse that you were looking for.'

Stacey sat with her hands stuffed broodingly in her pockets and lapels pulled right up. Then she spoke.

'When I was ten years old my father had an affair with another woman. And during that time, I watched my mother fall apart. Even though my father didn't suspect that my mother and I knew about what was going on, we watched him week after week following the same pattern. Each time, he would come up with excuse after excuse to cover up his infidelity.

What a complete fool he made of my mum. Yet, still, she kept the place going, running smoothly, efficiently. Sometimes, she would talk to me about the affair and break down, and when he came back home, she made me promise not to say a word about it to him or anyone. You see, she was so scared of losing him, and worried sick of seeing her only child's home fall apart, that she thought it was worth keeping quiet and putting up with it.' Stacey's head rocked bitterly.

'From that day on, I swore to myself that if I ever met someone, I would never allow them to do to me what my father had done to my mother.'

Will looked over and said meekly. 'I didn't know all that.'

'That's because I've never told anyone, I made a promise. Even to this day my father doesn't know that we knew all about his little secret all those years ago.'

'So what happened to the affair, did it just fizzle out?'

'Yeah, it came and went alright, and things went back to way they were before. But it took me years before I could ever trust my father again. It took years to be able to sleep soundly at night without worrying if some other woman would ever try and take my father away from us.'

Will didn't know what to say, he tried to think of something supportive but couldn't, so instead he just gave her a moment to herself. Yet, deep inside him, the question he had been burning to ask just seemed to pop out all by itself.

'I heard you were seeing someone else.'

For a second Stacey didn't reply, and he thought he'd put his foot in it, then her lips parted. 'Just a friend that's all. Except that he wanted more than I was willing to give.'

Will was content that that was out of the way, now he could move on. 'There's nothing you can do to change the past you know, Stacey? What is done, is done. And getting back to us, I know we had plans and all that. I know we had everything mapped out ready, but things don't always go to plan. That's part of life and instead of coming to a dead stop and giving up, you just have to re-route yourself, and carry on.

In prison, all I thought about was how I could get back with you. That's the only thing that kept me going. That was my light at the end of the tunnel.'

Will waited for a response, but didn't get one, so he continued...

'I know you find it difficult to understand my past, and the things I had to do to make a living, but that is all in the past now.'

'Yeah, but like I've said it was a bit hard to take in all that stuff about you working for an Organised Crime Agency.' Stacey huffed.

'Yeah, well, believe me, Stacey, it was no wonderland, I still get nightmares about some of the things I saw and had to do. If I had the choice to go back ten years, there's no way I would have gone through with it. I know some of the guys I worked with have had to have counselling. You really wouldn't believe some of the things people do, desperate people, people hooked on drugs and what they're capable of doing. They will stab you, kill you, even eat you to get at the things they need. It's a very scary world out there, you know, Stacey.'

Will went quiet for a moment, sombre. 'Have you ever seen an eight-year-old girl drug addict? A girl who has been injected with so much drugs to keep her quiet and unresponsive to the hands of a paedophile?'

Stacey glared at him, repulsed.

'Do you know the sounds she makes when the drugs hits her eight-year-old undeveloped brain? She makes a clicking sound like water dripping from a tap. Her little body convulses like an animal that has just been run over by a car.

Lying there, she looks like a brain damaged old dog that nobody wants or cares about. And every now and again, as her baby body is ravaged by the drugs and the grubby hands of that scum, she asks for mummy, and clutches that teddy bear's arm as tight as she can.'

Will lost his voice and had to turn away from her, his fist clenched into a white ball by his side, it took every bit of strength he had not to cry out with volcanic fury.

'Jesus, that's terrib...' Stacey couldn't even finish the word, but she dared to ask. 'What happened to her?

Will waited for the storm inside him to subside, then answered her. 'She died.'

For a while they sat in silence, both of them mourning for a child they had never known. Both of them feeling guilty for their own petty arguing until finally Stacey decided it was time to call it an evening. Courteously, Will walked her back to her hotel, and as they stopped to say their goodnights, he had to ask the million dollar question.

'So what do we do now Stacey? Is this goodnight, or goodbye?'

Stacey lowered her head. 'I don't know, Will. I honestly don't know what I want at the moment. I have so much that I need to absorb I...'

Words seemed to fail her, so Will took over.

'Stacey, I've waited for three long years for you, I can't wait any longer. I'd much rather you tell me now than have to wait another week just to hear you say that there will never be another chance for us.'

'I know, I understand that, but I just can't make a final decision like that tonight, not with all these things going around in my head. Just give me a couple more days to put all this into some kind of perspective. Surely if you've waited this long, a few more days aren't going to make any difference.'

For Will, he had no choice, he had to accept her request. Disheartened and frustrated, he watched her begin climbing the steps to her hotel, then stop at the front door.

'Will, the watch I bought you on holiday all those years ago, I thought it had broken. Why are you still wearing it? Why haven't you gotten a new one?'

Will flicked a look at the tired-looking contraption and simply shrugged.

'I don't know.'

Stacey stood there for a moment, then uttered a final goodnight before disappearing indoors. Will waited until the door had shut, then he left.

CHAPTER 13

Fifty-four-year-old Roy Evans lumbered up Marl Drive road in the Llandudno junction. He'd just spent the last half an hour in the labour club around the corner in deep negotiations with a good looking brunette. A price had been agreed, and a service was booked, but the assistance he required had nothing to do with anything seedy. The duty he was paying for would indeed be of a physical nature, but that was where the similarities ended.

Roy tugged on the filter of his Benson and Hedges, the thick cigarette smoke rolling out of his mouth like a long white tongue, and then being sucked back in again. He took another drag as if to try and ease his troubled conscience. Was he doing the right thing? Was he right to go along with it? Would it right the wrong that had been committed?

Yet, why should he be feeling this guilt now right, why these second thoughts, why the hesitancy? Four years ago, he would have used up all of his life savings to be granted this opportunity. Roy stopped in his tracks, as if ready to steel himself against a tidal wave of suppressed memories and emotions that were about to crash over him.

*

Four years ago, one Friday night, his son Reggie, a regular fast-cars, girl-shagging, normal-hormonal eighteen-year-old was out on his usual weekend booze-up. Towards the end of the evening, Reggie and his girlfriend staggered glassy-eyed into the Chinese chippy for a battered cod and chip supper on the way home.

As they amused themselves waiting for their order,

three tanked-up gorillas also wanting to satisfy the munchies, jostled vocally through the entrance door. Not wanting to get in their way, Reggie and his girlfriend stowed themselves away in the corner of the chippy.

With gruff voices from shouting all night, and reeking of Armani after shave, the three white shirted youths growled out their orders to the two petite Chinese girls behind the counter.

Hearing their loud drunken slurs, the Chinese girls furtively rolled their eyes at each other as if it was that crazy time of the night again. Beware of the wide-eyed morons. Nevertheless they nodded obediently as that was their nature, and got on with the orders. However, the inebriated trio still needed something to occupy their tiny minds while they waited for their meal. And like foxes to a farmyard it didn't take long for the juicy behind of Reggie's girl to grab their attentions.

The ugliest, and most depraved member of three gave the nod to his mates.

'Lovely bit of mackerel there.'

'Don't forget the salt and vinegar,' another one added and they all fell about wheezing in hysterics.

Reggie turned to his girl and told her to ignore them, then whispered deridingly that no girl would ever bother with three cheese dicks like them anyway. Reggie's girl gave a little chuckle which seemed to irritate Ugly Boy as if he sensed her derision, and he was quick to react.

'Hey, luv, I can't afford to buy fish tonight, so can I get some cheap cod by getting you to sit on my face?'

His two mates doubled over, thinking, oh what a riot their mate was.

Reggie's girl eyed him as if he was a lump of shit and told him to piss off.

'Piss off to you too, you slag.' Ugly Boy spat back.

Now they had gone too far and Reggie intervened. 'Hey don't call my girlfriend a slag.'

Ugly Boy tore his hands out of his pockets to show his

balled fists. 'Oh, yeah, and what are you gonna do about it?'

Reggie aimed a fuming finger. 'That's out of order!'

Ugly Boy and his pals began to edge closer, and sensing danger Reggie's girl stood in front of him to keep them apart.

Still feeling cocky and wanting to impress his mates, Ugly Boy stuck out his chest, but his Neanderthal forehead seemed to stick out even further. 'Think you're rock, do yer?'

'No trouble, no trouble,' one of the Chinese girls waved in alarm.

True, Reggie was scared but he wasn't going to show it in front of his girlfriend, so he tried to put on a bit of bravado. He moved her aside and confronted the yobs. 'Look, just get yer chips and do one will ya?' he cried, but the youths closed the gap until there was only Reggie's girl separating them all.

With his two mates beside him like two testicles supporting a penis, Ugly Boy wanted his pound of flesh. 'You wanna have a go, do yer?'

'NO TROUBLE!' the Chinese girl yelled again.

In desperation, Reggie's girl tried to haul him out of danger, but Reggie yanked himself free. He still wanted to stand up for himself.

'C'mon then, you want to try it?' Ugly Boy poked him in the chest, and Reggie's girl tried to wedge herself in between them, but got caught up in the jostling. Seconds later the fists started flying, and in the melee', she was sent tumbling to the ground. Reggie tried his best to fend off his three attackers, but it was simply too much for him, and he caught a swinging right hand to the side of the head staggering him. But it was the second paralysing blow, which put him down, and that's when they overpowered him. The three piled on top of him, raining kicks and knees into his head and body.

Reggie's girl screamed for them to stop, but it was like

shouting into a storm, as they pinned him against the bottom metal panel of the counter.

Meanwhile, one of the Chinese girls disappeared into the back to call the police, leaving the other standing at a safe distance behind the counter. Even where she was standing she could hear Reggie's head bouncing off the metal panel. All Reggie could do was curl into a foetal position, and pray they would soon stop. However, the sickening assault continued as Ugly Boy took a step back and kicked his head like a football which slammed against the counter panel with a deafening clang. It sounded like someone smashing it with a sledgehammer. Yet, it didn't stop there! Not fulfilled by the beating he had meted out already, Ugly Boy took to the air like he was jumping into a swimming pool, and landed both feet on the side of Reggie's head. Again, he did this, and Reggie's head split open, blood pouring over the hard tiled floor and pooling from the gaping wounds over his temples.

Fearing for her boyfriend's life now, Reggie's girl dived on top of him to try and prevent anymore damage being inflicted.

Finally, the three yobs had spent their fury and fled the chippy without their orders, leaving Reggie's girl sobbing hysterically over her boyfriend's limp body.

Reggie Evans was rushed to hospital with severe head trauma and had to undergo an emergency operation to remove blood clots and reduce swelling of the brain. After his operation, the surgeon had to put him in a coma-induced state to give his brain the chance to recover.

For three and a half weeks it was touch and go, but at last, Reggie started to show signs of improvements, and eventually he did pull through.

However, the severity of his injuries left him with irreversible brain damage which resulted in slurred speech and frequent memory loss. But at least he was still alive.

The perpetrator of Reggie's near-fatal injuries, Ugly Boy, a.k.a. one Jonathan Morris was arrested a week after the incident, and later convicted in court of grievous bodily harm with intent. He was sentenced to six years imprisonment, but released after three and a half due to good behaviour. Justice served, indeed.

*

The Wetherspoons pub stood at the bottom of Gloddaeth Avenue just off the north promenade. The enormous size of the building was due to the fact that it used to be subdivided for a cinema and bingo hall called the Palladium that was originally built in 1920.

Back in the 1999, it was bought by the Wetherspoons corporation and the whole building had to undergo major repairs and restorations in order to convert it into a public house. However, homage was paid to the old Palladium by retaining some of the decor. Still in place were the viewing galleries that flanked the stage, and inside they had put cardboard cut-outs of Edwardian dignitaries. And overlooking the main bar area, they even kept the upper cinema's circle, complete with the flip-top seats.

Inside the grand bar room, and celebrating his early release from prison, Jonathan Morris and company were sitting around one of the beer tables near the dining area. Morris had only been out of prison one week, and he delighted in regaling to his mates about how easy it had been doing the three-and-a-half year stretch inside. However, what he failed to include in his account was that on the first night he was locked up alone in his cell, he broke down and cried like a baby.

Draining his pint of Foster's, Morris stood up and claimed the next round, his treat to his loyal mates, who all cheered loudly. Threading through the hordes of drinkers, he finally made it to the bar, and waited to catch the young bar man's eye. But it was his eye that was caught when a stunning blonde girl turned to him at the bar, and he soon forgot about the drinks. Standing there in front of him, she had the look of a Play-Boy mansion bunny, with a bursting cleavage just dying to leap out and say catch me. Morris's jaw nearly hit the floor, no subtlety, no tact, no cool charm, he just salivated right in front of her. The woman read him straight away, and flashed that 'I like you too' smile right back at him. Morris let his eyes off the leach and licked his lips.

'So do you wanna drink?' he asked.

'Yes I do,' she purred. 'I've been watching you all night just waiting to get you away from your mates.'

Morris looked dumbfounded. Was this for real? Whatever, he couldn't wait to show his mates what he'd pulled. And he had only been out on the town for about an hour too, not bad.

'So do you want to join me and my mates at our table then or what?'

The woman inched closer, her come-and-get-me eyes, and the whiff of her *Gucci Envy Me* perfume causing a twitch in his trousers.

'I'm afraid I don't do groups, but I do a very good one on one,' she panted.

Morris's face scrunched painfully. 'I just can't leave my mates, not tonight.'

She leant a bit closer. 'Tell you what then, meet me in the Cottage Loaf around the corner in ten minutes. And then you can buy me that drink, and then I'll decide whether or not to take you back to my flat later.'

She turned around and wet his beak by brushing her pillow-soft arse cheeks up against his semi-hard on. As she left, she rolled her hips from side to side, and used her proud succulent backside as if to say suck on this. Overpowered by his boiling hormones, he almost grabbed the bar man by the throat to get his order in as quick as possible. When the tray of drinks were finally ready, he threw the bar man a tenner and didn't even wait for the change – not that there would have been much anyhow.

By the time Morris had sprinted back to his table

without spilling any of the drinks, he already had his excuse ready. Hastily, he plonked the tray down, and the glasses tinkled together. 'Listen lads I've just got to pop around the corner to pick up some weed from someone. We're gonna need some smokes later aren't we?'

His mates already supping on their pints, looked up at him dubiously. One of them spoke up. 'Don't be long then, or your gonna miss the next round.'

'Yeah, yeah,' he replied and followed his dick out of the rear exit of the building. Outside, he marched over towards the thrumming beat of the Cottage Loaf pub, passing the side road that lead back to the front of the Wetherspoons. Half way across the road, he heard a woman's voice call out to him, Morris turned to find the blonde woman waiting half way up the side street smoking a cigarette. As excited as a school kid, he scuttled over to meet her. Standing waiting, she watched him like a hawk and chimneyed smoke out from her mouth. When he reached her, she flicked her head towards the dimly lit, back alley.

'I've found a quiet spot so we can work up a thirst for our drinks afterwards.'

Morris grinned like a Cheshire cat, and led her by the hand down the grubby passage way. Seconds later, he had her pinned up against one of the yard walls, and was feverishly trying to ram his slug-like tongue down the back of her throat.

The whacking clump to the back of his head brought him down to his knees. Heavy duty adhesive tape was stuck over his mouth, and his muffled cries of agony, and bemusement were ignored. Next, he was held down on the cold gritty tarmac, with his hands held behind his back and his legs restraint.

Morris's glazed eyes bulged like billiard balls as they ran up the length of a tall black figure standing in front of him. Just like a trapped animal sensing extreme danger, he began to struggle frantically. The large looming figure took a step back, and that's when Morris realised exactly what he was in for. He tried to scream for help, but his muted cries were drowned out by the thumping music coming from the Cottage Loaf.

As the first kick came at him, he tried to turn his face away, but it caught him flush, and it felt as if a car had just ploughed into him. The second boot stunned him so much that he hallucinated he'd fallen out of his bunk bed back in the prison cells, and he almost pissed his pants. The final kick completely numbed his senses and filled his head with scary demons that dragged him down a metal spiral tunnel into a pit filled with mutilated bodies. Fortunately for Morris, he was now unconscious and spared the savage beating. When it was all over, Morris was left dumped in the grimy alley like a bag of rotting food. Slowly he began to rouse from his concussed sleep. His body moving in spasmodic jerks, he scrambled on to trembling hands and knees. Get up! Get up! The voice pounded in his head, as he fumbled around like a newly born foal trying to climb to its feet. However, on his third attempt he made it, but the world suddenly tipped forward again. He spewed vomit and blood from a mouth swollen as if it had a tennis ball in it, and wiped the dripping gunge with the sleeve of his white shirt.

In his head, a jack-hammer was going off, and he gripped his skull as if to try and stem the pain. Somehow, Morris was able to get back to his feet and manoeuvre his cumbersome, jerky body towards Goddaeth Street, the main road. There under the exposing orange street lights, the full extent of his facial injuries were displayed to passing members of the general public. At first glance, it looked like someone had plastered his face with a plate of lasagne. One reveller even thought he was masked up for a monster fancy dress rave.

Yet as he felt the black curtain of unconsciousness draw over him, Morris reached out a desperate hand for someone to help him. Then he collapsed, and was rushed to hospital.

As it turned out, Jonathan Morris survived this brutal attack. However, the road to recovery would be long and painful, and would require some corrective facial surgery, and wiring to hold his lower jaw together. The following week, the attack itself was reported in the local newspaper and used to highlight the shocking face of today's yob culture.

But as Morris recovered in hospital with a headache that would blight him every now and again for the rest of his life, he must have wondered what had happened to his blonde bunny girl? Did she get attacked too? Or was she a part of an elaborate set-up?

Suffice to say, she was the very least of his concerns, as he was unlikely to see her ever again. She was not his bit of skirt, and nor was she a true blonde.

The money she had received for playing her part in his assault went very nicely towards a plane ticket to Copenhagen to meet up with some comrades involved in another illegal organisation.

But while Mr Morris winces in great pain as he tries to suck up his tomato soup through a straw, he also might want to think about something else? How did it feel being on the receiving end of a senseless, barbaric pasting for a change?

And as for the vicious yobs who had beat him up, were they now wearing his blood as a badge of honour, just as he did after he put some poor chap in a coma back in a chip shop three and a half years ago?

No probably not! To the authors of Mr Morris's grief, (Tom, Charlie and Nigel with the paid assistance of one of Karen's former escort mates) the beating was simply a job they were paid to do, and next week they may be paid to do it to someone else. Nevertheless, justice had been served once more, and this time, it was sent with the compliments of Mr Roy and Reggie Evans.

*

Donna McMurphy (the loan shark victim) held out a piece of paper with a name and phone number scribbled on it. She paused for a moment then told herself that it had to be done. Fretfully, she tapped in the number on her mobile and waited for the call to connect. While the phone rang, she could hear a voice within saying to her that she still had time to change her mind.

The line clicked open.

'Yes, hello, is that Karen White?' Donna asked, as her palpitating heart rocked her body.

'It is.'

'This is Donna McMurphy I don't know if you remember me?'

'Yes I do, Donna, what can I do for you?'

Donna hesitated, and had to force herself to speak. "That bit of business we talked about a week or two ago, I've decide to accept your services.'

'That's fine, Donna, welcome aboard.'

Yet before she signed up for her club membership card, she first needed to know the cost of this so-called service. 'Exactly how much is the charge for your services?'

A price was relayed down the phone, and she rolled her eyes with dismay. It was expensive but weighing it all up, she figured she was still saving a fortune compared to what the loan shark wanted. Donna sealed her eyes to steel herself ready for such a committed decision. 'OK, I'll do it.'

Miss White got down to business. 'Great, can you spare me ten minutes of your time?'

Donna sat back in the couch and breathed a little easier. 'Yes of course.'

Over the next ten minutes, Donna imparted the necessary information including how much they owed the loan shark, and how much they had already paid. Plus a possible business address of the alleged loan shark, what day he usually called, and what time, and last but not least, could she get another loan as soon as possible?

By the time Donna had put down her mobile, she felt as if she had just completed an insurance quote. Drained, she flopped back in her couch, and wondered once more if she was doing the right thing?

The answer came right back at her: When you are clinging to the edge of a cliff and someone throws down a hand, take it.

*

His name was Simon Lewis, and he had been operating as an illegal money lender for about four years. He stood about five feet five inches, wore jam-jar glasses that made his eyes grow to the size of a bugs, and he always wore baggy tracksuit bottoms, to hide the balcony of blubber from all those late night takeaways. Simon was thirty-three years old and lived with his mother in a semi-detached bungalow in Abergele.

Because of his short size and be-spectacled appearance, he always felt that he never existed in the eyes of the female species, and in that respect, was as a bit of a loner. At school they used to tease him by calling him Penfold, after the character from the kiddies programme, *Danger Mouse.*

In his mid twenties, he used to work in a supermarket warehouse until an accident with a fork lift truck crushed his pelvis rendering him unable to work.

Of course, he ended up suing the company and received around twenty-five grand in compensation. It was with this tidy sum of money that he began sowing the seeds of his illegal loan-sharking empire.

Over the years, the majority of his clients were basically the weakest links in the chain, old people, junkies, or careless spendthrifts. Or, as he would describe them in his own callous way the easy pickings who can't fight back.

With intimidation and fear now his allies, he showed no remorse whatsoever when looking into the pleading eyes of an old woman handing over her heating money from her trembling liver-spotted hands. No pity whatsoever in seeing the pasty white fear in the face of a dried up junkie when he and his cronies came to collect. Yeah, try and call me Penfold now, you bastards. He would snigger as he swanned around in his brand-new BMW, or when his £300 pound-a-night hookers would sit on his face.

Saturday afternoon, shoulders back, chest out, arms splayed and not forgetting the gum, he swaggered over to his BMW parked in the Sainsbury shopping mall. Heading towards him was an attractive young mother pushing a pram, and as she passed he made a loud kiss so she could hear. To the young woman, he didn't even exist, or she simply pretended that he didn't.

Simon huffed smugly, and thought he could do better anyhow. He checked the time on his gold Cartier watch knowing that he was due to pick up his two gorilla-minders ready for a collection. Today, it was some dozy middle-aged woman and her gambling idiot husband who were well overdue for a bit of leaning on.

Reaching his car, he pressed the remote control alarm as conspicuously as he could so people would see the expensive motor he drove. The car bleeped, and blinked back at him like a devoted pet pleased to see his master. Simon opened the door, and squashed his ball of a belly down into the car, but before he had time to close the door, three more men dived in. Simon's face froze with outrage. 'Hey, what the hell?'

'Shut up, fat boy, and close the door,' the man beside him ordered, while the others watched from the back seat.

The fact that they were all wearing beenie hats and sunglasses suggested that this was not a social call and Simon lurched sideways to try and get out.

Two pairs of hands grabbed his shoulders.

'What's all this? Get your hands off me.'

'Shut up, Simon, and start the car, we're going for a little ride.'

'No we're not,' Simon cried, then felt the tip of a large hunting knife prod his fleshy abdomen. He froze.

'I'm not going to tell you again.' The man stared through the black lens of his shades.

Simon eyed the gleaming blade at his stomach, then hauled the door closed with a nervous sigh. 'So where are we going?'

'You drive and we'll tell you,' the man told him, and retracted the blade.

Simon gunned the ignition, gone now was the usual swagger, and back again was insecure old Penfold. He reversed out of his parking space, and headed towards the exit of the mall, the presence of these intruders muddying his concentration. Now his mind was racing at a hundred miles an hour and he wondered – how he would put it – what the crack was with these guys? Were they a part of another rival lending firm? Was it drug related? Or were they just up to plain and simple robbery? Or worse?

'Drive over to Towyn beach and we'll have that little chat?'

Simon cast a wary glance at him. 'What about?'

The man stared straight ahead. 'I'll tell you when we get there, I don't want to ruin your concentration and cause an accident.'

Simon wasn't sure whether he should be worried or not, but did as he was told. Soon after, they drove as far as they could up towards the long stretch of Towyn beach. When they stopped Simon hand braked and switched off the ignition. The first thing he expected was to feel the knife at his stomach again, or perhaps this time they intended to plunge it straight in. A film of perspiration beaded his forehead and upper lip.

Sunglasses unbuckled his seat belt, and turned to face Simon, the springs under the seat creaking under his weight. 'Right then, we know all about your dodgy loan-sharking business, Simon Harris, and the way you go about taking advantage of vulnerable people by giving them loans with ridiculously sky-high interest rates, and then profiting from their misery. Tut, tut, tut, very naughty of you.'

Simon's blubbery jowls shook in dispute. 'What's wrong with that? The banks are doing it every day, it's perfectly legal.'

'Is it now? And is it also legal to intimidate old people, and threaten to burn down their houses if they don't pay? The banks do that as well do they?'

Simon half-smirked like a school bully told off for stealing kid's packed lunches. But his arrogance changed the mood of his captors.

'Here's the deal, Simon, a couple, the MacMurphys owe you two grand, and you're asking for seven back, shame on you.' Sunglasses shook his head patronizingly.

A padded white envelope was handed over from the back seat, and sunglasses took it.

'There's fifteen hundred in here, £500 less for our expenses.' Sunglasses wagged it in front of him, and Simon snorted at the insult. 'No way.'

'Yes way, cos if not we'll drive your nice BMW out into the sea with you tied in the boot, and we'll leave you there. And what's more you better pray that the tide doesn't get any higher. Oh, and, yes...'

Sunglasses was handed a mini-camcorder from one of his associates in the back. He flipped out the small colour view finder, and angled it so Simon could see it.

'Ah, yes, here we are.' He pressed the play button.

On the playback it showed his two bloated minders sat in chairs with their hands tied behind their backs. Then the lens zoomed right up to their moon-shaped faces flushed with fear and alarm. In the background, someone could be heard telling them to speak.

'Yes we are guilty of using intimidation, blackmail and violence to recover debt payments from clients. And we are employed by Simon Harris.'

Simon turned his head away, his lip curling with fury.

Sunglasses told him. 'And after we leave you in the sea,

this will be handed over to the police with directions to your whereabouts of course. With a bit of luck they might get here in time to save you precious car. But I can't promise they'll be able to save you too.'

In the back, his two associates couldn't resist a tiny snigger. Sunglasses shook the envelope again. 'The MacMurphy's debt is now paid in full.'

Simon glared at his captors, then snatched the envelope out of his hand.

'Good boy, and don't make us have to visit you again, because next time, as they say in the Godfather, you'll be sleeping with the fishes.'

All three men exited the car leaving Simon holding the envelope and looking like he had just removed a rather large bottle from his behind.

Once again, justice had been served.

CHAPTER 14

Arms folded, they all stood in a semi-circle watching the demonstration given by Geoff and Guy. The team were having their third training session, and this week they were covering knife defence.

First Guy was the attacker, and Geoff the victim. Guy circled him assuming the role of a thug stalking his prey and waiting for the chance to strike. Geoff with all his karate savvy and knowledge tried to keep at a safe distance by constantly moving and feinting. Whenever Guy would try to move in, Geoff would flick out a kick to his knee caps. Every now and again Guy would lunge at him and Geoff would continue to strike the knee, and simultaneously block the knife hand.

This they carried on practising a few more times, then they switched to allow two more students to have a go. As they did this, Geoff and Guy the two main instructors stood aside, ready to shout out instructions and make comments as they went along.

First Brad had a go at defending against the knife, and the former Ninjitsu student used only arm blocks to fend off the attack, with the emphasis on twisting his palms inwards to protect his arteries. Geoff and Guy made mental notes of this. Then after Tom, Charlie, Phil and Mike all had their turn, it was time to comment on their efforts. Although judging by the looks of Geoff and Guy, it didn't appear that they were very impressed.

'OK, guys, relax.' Geoff told them and took the centre floor. He scratched his bald head with disquiet. 'We need work, lads. The majority of those attacks would have resulted with most of you getting cut to ribbons, or worse.'

The rest of the team accepted the criticism, while Tom couldn't help but share an indignant glance with Charlie.

'If we do have to confront this gang called the Wilkinsons, known by that name for obvious reasons, or any other knife-wielding maniacs out there, then we've got to buck up our ideas and get serious.'

He aimed his first comments at Tom and Charlie.

'You two were so flippant about that knife you'd have thought you were defending yourselves against someone holding a banana.'

Both of them took it on the chin.

'And you're both bouncers, so what does that say?'

Then he turned to Phil and Mike. 'You two were the complete opposite you were flapping your arms about so much you could have flown away to safety.'

The rest of the team found this quite amusing, but Geoff soon shut them up.

'Phil, you're a damn copper, you need this training. Even when you're out in the field you might have your pepper spray and your truncheon, but what if someone takes them off you, or you're off duty?'

Phil braved the remark.

'And Brad, I appreciate that you want to protect your main arteries, but the truth of the matter is that you arms are going to end up like chopped meat.'

Brad simply nodded.

Tom spoke up. 'Why then don't we just carry knives ourselves?'

Phil interjected. 'Because, if these new anti-crime laws come in, then you could be looking at five years for carrying an offensive weapon.'

'Yeah, but I'd much rather take that chance considering the alternative, wouldn't you?' He looked around for support, then Geoff took over again.

'Yeah, I understand that, and I also appreciate that martial art weapons are also considered illegal. But the truth of the matter is on the whole, knives are far more dangerous whether you're using, or sticking! I just detest the bloody things. I hate the look of them, the feel of them. In fact, it is probably the only weapon that actually feels just as dangerous holding one, as it does facing the pointed end. Everything about them is oppressive. The only thing knives should be used for is cutting up your food.'

Everyone listened intently.

Geoff paused to allow everyone time to absorb what he'd said. Suddenly someone knocked on the door of the warehouse. Frowning at the intrusion, Geoff marched off to see who it was.

Meanwhile, the class saw this as a chance to chill and gab about what Geoff had been talking about. Geoff turned the latch on the wooden door and pulled it open. Immediately, his face lit-up with amazement. It was Will.

'Will.'

'Thought I'd pop over and have a look, if that's alright?' Will shrugged innocently

'Yeah, of course, come on in!' Geoff beckoned him through.

Will closed the door behind him, and followed Geoff over to the team who all eyed him warily like a pack of wolves seeing a stranger enter their group. Except for Guy that is, who came straight over to shake his hand.

'Will, old mate it's been a long time. How are you?'

Will shook it heartily. 'Good, good. Nice to see you again, Guy.'

Geoff began the introductions. 'OK, lads, I'd like you all to meet a friend of mine and Guy's from the old days. Will Thomas.'

Everybody acknowledged him with a curt nod. Next, Geoff introduced every member in turn, and Will responded to each one with a civil grin.

Once the formalities were all done, Geoff gave them a bit of history about Will, and why he was here.

'Will has trained in martial arts for probably just as long

as I and Guy have. But his field of expertise lies in urban combat, and extreme martial arts, fighting styles that are geared more towards actual street fighting than the conventional art form itself. Plus he used to be a Mixed Martial Arts fighter.'

Brows of interest were raised, especially by Tom and Charlie.

'And the reason he has come here today, is because he has kindly agreed to sit in on one or two of our training sessions, and hopefully chip in and give us a few pointers every now and again.'

Everybody happy with this, Geoff resumed with the lesson, and tried his best not to feel intimidated by Will's presence. 'Right, back to the knife defence, where were we? Ah, yes, we've already established that any fool can be a danger with a knife in his hands.' He glanced over to Phil. 'Phil, can I use your assistance?'

Phil unfolded his hands with a why me, look on his face.

'When faced with someone threatening you with a knife, your main objective is to create as much space as possible between yourself and the blade. The first and probably safest option is, if you have the chance to run, then do so in the opposite direction as fast as you can.'

To Tom and Charlie, this was an insult to their egos.

'However, if your retreat happens to be blocked off, and you don't happen to have a weapon on you to defend yourself, then you have to react very quickly indeed. The longer you dither and hesitate, the greater the risk you will get stabbed.' Geoff nodded to Phil to begin the attack.

Phil lunged in with his imaginary weapon. In slow motion, Geoff side kicked him to the knee. Again he asked him to repeat the attack, and this time, Geoff froze in mid-kick. 'You see. At the same time I'm striking the knee, I am also blocking the knife with my lead hand, plus protecting my vital organs.' Geoff then glanced over to Will. 'Do you have anything to add to that Will?'

Will uncrossed his arms like a school kid caught day dreaming in class. 'Yes, yes, I agree.' He gave himself a second to focus. 'If you are threatened with a knife your first objective is to get the hell out of there.' He paused to gather himself. 'Even if you have a weapon yourself, don't use it play a game of who can stab the other first. Only ever use a weapon to defend yourself while you're planning your escape.'

Phil lifted his hand. 'So what do you think would be the best weapon to use against a knife then? Of course taking into account there are existing laws about carrying offensive weapons yourself.'

Will joined Geoff and Phil at the front of the class. 'Like I've just said, your main objective is to remove yourself from what could potentially be a fatal situation. Now with regards to what weapon you should use, my reply would be anything you can get your hands on that may help prevent you from getting stabbed. Or anything that can be used to disarm your attacker.'

Will slipped off his padded bomber jacket, and turned to Phil.

'OK. Phil, isn't it?' He asked.

Phil nodded.

'OK, Phil, you have a knife in your hand, and you want to stick me with it, go ahead?'

Intrigued, Geoff and the rest of the team looked on. Feeling put on the spot somewhat, Phil set himself ready. Meanwhile, Will stood relaxed clutching his jacket in one hand as if he was waiting for a taxicab.

Phil made a feint, then lunged in with his phantom knife. Yet as soon as he did, it felt as if he'd thrust his hand into a spinning washing machine, and he was thrown completely off balance. Luckily, he was caught by Guy and Brad standing nearby.

Phil regained his posture, and saw that his arm was gift wrapped with Will's jacket.

'Can I have my coat back please?' Will quipped, which

caused a few grunts of amusements from the team. Geoff's mouth twitched impressed.

Will explained. 'OK, that's how you open up your escape route. You may lose your coat in the process, but it's better than losing your life.'

Phil un-wrapped the garment and handed it back to Will who thanked him.

'Now if your escape route happens to be hampered like you have to scale a high wall to get away or something. Or you're trying to get away in your car and you can't get your keys out in time before your attacker get's to you, then you will need to disarm him. Will called for Phil to repeat the attack once more, and when he obliged, this time instead off flinging him off balance, he forced him down to his knees with an arm lock.

'From this position don't waste any time trying to grab the knife off him, as you might lose the hold and give him another chance. Always keep in mind that this bastard wants to stab you. He's willing to kill you, he's willing to take you from this world. Take you away from your mother and father, away from your brothers and sisters, or your wife and family.' As Will described all this, his face began to darken, his eyes widened and dilated as if he had suddenly become possessed. He glared down at Phil like he wanted to kill him.

Phil still bound by the arm lock and listening to all this began to feel a bit uneasy. Even Geoff and the team became a tad concerned at this sudden change in Will.

All at once, Will snarled like a wild beast and thrust down on Phil's elbow joint as if he was trying to chop a four by four. Phil clenched his eyes shut to steel himself against the impact, then he reopened them to find that his arm was still intact. Will looked down at him with a little smile.

'Sorry, Phil, couldn't resist it.'

Phil gave him a look of contempt while everyone else chuckled at his expense. Will helped him back to his feet, and unravelled his jacket for him.

After the joking had settled, Will proceeded to break down the defence technique in order to show the team exactly how he did it. Geoff and the team were evidently impressed by Will's self-defence tips, and the session ended with everyone greatly motivated by what they'd been taught. To show his gratitude, Geoff insisted on giving Will a lift home.

'Thanks for that, Will,' Geoff said on their way back to Will's flat.

'No problem, I enjoyed doing it. It brought back memories of the old days when I did a bit of teaching myself.'

Geoff felt a bit cheeky for asking, but did so while he had the chance. 'Listen, Will, our next session, I was planning to do a bit of technique training with the emphasis on power punching. It's not that I'm not confident enough with my own power, but I remember that you used to specialise in that department. And if you know a way that may give us some more zip in our punches, well now is the time we could really use it.'

Will turned to him with a crafty little smirk. 'What did I tell you all those years ago, Geoff? Didn't I tell you if you want maximum power you have to compromise traditional beliefs and move into the twenty-first century?'

Geoff replied sheepishly. 'I know, I know, but let's be honest about it Will, times have changed, and we are facing a very different beast out there now.'

Will relented. 'Yeah, I suppose you're right.'

'So do you want to help us out some more?'

'Maybe, we'll see? Thing is, although I did enjoy going through the motions tonight, I really don't want to get in too deep and start opening up old wounds again, if you know what I mean?'

He didn't, so Will had to explain.

'You have to be careful of the animal, Geoff.'

'What animal?'

'Let it always be your servant, and not your master.'

141

Geoff made him elucidate.

'Violence, carnage, aggression, fighting, when you begin down that treacherous path it can start to take you over. It's just as powerful as any drug out there. People in these occupational hazard jobs for instance, like bouncers, bodyguards, minders, believe me, they can tell you all about it. You see, unless you have that disciplined mindset that tells you that something is only a job, or there is definite justification in what you're doing. If you can keep that distinction, that separation, you'll probably be OK. If not, it may become a major problem.'

Geoff listened intently, but couldn't quite relate to what Will was saying.

'I've seen it so many times, Geoff. Timid people, mild-mannered people, they take a step into a violent world get a taste and then they get hooked. It's that adrenalin rush, and the self-gratification of conquering another human being. Then their appetite grows and grows, and they need more victims, more challengers to satisfy that lust for violence and glory. Finally, they can no longer help themselves – they will even do it for nothing, only personal satisfaction. That's when they become consumed by the obsession and they become completely de-sensitised to any remorse, any compassion, or any conscious thought for the consequences of their actions. They talk it, sleep it and even breathe violence. That's when you wake up one day and take a look in the mirror and you no longer recognise the beast staring right back at you. Your family don't even recognise you, or your friends. Finally you've become that Animal.'

Geoff didn't like the sound of that, and gave him a troubled look.

'And believe me, Geoff, once it has a grip on you, it takes incredible willpower to break free.'

'You don't honestly think it will ever come to that with us though do you?' Geoff asked concerned.

'It depends on how far you're willing to go with it Geoff.'

'But we're only talking about trying to protect ourselves here Will, not start World War Three or anything.'

'I'm not saying this is what's going to happen to you or any of the team Geoff. I'm just trying to warn you of the pitfalls and the dangers of what can happen if you choose to step into that world of violence. Don't forget I've seen it first hand.'

'Yeah, but what we're doing is extremely low-key compared to what you did.'

'Yes, I know that, Geoff, but believe me sooner or later you will know what I'm talking about, and I just want you to be aware of it. Like I've said if you trust you own judgement and believe in the justification of what you're doing then that will be your marker, your measure stick if you like. As a friend I'm just trying to give you a bit of advice that's all.'

Arriving at Will's flat, Geoff parked the car but kept the engine running. At first, Will seemed reluctant to want to leave as if he wanted to stay and chat some more, or maybe get something off his chest. Geoff then remembered about Will's meeting with Stacey, and felt guilty that he hadn't asked how it went.

'Sorry, I forgot to mention, Will, but how did it go the other night with Stacey?'

Will sat back and blew a long weary sigh. 'It's hard to say. I told her everything like we planned, and as expected she didn't believe me at first. Then we had a bit of a bust up, things calmed down, and she started telling me stuff about her childhood that I never knew before. Then I walked her back to her hotel and she said that she'd contact me in a couple of days to let me know if she was willing to start afresh.'

Geoff tried to sound encouraging. 'Looks like you got through to her then, especially if she confided in you like that.'

'Maybe, I don't know. I still haven't heard from her yet.'

Still wanting to know if Will would be around to help the team out, Geoff had to ask. 'If it's a no-go with Stacey, are you still going back to Warrington?'

'Yeah, I've been here nearly a couple of weeks now, all cooped up in that flat. The plan was to come straight down to Wales, spend a month or so here to patch things up with Stacey, and then take her back home with me. As soon as I got out of prison, all I wanted to do was get over here. I haven't even been back to my own home yet. Martin, the guy who's looking after my house must be thinking I'm never coming back. That's one of the reasons why I don't want to make any promises with these sessions, because I don't want to let you down.'

'Well, I'd hate to see you go back so soon, Will, not just because it's a great help to the team having you around to give us advice and that. But aside from that we haven't really had the chance to catch up and have a drink together, like the old days.'

'I know, I know. I tell you what, if I do end up having to go back home, before I go, we'll have a good knees-up just for old times sake, how's that?'

'It's a deal.' Geoff held out his hand and Will shook it.

As Will climbed out of the car Geoff tried to give him some last minute hope.

'I think Stacey still has something for you, Will, otherwise she wouldn't have turned up the other night.'

Will gave him a who-knows shrug.

'I think she will see sense and give it another go,' Geoff winked.

Will smiled and said cheers, before slinging the door closed.

'Let us know what she decides. Oh... and if you're interested, we're having the Christmas party this Saturday at the Kings' head, at 7pm.'

Will nodded and told him he'd come along if he could.

Unlocking the door to his flat, Will was greeted by his key jangling landlord in the hallway.

'Oh, ur, Will, a lady called for you about an hour ago. She said she'd try again tomorrow about seven pm.'

Will struggled to contain his disappointment, and forced an appreciative smile. 'Right, OK, thanks,' he replied, and disappeared into his room.

Closing the door behind him, he slumped against it, and gave vent to his frustration.

'Typical,' he groaned, 'if only I hadn't gone to Geoff's tonight.'

After wallowing in a bit of self pity, he took off his beanie hat and trudged over to the window, his thoughts now geared towards tomorrow night when Stacey said she would call again. He drew a weary hand across his face, saying to himself, Oh well, at least this time tomorrow, I'll know one way or another.'

*

That following evening at 7.04, the doorbell rang, which sounded to Will like an air raid siren. Stacey had arrived, and accompanied with such an intruding, offensive noise, it could only indicate bad news. With butterflies fluttering in his chest, Will dashed off to answer the door.

Outside, Stacey stood there looking even more fragile than she did the last time he saw her. Reading her negative body language made his heart sink, but he tried not to show it.

'Come in,' he told her catching the scent of her Ralph Lauren perfume as she followed him through. Will told her to have a seat on the couch while he stood leaning against the window table. He didn't even offer her a drink or anything as he just wanted to get down to the nitty-gritty.

'OK, Stacey, lets not beat about the bush any longer, do I go to the station and buy my one way ticket back home or not?'

Stacey coughed to clear her throat, 'Will, I haven't come here to give you any promises about a possible future with you. Your aim was to come back here to Llandudno to try and pick up where we left off, but that's never going to happen.'

The word, never, boomed in Will's head like someone had just dropped an atom bomb on to his city of hopes and dreams.

Stacey continued. 'So many things have happened to us in the meantime, too much water has past under the bridge. We're completely different people now.'

By now Will was already mentally packing up his backpack.

'Basically, what I'm trying to say is that we would have to start completely from scratch all over again.'

Perhaps it was because he was wondering what time the next train back to Warrington might be, but Will totally missed what Stacey was trying to say.

'Say again?'

'We should start again from scratch,' she repeated.

Suddenly sunshine burst through the dark clouds, and he nearly sang halleluyah. He double checked 'You're telling me you would like to start again?'

Her eyes softened for the first time since he'd been back. 'Why not?'

Will felt like giving her a massive bear-hug, but had to control himself, so he just stood there like a fool not knowing what the hell to do.

'But, Will,' she warned, 'short steps, OK? One step at a time.'

Will struggled, but managed to say. 'Whatever you want.'

Now, he asked if she would like a drink, and she agreed.

Stacey stayed with Will for about another hour. They talked about everything, the past, the present, but left out the future for now. The future, they decided, was something that would unravel all in good time.

At the end of the evening, Will insisted on walking her

back home, and on the way, she innocently asked where he was last night when she called round. Jokingly, Will accused her of checking up on him already, and told her he was only helping his old mate train some students, that's all. However, he didn't tell her exactly what they were training for.

Finally, Will left her at her hotel with the promise that they would meet up again in a couple of days. On his way back to his flat, Will felt like he was flying through the clouds, and in his excitement, he quickly sent a text message to his mate Geoff, which said... *LUKS LIKE I'M STAYING A BIT LONGER, THANKS TO STACEY.*

CHAPTER 15

The Broadway, Boulevards night club, stood on Mostyn Broadway Road. Formally, called the Grand Theatre, it was primarily a play house in its hey-day. Built with a red brick facade topped by low semi-octagonal towers, it once seated about a thousand people. In 1980 it finally closed as a theatre and was reopened as Revivals night club and later changed to the Broadway Boulevards.

It was Friday night at the Boulevards, and at around ten-thirty pm all the revellers were queuing up so they could party until the early hours. Standing on the door in their black crombie jackets, were Tom, Charlie and Nigel. All three were busy herding the flocks of people through, checking handbags, and looking for anyone carrying knives or drugs into the nightclub. Outside the temperature must have been touching freezing, and yet there were so many young girls in skimpy party tops waiting to get in.

'Jesus.' Tom muttered to Charlie as they let another partygoer through. 'Aren't these girls freezing their tits off or what?'

'They must be like packs of ice when they get home, mustn't they?'

Tom hissed a laugh and checked the next reveller through. Further down the queue Tom suddenly caught sight of a Shakira (the Latin American singer) look-a-like in a spotty jersey blazer, and tight leggings. She was standing chatting to friends, then turned to gaze down the tail end of the line as if she was trying to search for someone. As she did this Tom was permitted the glorious sight of her bulbous arse, something he imagined that would make the perfect cushion for him to sleep on over winter time. And to emphasise that fact, he decided to share his carnivorous fantasies with his chum Charlie.

'I bet she could keep you warm in the Winter?'

'Boom, boom,' Charlie replied.

Trouble – A red alert came over in their earpieces which were attached to their radios in their pockets. Tom elected to stay on the door while Charlie and Nigel went in to sort it out.

Moments later, both bouncers emerged dragging some unruly chap by the arms and then hurled him out into the street. The young man in a crumpled and torn cream flannel shirt, spun around to vent his drunken rage at the doormen. To everybody in the queue this momentarily took their minds off the cold lengthy wait.

'I've still got a pint in there,' he ranted.

For a moment, Tom thought he recognised the guy from somewhere.

Nigel, the ex rugby player took over. 'Well you shouldn't have hit that girl should you?'

At that moment, the yob's three other mates came out to see what was going on, and stood beside their pal. Feeling even more confident now, the lad pointed at the bouncers and threw another tantrum.

'These bastards have thrown me out and won't let me back in.'

His three mates, all virtually dressed the same as one another, began to join in and heckle the bouncers. Sensing hassle, Tom halted the queue going in, and stood as back-up for his fellow doormen.

Nigel raised his voice to match theirs. 'Look you've attacked someone and gotten into a fight that you caused. You even tried to fight us. That's three strikes, so you're out.'

All four knuckleheads barked in protest sounding like a pack of hounds, and then tried to get in Nigel's face. Immediately, Tom and Charlie stepped in to create a protective fence between them and the louts. But as far as

Nigel was concerned the four lads had already stepped over the line.

'Right, all of you are barred. Now sod off.'

The three bouncers then stepped back together and formed a wall by the entrance. Now that they had been given the shut-out, the lads continued with their shouting and posturing, and all claiming to be as hard as nails. Yet, none of them had the courage to step into the bouncer's territory. This was their protective barrier, their domain so to speak.

The four lads continued to slap their chests, and stick their necks out like chickens, all part of the bravado and swagger. Spurred on by the support of his mates, the lad decided to be the big man and challenge any one of the bouncers to a mano a mano.

Nigel sneered at the challenge and shared his contempt with his comrades, while the lad continued to try and goad them.

'C'mon, yer tosser, let's see how hard you really are?'

Nigel stepped forward and laid down the gauntlet. 'Piss off now or you're barred for life, the lot of you, and I'll call the police.'

Now the ball was in the lad's court, did he have the brass gonads to step over that line and have a go? Watching Nigel's back, Tom was itching to bulldoze in and totally obliterate this nobody, but he knew that would be playing right into their hands. Nigel then repeated the warning that he was going to call the police; surreptitiously laying the trap for these dead men walking.

The lad made a feint to see if Nigel would flinch, and show that he had a chink in his armour. But Nigel stonewalled him, and the lad's ego started to deflate like a punctured tyre. Evidently, his bottle was beginning to go, and not wanting to lose face, he resorted to verbal threats instead. Stabbing out a raging finger he snarled.

'You three are dead. You're all marked.'

Nigel simply stared through him and called him a silly

tosser, while the lad's head jerked like he was moving to an imaginary beat.

'We'll be sending some guys down to see you soon,' he growled. 'You three are already marked, some guys are coming down from the Wirrel to sort you out.'

Tom stepped forward, his lip curling with fury. 'Yeah, we'll see.'

'Go on piss off, you complete prat.' Nigel waved him off, and the lad started backing away feeling vindicated by the threats he'd made.

'Watch yer backs, lads,' he added as he and his cronies swaggered off back towards town.

Nigel turned to Tom and Charlie, shaking his head with derision.

For the rest of the evening, all of them had a bad feeling about the lad, and they kept a vigilant eye out for any passing cars that might be taking an unusual interest in them.

Towards the end of the evening they caught up with Snoopy, the doorman's secret grass, and asked him if he'd heard about any comebacks regarding the drugs. After all, he was the one who sorted out a buyer for their drugs.

Snoopy was actually a fitting name for this strange looking young man. He was short in statue with big ears like radars, and most of the girls thought he was kind of cute and cuddly just like the famous cartoon character. However, all Snoopy could tell them was that it could just be a case of misidentity.

Eventually, when the doorman knocked off for the evening at about 2.30 am, they paid particular attention when returning to Tom's girlfriend's car, parked on the prom. Fortunately, the coast was clear, and they made it back safely.

As for Nigel, they made sure he got picked up earlier by his girlfriend, so he was alright.

Back in the car, Tom and Charlie buckled up, and switched on the dashboard heater.

Tom snorted apprehensively. 'For the next few days or

so, I think we better come in your car, and keep some tools in the boot just in case.'

'Yeah OK, so what are we gonna do if it does have something to do with the drugs? You heard him, they're sending down some guys from the Wirrel, that's just outside Liverpool were we sold the damn drugs.'

Tom thought about it anxiously.

'Think we need the team as back-up just in case?'

'Yeah, don't really want to Geoff and the others involved but we're not going to be able to fight them on our own even with Nigel. That's if it is the drug gang.'

'So what are you gonna tell Geoff?'

'I'll just tell him that we've heard that the Wilkinsons might be planning an attack against us so we might need the team's help.'

*

Saturday night Tom and Charlie were marked down to cover the doors on the Wetherspoons pub. Nigel however, would remain at the Boulevards with his own weekend crew. This time they came to work in one of Charlie's old banger cars, and they parked it behind the Wetherspoon's building in the town hall car park.

During the evening, nothing out of the ordinary happened, just the usual drunken dispute to sort out, or escorting some poor alcoholic off the premises. In fact, it was considered by all on duty to be one of the quietest nights they'd had in a long while.

Last orders were about 11.30pm, and the process of winding down for another evening was well under way. Finally, after all the customers had been herded out, and the doors had been locked, Tom and Charlie stayed behind for their customary pint. They both remained there chatting with the other doormen and staff members until around 12.30am, then they called it an evening.

Outside, it was a pitch black early morning, and at the

taxi-stand nearby, there was only a trickling of night clubbers left. Tom and Charlie huddled inside their heavy crombie coats, their breaths immediately turning into mist, as they turned down the back street towards the town hall car park. Mid-way down, three figures suddenly appeared at the end of the road. Tom and Charlie stopped dead in their tracks, and looked at each other warily.

Behind them, at the top of the road, blocking them off, three more figures appeared, and were silhouetted against the orange sodium streetlights. Now they were completely trapped, and facing a bit of a situation.

Hearts hammering in their chests, and reading each other's minds, they elected to continue down towards the first three figures en route to the car park. No words, no last minute plans were spoken between them, they simply accepted what was happening and continued on. However, the three facing them, began approaching, and closing the gap even quicker. Tom threw a glance over his shoulder to check on the other stalkers and they too were following behind. But what was even more worrying was that the ones behind, seemed to have something glinting in their hands, probably knives. Tom and Charlie unbuttoned their crombie jackets ready.

Out of the dark hidden crevices of the side alley, two figures wielding baseball bats sprang at the first three assailants clubbing them unmercifully. Seeing that the cavalry had arrived bang on time, Tom quickly joined in to help.

As for the rear assault, two more surprise arrivals were already dealing with them, and Charlie doubled back to give them a hand. Yet, seeing that the odds had changed dramatically, one of the stalkers suddenly lost his bottle and fled, leaving his mates at the mercy of these crazed vigilantes.

Back at the bottom of the road, Tom seized his attacker in a head lock, coat still over the head, and charged at the concrete strut of the Wetherspoon's building smashing the lad into it as hard as he could. All he could hear was a muffled cry and the body went limp, and sagged to the ground. Tom let it drop, then stomped on the lump just to be sure.

Beside him, he heard the squawks of pain from the other attackers as they were being pummelled on the wet tarmac by the baseball bats. To Tom, it sounded like someone clubbing rolls of carpet. He then glanced behind to see how the others were getting on, and saw one of them being choked by a pair of nunchakus, while another was already cowering on the floor receiving a good kicking. Meanwhile, Charlie reappeared empty handed after giving up on the chase for the one who had chickened out.

Satisfied that they had taken control of the situation, Tom took his coat back from his attacker, and that's when he saw the gleaming blade lying on the ground. Repulsed by the thought that this piece of dirt was going to actually use it against him, he fished up the knife and gave him a few more furious kicks.

Mike and Guy, who had taken care of the first three assailants walked over to Tom, baseball bats swinging from their hands, and exhausted breaths steaming from their mouths. Tom acknowledged them with a nod, and glared down at the three lads lying unconscious at their feet.

'These bastards were planning to stick us with these knives. We should kill them for that.'

The three remaining team members, Charlie, Brad, and Geoff jogged back down the street to meet them. Shaking with fear and fatigue, Geoff clutching his pair of Nunchakus blustered to everyone. 'Come on, guys, we haven't got time to take any pictures, let's go! Police will be here soon.'

Everybody except Tom followed. Tom however, still brandishing the knife as if he couldn't let go of it for some reason, knelt down beside his sleeping attacker. The lad was about twenty, with wavy-blonde hair and looked like a harmless university student.

'So you've found out who we are have you? Well I'll

give you something to remember me by, pretty boy.'

He leant over and sunk the tip of the blade into the lad's cheek, then sliced down over the hard cheekbone and into the soft fleshy jowl. Dark viscous blood instantly filled the wound and trickled down his face. The lad barely stirred. Satisfied, Tom stood back up and quickly repeated the act on the other two slumberous attackers beside him. From the town hall car park Geoff shouted for him to move, and just before he did, he uttered ominously to his fallen victims. 'Next time, I'll cut your sodding balls off.'

CHAPTER 16

Halfway around the Great Orme, on marine drive, Stacey called for Will to stop. Exhausted, she bent over hands on knees and thought this was the closest thing to death she'd experienced since that spaghetti bolognaise had given her food poisoning some years ago. While jogging around the Orme with Will she had fooled herself into thinking that she was still as fit as she used to be. Yet despite her near collapse, Will was still impressed by her effort.

'Bloody hell, Stace, I really didn't expect you to get this far.'

He trudged over to her and leant against the stone wall. Her breaths settling, she straightened herself and sat up on the wall.

'I'm spitting feathers, I'm gasping for a drink of water.' She swooned.

'Won't take us long now, we'll be back down the other side soon,'

Stacey heaved one final breath and gazed behind at the spectacular view of the North Wales coast. However, despite the fact the skies were a bit dark and leaden, it was still an impressive sight. Stacey followed the landscape from the rolling Penmaenmawr mountains, right down to the rural towns and villages, of Llanfairfechan and across to Bangor and Holyhead.

'Magnificent, isn't it?' She cooed.

Will threw a glance back and agreed.

'Pity we weren't fortunate enough to have places like this to jog around when we started courting.'

Will smiled in accord.

'Strange that two people reared from the same town, should find each other in a place like Warrington don't you think?' Stacey added.

Will thought about it for a second, 'Well they say that in order to open your eyes, you have to broaden your horizons. And as ironic as it sounds, maybe if we'd stayed at home our paths may never have crossed.'

Stacey turned back and began fretting about those lost years. 'You don't think I've changed that much in four years do you?'

Will checked her out. 'No. The only difference is I can see is that your arse has gotten a bit bigger.'

She gave him a lethal stare, and clouted him across the thigh for his cheek. Will continued to wind her up. 'Being that we are using a public highway you should have a warning sign like those big lorries have saying, wide load.'

Stacey was so close to thumping him now that she balled her fist up ready, but Will was already off. When it was safe to return, Will sat back down beside her and couldn't resist a little chuckle. But seeing that she wasn't very amused, he tried to make his peace.

'I'm only joking, you have a lovely arse, honestly.'

Eventually, she forgave him, and they started talking about Christmas and what effect it would have on them. Stacey began chewing her nails as if something seemed to be bothering her. 'Will, for the last couple of years, I've spent Christmas with relatives in Saughall, Chester.'

'Oh?'

'Yeah, and we're all supposed to be going there again this year because we've already had the invitation.'

Will's spirits appeared to wane. 'So what you're saying is that you won't be able to see me over Christmas right?'

Stacey felt awkward then suggested, 'maybe if I asked my mum and dad if you could come with us?'

But Will dismissed the notion straight away. 'I don't think that'd be such a great idea, do you? I mean your mum doesn't really approve of me, and your relatives are complete strangers to me. It wouldn't be fair to everyone. I know exactly how they'd feel. You can't relax and be yourself when you have to entertain people you've never met before. Christmas only comes once a year and I wouldn't want to ruin it for them.'

Stacey could see his point, but still felt uncomfortable about the thought of Will spending this Christmas all alone.

'Maybe when I get back, we can go out and have our own celebration?'

Yeah why not,' Will replied and slapped his thighs ready to finish off their run back down the other side of the Orme. Meanwhile Stacey hauled herself off the stone wall and felt her poor tortured legs already beginning to stiffen up.

As they resumed their jog, Will, just by chance, noticed someone with a pair of binoculars standing high above the road on a rocky outcropping.

*

Geoff pulled up in his black car outside Will's flat and waited with the engine humming in neutral. A moment later, Will ambled down the entrance steps in his beanie hat and tracky's, then hopped in the car and they drove off.

En route to another team training session, Geoff opened up conversation by asking Will how things were going with Stacey. Will held up a fingers crossed sign, and Geoff smiled back at him before digressing.

'We had a bit of a run-in with some members of that Wilkinson's gang at the weekend.'

Will's face darkened. 'What happened?'

'Well, apparently Tom and Charlie had trouble with this pleb head on the door on Friday night, and he threatened them that they were going to get a visit. Straight away they thought of the Wilkinson's. So not wanting to take any chances, Tom phoned us the next day, and we set it all up ready for that evening just in case. Luckily they took the bait and we were there to back the lads up.'

'How did they come at you?'

'Three by three formation and they were carrying, but so were we.'

'Did you hurt them?'

Geoff gave him a little snarl. 'Oh yeah, we battered them unconscious and left them lying there on the cold tarmac.'

Will noticed this unusual aggressiveness in his old friend and stared out of the window with concern. Geoff flicked a glance at him.

'What's up?'

'Be careful, Geoff, that won't be the end of it, you know?'

'Why do you think they'll come at us again?'

Will answered with a look of caution, and Geoff responded with classical male bravado.

'Fine if they do. We'll be waiting for them, and in the meantime we'll be training like hell to prepare for them.'

'Geoff, you can't have this shit coming at you all the time especially with knives, you've got to put a stop to it now.'

This irritated Geoff. 'What else are we supposed to do just give in and let them win?'

'Nobody wins in these situations, Geoff. Look I'm not saying it's not right to train yourself ready to fight, of course you should, everybody should. Everybody should be armed and ready to stand up for themselves and defend their castles against the threat of an enemy. But if someone has a vendetta against you, that's a different story, they're not going to give up until they get you. And it doesn't matter how strong you become, or how hard you have trained, they won't come at you at your strongest, they'll come when you're at your weakest. Even the worms defeat the tiger in the end. Nobody is indestructible.

'So what are you saying? What would you suggest?'

'Don't keep waiting around for your enemies to call on you, Geoff. Never give them that kind of advantage. If you keep giving them the first shots like that, eventually they're going to get lucky. In my opinion you have three choices, first you could go to the police, which is the easiest and probably the safest way out of this.'

Geoff could hardly believe his ears. 'Go to the police? You honestly think we can trust them to sort it out? The police will probably end up arresting us for trying to defend ourselves, and we'll end up becoming a laughing stock.'

Will switched straight to option 2. 'You can fix a truce with this gang and end it amicably.'

Geoff shook his head. 'There's no way the team will agree to that after everything that has happened so far.'

Will tried the last and most desperate option. 'Or you can find out who the leaders of this gang are and take them out?'

Now, Geoff thought that was more like it, but Will warned him.

'That is a last resort option, only after everything else has failed. But if you do decide to take that road, then there are many dangers that come with it. OK, you crush your enemies and take control. Then you become the top dogs and you might rule until someone else wants a shot at the title. And believe me, Geoff, there will be many contenders. You will spend the rest of your life looking over your shoulder, always on standby, always waiting for that next challenge that might be just around the corner. And that is another route to becoming that animal I was talking about.'

'Well I think we should go after them.'

'Well I don't, Geoff. My advice to you while there's still a chance before it escalates to the next level is to try and seek a truce. If all this carries on the way it's going, someone is going to get killed.'

Geoff looked on bleakly, 'I think it's gone too far already, Will. I honestly don't think we can just turn it off like that.'

'Yes, you can, Geoff. Anyone can back off if they want to. The only thing that is stopping you from doing it is your ego. Listen, it's not always about beating the next guy to prove how tough or how great you are. The most important victories and accomplishments are the ones that come from inside.' Will tapped his chest to emphasise the point. 'That inner ability or strength to override those corrupting emotions is what really defines a true man. Our biggest downfalls in life are not the obstacles we face, or the enemies who challenge us, the hardest battles we have to encounter are the ones with ourselves. Our own minds, our conscience. You can defeat all the armies in the world, but it will never compare to the triumph of defeating that enemy within − your fear.'

Geoff couldn't help but smirk. 'What is that, Zen Buddhism or something?'

Will didn't appreciate his humour. 'All I'm trying to say is that you only need to fight when your back is against the wall, and there is no other way out.'

'But, Will, I find that hard to accept after hearing about all the things you used to say when we were young. The old Will would be leading an assault straight into their lair now and wouldn't take any prisoners. And what about all the people you have wasted while you were working for the Serious Crime Agency or whatever? Now all of a sudden you've turned into Stars on Sunday preaching peace on earth, what's going on, have you been born again or what?'

Will took a long deep breath as if he was indeed trying to draw strength from the Lord God Almighty. 'Geoff you're absolutely right, I have changed! At one time in my life I thought the only way to beat violence was with violence, out there pain was the only truth those scumbags knew. But there's a saying: there's nothing like the sight of a battlefield after war to inspire peace amongst kings and generals. And it's only now after everything I've seen and done, I can honestly appreciate the futility and pure waste that violence creates.'

'So why are you helping to train us then?'

'You asked for my help, and I agreed to do it, and everything I teach you comes with a specific warning. But perhaps the only way you will find that peace on that battlefield is to experience all the blood and guts for yourself. I really don't know! Everybody has to find their own path. All I can say is that for me personally, I have seen enough violence to last me a lifetime. Don't get me wrong, I don't mind training you and the team, because if you haven't got the proper tools to defend yourself, then you will be vulnerable and I would hate to see any of you get hurt. But technically speaking, in actual street combat situations, you're all still only novices.'

Geoff nodded resignedly.

CHAPTER 17

THE CHRISTMAS OUTING

The venue they chose for their Christmas get-together was one of the oldest public houses in Llandudno, The Kings's Head, situated at the foot of the Great Orme. The pub itself was first made famous in 1844, when the decision to build it was based on the suggestion made by a Liverpool architect after he proposed that it would make an ideal watering hole.

Almost everybody was in attendance at the Christmas outing, except of course for Will and Stacey, plus Guy who had already informed them that he was running a bit late. The rest of the team, and their wags were sitting in the upper circle overlooking the bar.

In between chit-chats with the guys, Geoff took a sup of his Guinness and watched contentedly how everybody seemed to interact so effortlessly. Even the wives and girlfriends who had never even met before, rabbited on like long lost school pals.

Charlie's missus, Clare who was just a notch above average looking and had a blonde bob haircut, was chatting with Geoff's wife Jan about clothes (what a surprise) But what really interested Geoff about Clare was that whenever she described something, she always seemed to pull the strangest expressions as if she was actually tasting her words. Weird!

Mike's fiancée Sienna, a heavy-set coffee-skinned black girl, had the most astonishing shade of brown eyes he'd ever seen. She was having a tete-a-tete about holidays with Phil's wife Norma. However, Tom had arrived without his girlfriend Karen, and when Mike enquired where she was, he replied that she would be coming later.

Geoff suspected that perhaps they might have had an argument and Tom was embarrassed to admit it.

Then there was Brad, the only other member of the team who had arrived unaccompanied. Yet by the way he was eyeing up all the young ladies swanning around the place, he was certainly looking to remedy that. Not wanting Brad to feel left out, Geoff leaned over to chat with him.

'Hey Brad?' He almost had to shout over the din, and Brad raised his brow in response.

'So how long have you been living in North Wales?'

'About two years now. I'm originally from Brussels, but my family moved to Cardiff when I was six. Then I came up here to look for work.'

Geoff was curious why Brad hadn't picked up a South Walien accent, but didn't mention it. 'Are you settled here now then, or are you planning to move on?'

Brad gulped down a mouthful of Magner's cider. 'Yes, I'm settled for now, and I'm considering going to tech here to study psychology.'

Geoff nodded with admiration just as he spotted Guy and his wife, enter through the door. Geoff waved down at him until he caught his eye. Guy thumbed back up his glasses and led his wife up towards them. Although Geoff and Guy had known each other for a number of years, Geoff had only been introduced to his wife, Joyce, just the one time. That was ten years ago, and those first impressions still remained.

With regards to that first meeting with dear old Joyce, Geoff found that as hard as he tried, he just couldn't seem to warm to her. Although, this certainly wasn't an indication that he disliked her in any way, he merely put it down to the fact that because she was so shy, she probably had very limited social skills.

Geoff always felt that she belonged to a certain breed of woman, whose sole purpose in life was to have a short courtship, marry, settle down, and that's it! She was a throw-back to those old-fashioned post war-time wives, who hardly ever used to go out, except to shop for their families. They hardly ever socialised except when there was a wedding, or funeral to attend to, and they only ever made love for one purpose alone, procreation.

Not that there was anything wrong with this, different strokes for different folks etc. Maybe she was simply born in the wrong era?

Yet to be fair to her, in her prime she was an attractive woman, not in a glamorous sense, but in today's lingo, what we term a yummy-mummy. The problem was she never realised how attractive she was, or simply, it was never that important to her. Geoff found himself pondering about this all over again.

Shame, Geoff sympathised, as she clung to Guy's arm like a lost child as they reached the group. Looking at her now as she approached middle-age, she reminded him of a beautiful garden rose that had always been kept in the shade and never had the privilege of basking in the sunlight. Geoff stood up from the table to greet them, and tapped Guy heartily on the back. As for Joyce, he planted a respectful peck on her warm, scented cheek. In a way, Geoff could feel her agony, her pain, her torture at having to step out of her safe little world and expose herself like this to the prying, critical eyes of her peers.

Soon the next round of drinks arrived, and everyone clanked their glasses together. The place itself, appeared to be filling up quite a bit now, and new arrivals had to cluster together by the entrance until they could find a spot to stand or sit. Geoff looked over the wooden balustrade and jeered at the sight of a group of tarty looking women wrapped up in Christmas tinsel. By now the noise levels were rising to an almost deafening babble.

Geoff felt a tap on his arm; it was Tom, so he leaned over to hear what he wanted. Tom's face was becoming a tad flushed, and his eyes were already beginning to glaze over with effects of the alcohol.

'Yer mate Will not coming then?' He asked.

Geoff shook his head. 'Got women trouble to sort out.'

'Where the hell did you dig him up from?' Tom was almost shouting now because of the noise.

'He's an old friend and training partner.'

'Yeah, but what's he all about?'

Geoff blew heavily. 'That's a long story which I don't think we could get through in one evening.'

'Well, what was he a boxer or something?'

'No, not at first, he started off as a karate student just like you, then he began delving into other styles, exploring other methods of self defence to see what they had to offer. In the end he picked what he wanted from everything he'd learned, and formed his own way of fighting.'

'What like *Bruce Lee?*' Tom jeered.

'Not quite.'

Charlie chimed in. 'Sort of, wos his name, Frankenstein, taking the best body parts and building the ultimate human being?'

Geoff smiled at his analogy. 'Exactly.'

'Think he's ever killed anyone?' Tom asked morbidly.

'I don't know about that. But whether he has or not, he doesn't do it anymore.' Geoff replied diving into his Guinness to duck out of any more stupid questions.

'I think he has.' Tom winked knowingly.

Geoff swallowed a mouthful, and put his pint back down. 'Why do you think that?'

'Because he's got that look.'

'What look?

'Like he doesn't give a shit. Like he could stomp on you as if you were a spider, and then carry on eating his cornflakes.'

Geoff took another swig to hide his derision. Behind their group, a handful of folks at another table began singing Christmas songs, and one or two of Geoff's lot joined in. After the songs, and the cheers ended, most of the women visited the ladies while others nipped off to the bar for refills.

Mike, the only coloured member of the team, came to sit by the lads, and Geoff saluted his arrival. Taking advantage of the opportunity he decided to get a bit of background on his team member.

'Hey Mike, how did you get hooked up to these two then? (meaning Tom and Charlie)

Mike shrugged bashfully. 'Oh, I was training for the marines and got discharged for beating up another trainee.'

'Why was that?'

'He kept on harassing me and making comments about the colour of my skin. So in the end, I waited until he was on toilet cleaning duties, then I did a crap and used his head as a bog brush.'

Although Tom and Charlie had heard this story before, they still couldn't help giggling like a pack of hyenas.

'Nice,' Geoff remarked.

'Yeah, so I came out of the marines and went to stay with my girlfriend Sienna in Llandudno, and based on my recent faux pas...'

'Ohhh.' Tom mocked his fancy turn of phrase.

'She suggested that I'd be better suited channelling all that pent-up energy and hostility into becoming a doorman. And that's where I met tweedle-dee and tweedle-dum here.'

They both gave him a look for his cheek. Nudging Geoff's arm, Brad nodded down to puny-looking Guy getting jostled in the queue for the bar. All of them craned their necks over the wooden balustrade and found it amusing to see him being bounced around like a rugby ball in a scrum.

Geoff sat back with a note of caution. 'Yeah but they'd soon start flying if he began to throw that hip of his.'

Tom sneered. 'To look at him you'd think he'd get beaten up by a gang of field mice.'

Geoff raised a brow. "Once, in our youth when he wasn't throwing petrol bombs, he was throwing six foot four guys out of the Boulevards.'

Everyone found this difficult to believe.

'Oh yes, once this nipple-head, another bouncer at a club in Rhyl, was on a night out showing off to his girlfriend and all the other bouncers that he was the top dog. So what does he do? He picks on the smallest guy in the place and accuses him of spilling his drink. Even though Guy was nowhere near him, he still apologised and offered to buy him another. But that wouldn't satisfy this chap's ego, and he expected Guy to crawl on his hands and knees like a dog.'

'Cheeky bastard,' Tom huffed, checking that none of the women had heard his language.

'Anyhow, Guy tried to walk off and the chap grabbed him by the collar. Next thing this sixteen stone tower of a man was wind-milled over and crashed into the table full of drinks. What a sight! And there was little Guy standing over him.'

'So what happened then?' Brad asked.

'Well, he didn't stay around waiting for him to get back up, he was off, job done.'

Phil the copper then arrived with a fresh tray of drinks, and everyone welcomed the sight of more Christmas cheer. Later Geoff collared Phil for a quiet word and asked about the possibility of acquiring some stab-proof vests for the team. Phil blew hard at the request, but said he would try his best.

Towards the latter part of the evening, most of Geoff's party were becoming a little worse for wear. By now everybody had on their beer goggles, and there were the usual teary sniffles from some of the women, (namely Phil's wife) who had drank just a bit too much vodka and orange. Now they were down to their last round of drinks.

Standing by the entrance to the toilet, Brad was chatting up a cute-looking brunette in a stripy jacket, and a short denim skirt. From their balcony table, Geoff and Guy smiled admiringly. 'Fair play to him, nice to see him making the effort.'

Guy thumbed his glasses back up. 'Yeah, especially after he caught his fiancée cheating on him a couple of years ago.'

'Shit, what did he do?' Geoff asked.

'He jumped straight on the chap she was with, but unbeknownst to him, he turned out to be a judo brown belt.'

'Did he get beaten?'

'No, no, he managed to survive, just. But for a while he said he was getting tied up in knots. That's why he came to my dojo and started learning the art.'

Listening to this, Charlie, bleary-eyed, joined in on the conversation.

'I was thinking of starting judo classes once,' he slurred.

'I didn't know that?' Guy replied.

'Yeah, me old man, used to do a bit in his youth, before he hit the bottle that is. And he started to, you know, teach me a bit.'

Guy nodded, interested. 'So did your father pick it back up later on in his life?'

Charlie's glazed eyes dropped to the beer-spilt table. 'Naw, the drinking saw that he never got the chance again, boom, boom.'

'Sorry to hear that,' Guy said flashing Geoff an uneasy glance.

Finally the Christmas night out began to draw to a close, and couple by couple they started to depart. With only a handful left, and with their taxi waiting outside, it was Geoff and Jan's turn to bid everyone good night. Tom, still tanked up, but coherent enough, stood up and gave Geoff an almighty bear hug. Geoff strained in his tight embrace, and waved to everyone else before lumbering out of the King's Head clutching his wife's hand. Feeling fuzzy-headed himself, but not completely cabbaged like some of his chums inside, he flopped in the back seat of the taxi with Jan. The taxi was warm and cosy, and had a sobering scent of tobacco about it. As they pulled off, Jan leant her weary head on her husband's shoulder.

What a night, Geoff said to himself, not only did everyone thoroughly enjoy themselves, but they also got to know a bit of history about one another.

First there was Brad from Brussels and the judo lesson from his cheating girl's lover. Then there was Mike getting discharged from the marines for using someone's head as a toilet brush. And last but not least, they had Charlie who lost his judo teaching father to the bottle. What a motley crew of neighbourhood watch avengers.

Geoff felt a silly smile grow on his face and thought that on the whole it turned out to be a cracking evening. Shame Tom's girlfriend, Karen, didn't show up though?

CHAPTER 18

Defiantly, she drew back her nylon curtains, wanting them to know they were being watched. Mrs Roberts was a sixty-four-year-old widow who lived alone on a housing association estate in the junction, alone that is except for her six-year-old white terrier called Tibby.

Until recently she also had a ten year old black moggy called Thomas, but *they* had caught him, and hung him to death on the branch of an old oak tree in the field nearby. Sadly, she only found about that when one of her neighbours had discovered it while out walking their dog. Unfortunately, she couldn't prove *they* had murdered her cat, but she knew it was them alright.

Poor Thomas! How could anyone do such a thing to an innocent creature like that? Even though that was three months ago, she still missed Thomas terribly. Every morning, the sight of his empty food dish waiting under the kitchen table would break her heart.

Now all she had was Tibby, and if anything should happen to him as well, then that would be it. They might as well do her a favour and put her out of her misery too.

Just how much longer was this torture going to continue? How much more did they think she could take? Hadn't she suffered enough already? All she did was report one of these sink-estate yobs to the police after catching him trying to steal an expensive ornament from her back garden. Yet when the police eventually caught their suspect, just by chance they discovered that he had drugs in his possession, and that was the only reason he was charged.

Now these vengeful thugs were intent on making her pay for grassing on one of their mates. For the past six months, every Friday and Saturday night, after they had tanked up on a couple of litres of Strong-bow cider, it was straight over to Mrs Roberts for her weekly dose of torture. These youths, these feral yobs ranging from about fourteen- to seventeen years old would stand on her front lawn shouting obscenities, throwing empty cans at her window. But what would really get her goat was when they threatened her with what they were going to do to her precious dog. That's when she showed her defiance to them, and refused to give in. So why didn't she simply call the police? First, Mrs Roberts knew only too well the futility of calling the police. During the last six months, she had reported these pests on numerous occasions but as usual, no action could be taken until an actual offence had been committed. Number 1, by the time they got around to responding to the call, the yobs would be gone anyhow. Number 2, If the yobs knew that she had called the police, it might antagonize them to do even worse.

So why didn't the neighbours intervene? Answer, they didn't want to get involved for fear of retribution by the young thugs.

Mrs Roberts glared at them from her living room window. To the youths outside, she looked like an illuminated waxwork dummy. They jeered, called her a fat slag, and one of the cheeky buggers even bared his backside at her. The ring-leader of these social misfits was a seventeen-year-old lad with short bleached blond hair, who wore a single ear ring. His name was Mongoose, because his face looked pinched out in a kind of snout.

Arrogantly, Mongoose eyed her from her lawn and glugged on his bottle of cider. Mrs Roberts's head shook with contempt, and her terrier, Tibby, yapped at her feet as if he was telling her to ignore them. As if complying to her dog's command, she released the nap of the curtain, and went to sit back on her leather two-seater couch. Satisfied, Tibby leapt up on her, and curled up by her side. Mrs Roberts began stroking his soft white fur more out reassurance for herself than a show of affection for her pet. In an attempt to take her mind off the ruffians, she tried to focus on the TV, but it didn't seem to be working. Inside, her heart was still racing, and she had that awful gnawing dread in the pit of her stomach imagining what the yobs could be doing outside her home.

As time passed, her couch became a seat of brambles, and she was itching to go to the window and check on the hooligans. No I mustn't, she told herself. Besides, should she need something for self defence, there was always the nine iron golf club that she kept behind the living room door. (one of her late husband's clubs from his old set) Trying to relax again, she turned back to the TV in the hope of forgetting about the yobs

Crash. The racket came from the kitchen. Mrs Roberts bounded up from her couch and dived for the club behind the door. Tibby yapped in alarm, but she ignored him and tore through the hall to the kitchen, club in hand.

Throwing the door wide open, and slapping the light switch on, she discovered to her horror that Mongoose was crouched half way through her broken window above the sink. Screaming more out of fear than anger, she flew at him swinging the club wildly, first catching the ceiling light shade which smashed to the floor. Mongoose tried to scarper back out of the window like a filthy rat caught in the dustbins, but Mrs Roberts caught him with a glancing blow on the small of the back. Mongoose let out a rat-like squeal and disappeared back into the darkness.

To try and cut him off, she bolted through to the front, the fear and adrenalin affording her some manoeuvrability for her size, and age. Outside, only a few of the gang remained, yet Mongoose was nowhere to be seen. Now directing her fury at these smirking little yobs, she marched over to them wielding her club.

'Go on sod off you bunch of evil bastards. Get away from my home,' she cried, threatening to whack them one.

Quickly they dispersed with a new found wariness of this old woman, with a golf club.

Then it suddenly dawned on Mrs Roberts that while she was out in the front, Mongoose may have doubled back, and re-entered through the kitchen window. Gasping in panic, she dived back indoors and reached the kitchen which lay empty except for the shards of smashed glass, scattered on the window ledge. With her breathing laboured, and her heart banging in her chest, she tried to calm herself down so as not risk having a cardiac arrest.

However, the respite was short-lived when her attentions turned to her beloved dog whom she hadn't heard yapping for a while.

'Tibby?' she cried, completely oblivious of Mongoose now. 'Tibby, Tibby?'

She flew into a lather beginning to scour the entire downstairs, but there was no sign of him. She noticed the front door was wide open, and suspected that he might have got out, so she rushed out on to the lawn. Still there was no joy, but at least the yobs had gone for now, but they would be back.

'Tibby? Tibby?' she cried scanning the small cul-de-sac, but he was nowhere to be seen.

In her mind she began to imagine all sorts of terrible things that may have happened to her beloved pet. Perhaps they have taken him, she fretted. Just then another possibility provided her with some meagre hope, maybe Tibby had run upstairs and hidden under the bed like he did once when the man came to fix her washing machine. With that, Mrs Roberts trundled up the stairs to check, praying that Tibby's joyful yap would put an end to her torment. Upstairs, she looked everywhere, under the bed, in the dressing cupboard, even in the bathroom, but it seemed hopeless.

Crushed, she slumped head in hands on the edge of her bed, and was just about to succumb to her overwhelming misery, when a knock sounded on her front door. Raising her head with the possibility that someone might have found him and brought him home, she raced back downstairs to find two police officers standing in her open doorway. Maybe one of the neighbours had called the police on her behalf, thank God, she thought.

The young female officer began to address her. 'Mrs Roberts we understand you've had a bit of a disturbance?'

Mrs Roberts heaved a weighty sigh. 'Yes, those bloody thugs tried to break into my home, and I think they've stolen my dog.'

The two officers flashed awkward glances at each other, then the male officer took over.

'Actually, we're here in response to a reported assault.'

Mrs Roberts looked at them confused. 'But I haven't reported anything yet.'

'No, the report was made by a seventeen-year-old youth who claims that you attacked him with a golf club.'

'Yes, that's right, I caught him trying to break in through my kitchen window, that's why I attacked him.'

'Well, the report that we received was that a couple of youths were talking outside in your close, when you stormed out with a golf club, then attacked one of them, and threatened the others. We have witnesses to support this claim.'

Mrs Roberts couldn't believe what she was hearing. 'Those fiends, or yobs, as I would prefer to call them, have been harassing me for the past six months. They stand outside my home drinking alcohol, throwing empty cans at my house, and use terrible foul language. Then they tried to break into my home, and that's why I attacked one of them.'

The young female officer interjected. 'Well, like we've said, the only report we've had is of an assault committed by you on these premises.'

Mrs Roberts's began to lose her patience. 'What about all of the harassment I've suffered over the past six months? What about the breaking and entering?'

'Of course, if you wish to report a break-in we will investigate. But for now we have to clear up this complaint of an assault which you have already confessed to.'

Mrs Roberts glared at the two officers indignantly. 'So you mean to tell me that this scum can get away with harassing me as much as they want, break into my house, steal my dog, and because I have to defend myself, I'm the one being charged?'

'Like we've already told you, Mrs Roberts, we will look into your complaints in due course, but first we have to sort out this accusation of assault.'

'Oh, of course,' Mrs Roberts retorted bitterly, 'the criminal's rights must come first, mustn't they? Over the last six months I have made dozens of complaints about the behaviour of these estate yobs, and what have you done about it? Nothing! Yet as soon as one of these hooligans make a complaint, you're here like a shot.'

'But an assault with an offensive weapon is serious, Mrs Roberts,' the female officer retorted.

'So is harassment, breaking and entering, and stealing a pet,' Mrs Roberts hit back.

'I understand, Mrs Roberts, but I'm afraid first things first, we must ask you to accompany us to the station to make a statement.'

All this had become too much for her now, and Mrs Roberts began to cry.

'What about my poor Tibby? What have they done with him?' she sobbed.

'We'll find your pet, Mrs Roberts,' the male officer leant towards her. 'Listen, we understand your frustration we really do. We'd like to nail these thugs just as much as you, but the problem is that they are still minors, and until we have concrete proof they have actually committed a crime I'm afraid our hands are tied.' Then he signalled to the waiting marked Honda CR-V. 'Please, if you will?'

What's the point, she thought and reluctantly, she got herself ready. While she did, the officers sorted out a 24

176

hour glazer to board up her kitchen window until it could be repaired the next day. When all this was in hand, she locked up her home, and climbed into the back of the police car feeling like a criminal and was escorted down to the police station. Justice, thy will be done.

*

About an hour later, the police drove Mrs Roberts back home, as yet no charges had been made against her, but she was informed they would soon be in touch. Be in touch, she thought, at the moment she couldn't care less, she was more concerned about the welfare of her beloved pet. And the only thing that had kept her going down at the station was the possibility that when she returned, Tibby might be waiting for her on the front door step, with his tail wagging behind him. Unfortunately though, he wasn't.

Gloomily, she re-entered her home and tried to bring some life back into it by turning on as many lights as possible. She lumbered into the kitchen to make herself a cuppa, and saw the boarded-up window, thankfully, the smashed glass had been tidied up for her. She began filling up the kettle-jug, and as she waited for it to boil she noticed the crumpled light shade put on top of the fridge freezer. Then it suddenly dawned on her that around this time of the night, Tibby usually had his supper from the fridge, a couple of slices of honey roast ham. Mrs Roberts began to cry again, she didn't care about the trouble with the thugs, she didn't care about the charges of assault she could be facing, all she cared about was Tibby.

That night in bed, Mrs Roberts had never felt so alone since her husband Alf had died five years ago. And the corner of her bed where Tibby usually slept, looked so cold and empty.

Every now and again just as she was on the verge of stealing a couple of winks of sleep, she thought, she could feel Tibby's soft warm body at the end of her bed. Once during the night, she even imagined she could hear him yapping outside the house, but when she opened the bedroom window to look down, there was nothing.

The following morning, Mrs Roberts decided that today, she was going to initiate an intense search for her pet, starting with door-to-door enquiries. She had to try at least. Upstairs, while she tidied her bed, she heard the letterbox flap shut, and supposed it was the postman delivering. But when she came back downstairs, she found a small card lying on her doormat. She bent down to pick it up, and heard the tired bones clicking in her legs. She turned over the card, it read:

WE HAVE BEEN ALERTED TO YOUR PROBLEM. IF YOU REQUIRE OUR SERVICE PLEASE CONTACT THIS NUMBER?

Mrs Roberts drew her head back bemused at the message and what it could possibly mean. Was it referring to her lost pet, or did it have something to do with her trouble with the yobs? She shrugged helplessly and figured, what the heck, haven't got anyone else to turn to, why not? So she went into the living room, picked up her cordless phone, and punched out the number.

That Saturday evening, because of the heat from the police, Mongoose and his gang kept well away from Mrs Roberts's house. Instead, they were content just hang around the entrance to the housing estate, beneath the orange glow of the sodium streetlights. There they happily swigged on bottles of lager, and gloated at their victory over Mrs Roberts last night.

Mongoose, feeling like the exalted leader of the mafia, leant idly against the wooden perimeter fencing, and took another mouthful of lager. Just to amuse himself, he waited for one of his lesser gang members to move into range then spurted it out all over him. Insulted by the gesture, but not wanting to incur his leader's wrath, the lad gamely chuckled along with the others. The next mouthful, Mongoose swallowed for himself, then he addressed his soldiers.

'When the heat dies down a bit, we'll chuck one of those silver dart rockets through her letterbox. But we'll snap off the guidance stick so it will spin around throwing off sparks, and hopefully burn her house down.'

All of them snorted in delight.

'How's yer back?' one impressionable member asked.

'That's nothing. I was just using that as an excuse,' he sneered, putting his mouth back to the bottle, and secretly hiding the fact that he squealed like a rat when he got hit from the club. 'Anyway that's nothing compared to what I'm going to do to her and that mutt.'

Further up the road, a navy blue escort van headed towards the estate, and Mongoose alerted his gang. 'Let's pelt this van with bottles for daring to come on to our patch.'

Ready to do whatever their leader said, they concealed their bottles by their sides so the driver wouldn't see what was coming. As soon as the van was in range, they all hurled their bottles at the van, one or two of them completely missed, but some smashed against the rim of the roof, sending shards of dark green glass everywhere. The van screeched to a halt, and the gang tried to scarper back into the estate, Mongoose and one of his soldiers bringing up the rear.

'Got yer.'

Mongoose and pal ran straight into a human wall, two six foot slabs of meat with balaclavas. The two men literally carried the struggling lads over to the van, which now waited with the back doors wide open. The two prisoners yelled and writhed to try and get free, but they were slung into the back before they even knew it, then the two men got in with them. The doors were quickly slammed shut, and the van skidded off down the road.

Behind them at the entrance to the estate, one or two of the gang members dared to poke their heads out wondering what the hell was going on, and where had their leader been taken.

A couple of miles away under the dark canopy of night, five figures (three men and the two teenagers) stood in the middle of a farmer's field. The two lads already stripped down to their waists, and hands tied behind their backs were forced to lie face down on the icy grass. Standing over them, one of the men held a long tapered piece of birch wood by his side. Thinking they were going to get raped, Mongoose turned his head in protest.

'Let us go. We'll do you for this, you better not touch us you queers.'

'Queers?' one of the men questioned. 'What do you think this is, a gang bang?'

'Don't you worry,' said another. 'That's the least of your problems right now. And besides, you're not even our types.'

Before commencing whatever they were going to do, one of the captors holding the birch wood turned to his mates and asked. 'What do you think, fifteen to start off with?' And they readily agreed.

Mongoose strained his head to look around. 'Fifteen? Fifteen what? What are you up to?'

To shut them up, insulation tape was plastered over their mouths. Mongoose and his mate grunted angrily behind the tape, then Mr Balaclava whipped the air with his birch stick just to get his stroke. Phew, Phew. First in line was Mongoose's mate, for Mongoose, they wanted him to suffer the mental torment of knowing what he was going to get. Mr Balaclava took his aim and struck the shivering white flesh before him with a cruel thwack. The lad squealed into the tape, again he struck him, and again, thwack, thwack. Listening to the high pitched wail of his mate was becoming too much to bear, and Mongoose tried to bury his face in the grass to escape from it.

When the punishment was over, the lad's trembling body displayed a dozen red welts that were clearly visible even in the dark. However, the lad tried to hide his tears of shame and agony by pressing his face in the cool grass. Now it was Mongoose's turn, and he sealed his eyes with dread. Before the lashings began, Mr Balaclava paused.

'OK, because you are the ringleader and we are so impressed by your lovely charm, you will get twenty strokes.'

Shit, Mongoose cried under his breath, and clenched himself ready.

The first whack stung like someone snapping a long piece of elastic against his skin. The second and third lashes were a bit stronger, and made it feel like his flesh was beginning to tear apart. By the fourteenth slash the pain was becoming unbearable, and he was having trouble catching his breath in between strokes. The agony he was now suffering, coupled with the terrible thought of what was happening to the flesh on his back, made him start to sob. So tense was his whole body, that by the twentieth and probably hardest lash, he squeaked and farted at the same time.

Mr Balaclava, exhausted after administering the punishment, finally stopped, and Mongoose's body went limp. As quietly as he could, Mongoose cried into the soggy grass, his bloody, quivering back looked like a couple of Bengal tigers had been fighting on it.

'Right, Mongoose or whatever your name is, if we hear of you or any of your rat mates hassling anyone else on that estate, the next time it will be fifty lashings. You got that?'

Mongoose nodded his head slowly.

'And another thing, if those charges don't get dropped on Mrs Roberts, and she doesn't get her dog back tomorrow completely unharmed, then we're going to find you again. We know where you and most of your rat pack mates live so watch out?'

Mr Balaclava squatted down beside him. 'Not as tough as you think now, are yer?'

Mongoose didn't answer.

Mr Balaclava straightened again. 'Next time you dish it out on some innocent old woman, or any other honest citizen you just want to hurt for the hell of it, you just remember what you've just had?'

Both lads were un-tied, and left alone in the dark field with their lacerated backs and bruised egos. In the distance they could hear a flock of sheep calling each other in one of the nearby fields. Never again would that sound be so soothing to them.

*

The very next day, the police called round to Mrs Robert's house to inform her that the charges of assault filed against her had been dropped. With regards to her lost pet, after questioning Mongoose and some of his gang, they had emphatically denied ever stealing him. But they assured the police officers that they would be more than happy to join in with the search. Flabbergasted by the news, Mrs Roberts thanked the officers for calling, but stressed that she could not rest until her beloved pet had been found.

However, tea time that day her prayers were answered when Tibby turned up bright eyed and bushy tailed in the charge of a very benevolent young couple. Apparently, early in the morning, Tibby had wandered into their garden in Marl Drive a couple of hundred yards down the road. Thankfully, he still had the identity tag on his collar, so he could be returned home.

Poor old Tibby must have been wandering around all night without any food or drink. Not to worry though, the caring young couple had given him a good feed before they brought him back home. In her ecstatic relief, Mrs Roberts offered them a reward for their kind hearted deed but they wouldn't accept it.

So at last, it was a happy ending for dear old Mrs Roberts, justice had been served.

CHAPTER 19

Will and Stacey, exited the multiplex cinema in the Llandudno junction, having just watched the new *Christmas Carol* feature film. Their next stop was the Pizza Hut for a couple of sit-down 8 inch pizzas with garlic bread. Tonight was their way of spending some quality time together, before Stacey headed off with her parents to spend Christmas with relatives.

Inside the Pizza Hut, Stacey did all the ordering as Will had never been into one these places before, and to him, trying to understand the menu was like reading directions in a foreign airport terminal. After the waitress had taken their order, Will shook his head with frustration.

'Good job you were here otherwise God knows what I would have ended up ordering.'

Stacey smiled amused. 'It's quite straight-forward once you've done it a couple of times.'

'Couple of times?' Will asked inquisitively. 'Is this where you used to come with that chap from your college?'

'Once or twice, yeah.' She shrugged like it meant nothing.

Will paused, his curiosity getting the better of him now. 'So just for the record, exactly how serious did the two of you get?'

'We only saw each other for about six months, that's all. It wasn't serious as you put it.'

Will put up his hands in defence. 'Hey, don't worry, that was before I came back on the scene, back then you were a free agent so you don't need to feel guilty about it?'

'I'm not feeling guilty about it. We just had a bit of a relationship and then it fizzled out, that's it.'

'Just like that?' Will teased her.

Stacey gave him that look which said, you're not going to give up are you? So Will eased up a tad.

'Honestly, it's OK if you prefer not to talk about it, all I'm doing is putting all our cards on the table that's all.'

Stacey gave in. 'OK, in the end he started to get a bit too clingy for my liking. And I wasn't ready for any of that.'

'What do you mean, he wanted to marry you?'

'He wanted to get engaged, but it wasn't just that, he was very insecure and paranoid as well. He wanted to know where I was all the time, who I was with, and what I was doing. It drove me mad in the end.'

'So what did happen in the end?' Will asked elbows on the table, hands crossed under his chin.

'In the end it got so bad that he started popping up wherever I went, it was a bit creepy. And then he started accusing me of seeing other people behind his back. He even tried stopping me from seeing my friends because he thought they were a bad influence. Once he even tried to get my mum and dad to phone him up whenever I went out. He used to get crazily jealous of me.'

Will's face darkened. 'He didn't ever hit you or anything did he?'

'No, no. He didn't beat me, but towards the end, he did grab me a few times. But getting back to the paranoid thing, after he started asking my parents to spy on me I thought that's it, I've had enough. And even after I finished it with him, he still used to follow me around. It almost got to the point that my dad threatened to go over to the college to see him, but I persuaded him not to. Instead, he phoned up the college to complain about him, and warn that if he didn't stop, we were going to get the police involved.'

'So what was he in this college then, a student like you?'

'No, he was one of the tutors on one of the courses I was on.'

'Sounds like a guy who's spent too much time living at

home with his mother, like Norman Bates. You didn't ever take a shower in his presence did you?'

'No,' Stacey groaned. 'But he does live at home with his mother, or he used to, I don't know if he still does?'

Will smiled at the coincidence.

'But all that is history now.'

'Yeah, just as long as he knows that.'

Stacey looked up at him. 'Yes, he does know that, and I don't want to suddenly hear that he's been in a mysterious accident or anything.'

'I don't even know who he is anyhow,' Will conceded. 'Plus I don't do that sort of thing anymore, remember? And besides, I don't want to jeopardise my parole either.'

'Yes!' Stacey emphasised. 'So behave yourself. I don't even agree with you going to all these training sessions with your mate, it might trigger that aggression in you again.'

Will frowned back at her. 'Don't worry, I'm not going down that road again, I'm just helping my old mate with his students, just giving them the benefit of my experience.'

Somehow Stacey still didn't look convinced about all that, but she let it go. Will, on the other hand was thankful that he didn't have to tell her the real reason why he was helping to train Geoff's team.

Finally their pizzas arrived and they both looked forward to tucking in. However, outside in the car park facing the pizza hut, someone sitting in their car appeared to be taking a particular interest in their dinner date?

*

'Fear is the warrior's best friend,' Will lectured the team as they sat listening on the rubber scrimmage mats. This was their fifth training session, and the last before the Christmas recess. Once again, Will had succumbed to the request of his old pal Geoff by taking another class. Deep in meditative

185

thought, Will dressed in a navy tracksuit paced up and down in front of the class.

'You see in conventional martial arts, they don't really prepare you for the effect that fear has on the mind and body. And in all honesty, this is imperative.' Will raised an admonishing finger. 'It doesn't matter how hard you train, or how fit and strong you are, if your mind isn't prepared for the fight, then the battle is already lost. I have heard of many good fighters actually run from a street encounter simply because they're bottle has gone. I know a lot of you are probably familiar with the term fight or flight. But what actually does this phrase mean? Back in prehistoric times when man was faced with fifteen foot dinosaurs with mouths the size of a car's boot he was given this sudden, explosive energy to run for his life. You've all heard the phrase, so scared that you've pissed or shit yourself. Well that is in fact very true, and the reason this happens is because it's nature's way of making the body as light as possible in order to gather as much speed necessary to run away from the enemy.

However, if a retreat is not possible, then the adrenalin will be used to prepare the body to fight. This includes anaesthetizing the body to pain, making the body faster, stronger, and providing you with the essential tools to help survive your encounter. All that sounds pretty good, doesn't it? But the downside to this wonderful gift is the troubling symptoms that occur, and what effect they can have on the mind and body. For instance, when we encounter extreme pressures, or a great fear for something looming, then the adrenal glands are triggered, and release stress hormones into our bloodstream. It's that adrenalin that revs you up ready for action, but many people are fooled into believing that this surge of energy is their body's way of telling them that they are shit-scared, and they should run for their lives. You have all at one time or another experienced these tell-tale symptoms, especially if someone has challenged you to a fight. They include, tunnel vision, body trembling, legs feeling like lead, a quiver in the voice, nausea etc.'

Everyone nodded in agreement.

'But when you feel these symptoms, instead of helping you, what does it make you feel like doing?' Will asked the team.

'Run like hell,' Guy spoke up, and Will zapped him correct with his finger.

'Run, exactly. And that is what many people do because they don't fully understand what is happening with their bodies.'

Tom raised his hand. 'So what are you saying then, should we run, or stay and fight?'

Will thought he was missing the point. 'That depends entirely on the person and the circumstances. All I'm trying to do here is explain what is happening to your body during those stressful moments. And that you should accept and use these factors to your advantage instead of letting them defeat you.'

Tom jumped in again. 'So how do we use them to our advantage then?'

'As I've said, accept what is happening to you, understand it, even prepare for it to occur. It's simply your body's own natural way of arming you ready for battle. It's a help not a hindrance, it's as natural as eating and breathing. When you're hungry – you eat. When you're thirsty – you drink, and when you're scared – you fight. Adrenalin makes you sharper, faster and stronger, use it, control it, harness it. Fear is the ultimate friend of the true warrior.'

Brad raised his hand. 'I understand what you're saying, but I've felt that fight or flight fear quite a few times and I've tried to suppress it, but you can't, can you?'

Will looked at him with amazement. 'Why do you try and fight it? It's a necessary tool so use it. If I gave you a weapon to use in a battle, would you waste time wondering if you should use it or not? No, you would say thank you very much that'll do nicely.'

Tom put up his hand again. 'Yeah, but when you're in that position and you get the shakes, the quiver in the voice, and the sheet-white look of fear, it doesn't actually paint a very good picture of confidence, does it?'

Will smiled, impressed by Tom's question. 'That is a good point.'

Tom preened himself, and got a mocking shove from Charlie.

'That is where the experienced fighter comes in. You see, you will never be able to suppress all those physical symptoms, even the most seasoned fighters get them. But with practice and experience you can learn to control them.

Geoff looked at his watch, it was that time already. 'OK, Will, that'll do us, I think.'

Will was content to hear that, and everybody began stretching and climbing stiffly to their feet. Charlie groaned as he clutched his aching back.

'My effing back, is killing me.'

Mike chimed in. 'Too much doggy style that is.'

'Well, you weren't complaining about that last night boom, boom.'

'OK, guys?' Geoff addressed them all. 'We've all got two whole weeks off now for the Christmas recess. We'll start back training, the first Thursday in the New Year. But...' Geoff crossed his fingers, 'should anything crop up, any emergency, the twenty-four-hour-call out still applies.'

Tom furtively rolled his eyes. 'Great.'

'OK then, so all of you have a good Christmas, don't get too drunk and let's hope that we don't have to see each other's ugly mugs until the New Year.'

Everybody gave him a look for his cheek, then wished each other the best before departing.

As Geoff drove Will back to his flat, Will asked if he could be dropped off at the Londis store as he needed to pick up some last minute items. Geoff did as he was asked, and pulled up outside the shop.

'Listen, Will, if you don't want to be by yourself on Christmas day you're quite welcome to spend it with us. I mean it's not going to be much fun moping around your flat all by yourself you know?'

'Don't worry Geoff, by the time I've had my run, showered and sorted myself out, the day will be almost gone anyhow.'

Geoff reluctantly gave in. 'OK, have a good one then?' He reached across to shake Will's hand. 'Don't forget if you change your mind, let us know.'

'I will, cheers.' Will said and shook it.

Slinging the car door closed, Will made his way towards Londis and Geoff tooted him as he drove off.

Later as he re-emerged from the store carrying his bits and pieces in a plastic bag, Will headed across the road towards his flat. As he did so, he noticed a short medium-built man in a duffel jacket standing outside seemingly waiting for someone. Will reached the other side of the road and the man approached him.

'Excuse me?'

Will stopped and eyed this dodgy-looking man with straight fair hair that curled up by his neck and ears like a badly fitted wig.

'Yes?'

'Does your name happen to be Will Thomas?'

'It does.'

The chap got right down to business. 'And you're seeing a woman at the moment called Stacey Williams?'

The penny dropped and Will got his first look at Stacey's ex. 'Yes that's right.'

The chap nodded, agitated, his adrenalin surge already giving him away.

'Well, my name is Peter Jackson and Stacey and I are more or less still an item. You think it's OK to steal another man's woman, do you?'

Will tightened his grip on the plastic bag as if he was going to hit him with it.

189

'Who's stolen what exactly?'

'You've stolen my woman.' The man pointed a loaded finger at him, his mouth quivering at the corners.

So far Stacey's ex was living up to all Will's expectations. Will looked him up and down and saw a short college bookworm with childlike manicured hands that probably couldn't rip their way out of a paper bag.

'Really?' Will replied. 'Well, from what Stacey tells me she broke up with you a long time ago, so what business is it of yours who she sees right now?'

'Stacey has not broken up with me.' The chap almost stomped his foot like a child throwing a tantrum.

Will was on the verge of feeling compassion for him. 'I think she has, mate, otherwise we'd have met each other a lot sooner.'

The chap took that as a warning. 'Oh yeah, and what's that supposed to mean?'

'Think about it, two's company, three's a crowd. And besides, Stacey and I were an item long before you ever came along. So it's not as if she's just jumped straight into the arms of someone else on the rebound. And as well as that, I came back for her because we already have a lot of history together. You only saw each other for six months.'

'Seven,' he corrected.

'Seven, was it? I thought you said you hadn't broken up?'

The chap tried to back track. 'Seven until you came along then.'

Will smirked inwardly. 'But apart from that, if Stacey had told me that she was happy in another relationship, I would have gladly put up my hands and left her alone. But she didn't say that, so I haven't actually stolen anything from anyone. You just need to accept that it's over and move on mate.'

Will hoped that that would end it, and he could continue indoors. But he was wrong.

'Oh yes, Will Thomas, I know all about you alright.' He said, and that made Will stop again.

'Stacey told me all about you when we were together. Enjoy you time in prison did you?'

This irritated Will. 'No, actually, I didn't! I served my time, paid the price and my debt to society has been settled. What's it to you anyhow?'

The chap gave him a drilling stare. 'You're just a no-good thug!'

Had this incident occurred some three years ago, the old Will would have seized this annoying little parasite by the oesophagus and almost choked him to death. But that terrible fire no longer burned within him. What was once a raging inferno was now a cold, burnt-out furnace full of dead ashes.

Seeing that his insults weren't having much effect on Will, the chap pushed his luck even more. 'Yeah, you're just a thick headed animal scum.'

Will laughed to himself he knew that no college bookworm like him would go to such lengths to pick a fight with some thug unless he had an ulterior motive. It was blatantly obvious to Will that this idiot was just trying to goad him into attacking so he could charge him for assault.

'Really?' Will replied and turned to walk up to his flat.

The chap made a grab for Will's arm, any other time that arm would be broken but Will wanted to see just how far he was willing to go.

'Don't you walk away from me,' he blustered, eyes bulging and face white with fear.

To Will's trained eye, an attack was definitely imminent, yet he was still prepared to take one just to see if the chap had the guts to do it.

Just to push him over the edge, Will muttered, go home, you're mother's calling you. Then he purposely turned his back.

Whack, the chap Judas-punched him to the side of his right eye. The blow felt hollow as if he'd been hit by a woman's empty handbag, Will spun around like a Spanish bull finding a terrier nipping at his leg. The chap stepped back as if he was expecting to get hit. But this particular bull didn't charge. Instead, Will breathed in calmly through his nose, and uttered almost triumphantly, nice try arsehole, and coolly ambled up the steps to his flat.

The chap watched amazed as Will disappeared indoors without a fight, then the reality of what he'd done begun to set in. He swung around, and walked off hands stuffed inside his duffel jacket pocket so no one could see them shaking as if he had a palsy.

Back in his flat, Will slumped on to his couch, clutching a folded wet towel to his slightly swollen eye brow. He was neither angered nor saddened by the incident, he simply viewed it as part of the price he had to pay in order to keep Stacey.

However, thinking about it, he was a bit cheesed-off that she had told her ex all those incriminating things about him. Tomorrow evening, he would be seeing Stacey one more time before she flitted off to relatives for Christmas, and Will wondered if he should mention all this. Removing the wet towel from his eye, he glanced over towards the bed at the box of *Gucci* shoes that were waiting to be wrapped.

*

Will and Stacey's last night together was intended to be a simple cosy night-in, but whether or not that might be soured by what he had to tell her, remained to be seen?

As Will greeted her at the door to his flat, Stacey's face became a mask of concern.

'What the hell happened to your eye?' she gasped.

Will told her to come in first, and she marched straight in carrying a plastic carrier bag.

Will closed the door behind her, and she waited uneasily for answers.

'I had a visit from your crazy ex,' he told her as he went to sit on the arm of the couch.

Stacey's face blazed with rage. 'And he did that?'

Will nodded.

'Why?'

'Because he was trying to goad me into hitting him so he could get me done for assault and prove to you that I am still just a vicious thug. And then hopefully, you would feel sorry for him and give him another chance.'

'And did you hit him back?'

'No, I didn't. I walked away from him.'

Stacey was dumbstruck, but probably more so at the fact that Will hadn't retaliated and put her ex in hospital. Somewhat relieved, she went over and checked his eye like a protective mother. The injury itself wasn't that bad, only superficial, just a minor swelling under the brow, with a speck of red on the corner of the eye-lid. Stacey stood back with her head tottering.

'I can't believe he would do something so stupid.'

Will stared back at her, remembering what her ex had said about him. 'Why did you tell him that I went to prison and all that?'

'What do you mean?'

'He said you told him everything about me.'

'I didn't tell him everything, all I said during our relationship was that you had a bad temper which was what got you put away, that's all. In fact I told you a hellava lot more about him than I ever said about you.'

Will thought about it for a second, then decided to forget it, after all why the hell should he believe that little twerp? Changing the subject, he nodded towards the bag she was holding. 'What's in there?'

She gave him a sulky smile. 'I've brought you a Christmas present.'

Will snorted in appreciation. 'What is it?'

'You'll have to wait and see in a couple of days, won't you?' she said, placing the bag next to the window table out of sight for now.

Will, couldn't resist teasing her a bit. 'I haven't got you one, you know?'

Stacey shrugged, as if she was pretending not to care. 'That's alright.'

Will enjoyed knowing that if that was really true, she would never let him forget it for as long as he lived.

'Yeah, of course I have. It's in the kitchen in a bag, I had a bit of trouble wrapping it though. How the hell do you women cope when you have a massive family to wrap prezzies for?'

'It's a woman thing, a man wouldn't understand,' she replied, trying to get a sly peek in the kitchen.

Settling down for the night, Will provided the drinks and they cosied-up on the couch to watch one of the Christmas films on the box. During the evening, Stacey began to lean on him, and rub her head affectionately on his arm, and it reminded him of old times. It felt so good to have her back in his life, back together in they're own little world. It was like they were twins embryos safe in a protective womb. How he wished she could stay with him over Christmas. Stacey then groaned.

'What's up?' Will asked.

'I've got one more keep-fit session tomorrow before Christmas and I really can't be bothered.'

'Discipline.' Will lectured.

'It's the last one and I bet Jenny the instructor, is really going to put us through the grinder.'

'Can I pop by and watch all of your arses wobbling as you're jumping up and down?' Will teased her, and got an irate stab in the ribs in reply.

At the end of the evening, back at Stacey's hotel Will handed the Christmas present to her in a plastic carrier bag. Stacey thanked him for it, and promised she would ring him whenever she could. As Will nodded, she leant towards him, and kissed him softly on the lips, a peck that lingered for a couple of seconds, and gave away her strengthening feelings. But for some reason she broke off the kiss, and headed off up the steps to the front door. Will watched her and waited for one last goodnight. With her hand on the door handle, she turned to him.

'Will I'm proud of you. Not hitting my ex showed a lot of spirit.'

'So there is hope for me then?'

Stacey smiled back and replied. 'Yeah, I think there might be.'

Then she disappeared indoors. Will smirked to himself, but as he left he began to dread the thought of returning to his flat without her.

*

'Reaching up... pulling on the rope...and down.' The pretty, blonde female instructor, shouted to the rest of her class.

Stacey, wearing her long, grey t-shirt and black leggings, pulled on that imaginary rope. Thirty more seconds of this and I am going to collapse, she thought.

'Annnd... stop.' The teacher called.

The class of women, ranging from all ages, all swooned and thanked God it was all over until next year.

'That's it girls, well done. See you all in the second week in January. And as a reminder, if there's anyone else still interested in the New Year's charity run please let me know as soon as possible. Have a good Christmas and see you all in the New Year.'

Although, everyone wished her same in return, Stacey and her class felt like telling their teacher what she could do with her charity run after putting them through all that torture.

Almost crawling on her hands and knees, Stacey made it back to her backpack and whipped out a white towel to pat at the film of perspiration on her face.

'Why the hell do we do it?' One barrel-shaped woman turned to her.

Stacey rolled her eyes back at her. 'Strawberry cheesecake.' She replied.

'I blame Toppolina's Pizza on Friday nights and Lorraine

Kelly in the morning.' Another pot-bellied woman chimed-in, and they all shared a little chuckle.

Exiting the fitness centre Stacey was still nattering to the barrel-shaped woman when someone stood in front of them. It was Stacey's ex; Peter Jackson.

'Stacey, can I have a word?'

Stacey turned and smiled at her gym buddy. 'I'll see you in the New Year, have a good Christmas.'

'OK, luv, you do the same.' She replied and left them to it.'

Stacey sighed irksomely, 'what do you want Peter?'

'I hope you're not serious about that Will guy.'

Stacey shook her head and stormed off, Peter followed behind.

'Stacey, he's only going to hurt you again, can't you see that?'

Stacey halted angrily. 'Oh, yes, and what the hell did you think you were doing going to his flat like that?'

'I just wanted to see what kind of guy he was and tell him not to hurt you again that's all.'

Stacey huffed with contempt. 'Rubbish, you went there to provoke him into hitting you so you could prove once and for all that he's a no-good thug. And when that didn't work, you hit *him*.'

'No, I was just defending myself from him, he threaten...'

Stacey cut him off. 'Didn't you realise the danger you were putting yourself into when you hit him? He could have crushed you like a grape and would have had the right to do so because it was *you* who attacked him.'

Peter struggled to find an explanation and Stacey held up a flat palm to stop whatever he was trying to say. 'Listen, Pete, just stop interfering with my life. We're not together anymore so it's no longer any of your concern. Just get over it, OK?' Then off she marched leaving him looking deflated.

CHAPTER 20

Christmas Eve, Tom, Charlie, Mike and Nigel were standing on the doors of the Wetherspoons pub. Outside, the icy December wind was whipping up to a steady thirty miles an hour gale. But this Baltic storm didn't seem to deter the Christmas revellers. Especially, the young ladettes, who swanned about in their skimpy party tops and killer heels to risk certain hypothermia in the quest for the ultimate yuletide rave.

'Jesus Christ.' Tom nuzzled down into the neck of his heavy reefer jacket, and stomped his feet like the old fashioned bobby on his beat. 'It's going to be a looooong night.'

Speaking too soon, a fracas errupted from inside the foyer, and all the doormen dived through the entrance to investigate. Inside, two warring lads were screaming in each other's faces – probably because of some girl they both liked. But when the bouncers intervened, somehow it was like showing a red rag to a bull.

Nevertheless, it didn't take long for Mike and Nigel to restrain the two combatants. That was until one of their mates took umbrage to the bouncers' interference and tried to lay one on Mike, and what a mistake that was. In a flash, Tom and Charlie leapt on to the miscreant like two Rottweilers on a ten-pound steak. They both carried him out headfirst and dumped him on the cold cement pavement with a loud humph. Tom then knelt on the lad's head with one knee while Charlie kept a hold of his legs to stop him from trying to kick them. The lad's face grimaced under the weight of Tom's bony knee squashing his head against the pavement. But they kept up the pressure until he had calmed down, and when he did, Tom released his knee, and gripped him by the lapels of his silky shirt. 'Don't you ever attack one of my men again, do you understand me?'

'Well, don't hit my mate then,' the lad argued.

'I don't give a shit,' Tom snarled, shaking him hard enough that the back of his head bumped the concrete.

'Hey, hey, that's not necessary,' one of his frumpy girlfriends protested, but Tom ignored her.

'Do I make myself clear?' Tom repeated the shove to underline his authority and the lad meekly agreed.

Tom let him go and stood over him while the fat girl helped him back to his feet. Just in case there was any more trouble, all four bouncers stood back on the door to form a barrier. Ironically the two lads who had originally started all this were now shaking hands, and tapping each other apologetically. They were no longer a worry, the bouncer's problem was now the plump girl who was determined to make her point about Tom's heavy-handed treatment.

With a face that looked like her make-up had been jetted on through a fire hose, she waddled up to Tom. 'I'm going to make a formal complaint about the way you handled my cousin.'

Tom rolled his eyes like he'd heard this a million times before.

'There was no need for any of that, he's not a violent person and didn't deserve any of that, it was well out of order.'

Tom quickly hit back. 'Yeah, and so was he for attacking one of my men, you're lucky we don't ban him indefinitely for that.'

'He didn't hit him, he was just trying to help that's all.'

'Listen, he tried to land a blow on one of my men, I saw it, we all bloody saw it, so stop trying to make excuses.'

'No he didn't.'

Tom couldn't tolerate this stupid woman any longer.

'Just go away you silly bitch, you wouldn't know your arse from a hole in the ground.'

The woman's jaw dropped open. 'I beg your pardon?'

'You heard.' Tom turned away from her, but she tried to get in his face.

'How dare you speak to me like that.'

Tom was really beginning to lose it now. 'Listen, just piss off, OK? You people you're all the same. You're quick to turn your cheek when one of your own are dishing it out, but when they get a taste of it back, you don't damn well like it, do you? Now for the last time, piss off!'

The woman was speechless, then the lad she was trying to stick up for, tried to drag her away himself, and that seemed to set her off again. Tom shook his head and watched as the lad hauled her away like a dog owner trying to drag his vicious mutt from a fight.

When she had gone, the other doormen started to tease him, Charlie getting his oar in first. 'Won't be getting a Christmas kiss off her then,' he scoffed, and everyone chuckled.

'Fat bitch,' Tom seethed, then quickly changed his tune when he saw Snoopy (the doormen's grass) jogging over from the taxi stand towards them.

Snoopy made an amused frown. 'Who's your friend?'

Tom's look said, don't even go there, then he pulled Snoopy to one side away from the other doormen. 'So what have you got?'

Snoopy waited for a couple of lads to pass by, then disclosed what he knew.

'The chap who I got to do the deal with the drug gang always goes to the Ship Inn pub on a Sunday night for a quiet drink.'

'Alone?' Tom asked.

'Well, he usually has one or two with him, but that's when he's most exposed, that's when he's least covered.'

'OK, cheers.' Tom tapped him, and checked that no one else was listening.

'Don't forget, we'll need you there to point him out to us. You'll get a little extra present in Santa's stocking this year. Keep us informed.'

Snoopy flicked the end of his nose with his thumb, a habit he always did whenever things were going right for him. Leaving Tom, he had a bit of a joke with the other bouncers before slinking off inside for a few drinks.

Meanwhile, Tom sidled up to Charlie and said out of the corner of his mouth.

'Sunday nights, this guy who got that gang for us goes to the Ship Inn pub in Rhos-on-Sea, we'll get it sorted this week. Hopefully we might be able to work out a deal so we can get those scouse maniacs off our backs once and for all.'

'Do you know who he is?' asked Charlie.

'No, Snoopy's going to introduce us.'

Mike just happened to pick up the end of their conversation. 'So, what are you going to get sorted?

Tom gave Charlie a sly tap to keep him quiet and thought up an excuse quickly. 'The Wilkinson gang, one of the leader's will be there on Sunday night at the Ship Inn so me and Charlie are going down there to see if we can call some sort of a truce.'

'Better give Geoff and the others notice.'

'Naw, I think we'll leave them out of this one.' Tom replied.

Mike frowned confused. 'What about the team?'

'I think we might be able to sort this one out without the team.'

'Are you sure about that?'

'Yes, Mike.' Tom snapped. 'And don't you go mentioning it to them either.'

Mike didn't like the sound of that, but judging by Tom's reaction, he kept quiet.

*

Buried deep in Christmas tinsel and coloured baubles, Geoff was sitting in front of the TV vegging-out to yet another adaptation of *A Christmas Carol*. That was until his interest was diverted by the conversation Jan was having on the phone with her mother. Apparently, Jan's father had caught a bout of the flu, so their annual Christmas dinner get-together would have to be cancelled. What a shame, Geoff mumbled to himself relieved that he wouldn't have to sit at her parent's house for a whole four hours with a smile glued on to his face, listening to how cute Jan was when she was a baby. Or hearing the same old boring story about how Jan was always expected to marry a musician with truck loads of money.

Geoff sat listening with one ear as Jan promised to ring first thing in the morning to find out how her father was. She clicked off the phone and tutted with disappointment. 'That's a shame, poor dad with the flu over Christmas.'

'Yeah, shame.' Geoff had to bite his lip to hide his amusement, and Jan picked up on his sarcasm.

'Oh yeah, you really sound broken-hearted.'

'I am, honestly; that's spoilt my whole Christmas now.'

Jan gave him a waspish look. 'It can be dangerous to get the flu at his age you know?'

'I know, I know,'

Jan's shoulders sank dejectedly, and she sighed, 'we'll just have to have our own quiet little Christmas get-together, won't we?' Then she nipped through to the kitchen to make a cuppa.

Geoff waited until she had left the room, then broke into a silent cheer.

Jan shouted through. 'I know you're laughing.'

*

CHRISTMAS DAY

By midday, most of the houses across Britain were cluttered up with Christmas wrapping paper and empty cardboard boxes. Kids were fighting over their toys, and mums were already in the kitchen steaming out the place cooking Christmas dinner.

However, being DINKYS Geoff and Jan were spared the burden of parenthood, and the threat of bankruptcy that came with it at this time of the year. Alternatively, they both enjoyed a quiet modest morning opening up their handful of gifts and kicking back with a glass of brandy. And there wasn't a screaming kid in sight.

Later on that afternoon, Jan had planned to have a small buffet for the two of them, and this suddenly gave Geoff an idea.

'Listen, Jan, being that we're not making such a big thing about Christmas dinner, how about if I ask Will to join us this afternoon for our buffet?'

Jan's face froze in mid-sip. 'I don't know, Geoff. Do you really think that'd be a good idea?'

'Yeah, why not? I mean he'll be sitting there alone in his flat now, and we're not doing anything special, so why not ask him over? It'll only be for a few hours, and it'll be the perfect chance for you to meet him.'

Geoff could see that she wasn't completely comfortable about this, but he worked on her until finally she relented. 'Besides, he might not even want to come,' he said, draining the last of his brandy and standing up ready to go.

Jan almost choked on her drink. 'What, you mean right now?'

'Well, yeah, I'll have to go and pick him up, won't I? And if I phone him he's just going to say no.'

'So why force him to come then?'

'Because if I go down there personally, he'll know I'm actually making an effort and not doing it out of moral obligation. You see, he'll say no because he doesn't want to intrude, but deep down I think he'd be glad of the company.'

'OK, Doctor Freud.'

Geoff humoured her, then went to fetch the car keys from the top of the hall cabinet. Meanwhile, Jan enjoyed one last sip of her brandy before preparing to tidy-up for their imminent guest.

Geoff pressed the doorbell to Will's flat and within a minute it was answered. Straight away, Geoff noticed the slight swelling on Will's eye, and the thought of his old pal ever getting a shiner shocked him to the core.

'What happened?'

For a second Will had completely forgotten about the injury.

'Oh, yeah, come on in. I'll tell you inside.'

Inside the flat, Will went to sit on the arm of the couch while Geoff stood waiting to hear what had happened.

'Stacey's ex paid me a visit the other day, and thanked me personally for trying to steal her off him.'

'Cheeky bastard, did you...?' Geoff gesticulated with his fist.

Will smiled back amused. 'No I didn't do anything.'

Annoyed at this, Geoff asked why.

'Because that was his intention all along, it was a trap.'

'A trap?' Geoff puzzled.

'Yeah, he wanted me to retaliate so he could get me done for assault, and then ruin my chances with Stacey.'

'So who the hell is this guy?'

Will shrugged. 'Just an obsessive ex who is willing to try anything to get her back.'

'And does Stacey know about all this?'

'Oh yes, she's pissed off about it too.'

Geoff rattled his car keys with agitation. 'Want us to sort him out for you?'

Will smiled appreciatively. 'Not necessary, Geoff. In fact he actually did me a favour.'

'How's that?'

'Well, the simple fact that I didn't respond proved to Stacey that I have changed.'

Geoff saw his point of view, then Will picked up his tray of food and went to sit at the window table, he nodded towards the couch. 'Have a seat, Geoff.'

Feeling a bit guilty for disturbing his meal, Geoff did as he was told.

'So to what do I owe this pleasure on Christmas Day? Shouldn't you be tucking into your own lunch round about now?'

Geoff noticed Will's pitiful plate of supernoodles and replied, 'Stacey's parents called off the dinner because of flu, so Jan and I were wondering if you would like to join us for a little buffet this afternoon?'

Will's first reaction was to politely refuse, but being that Geoff made the effort to come all the way down here, he found it difficult to say no.

'You sure about that Geoff? I mean doesn't Jan mind?'

'No not at all, In fact she's preparing it all right now.'

Will gazed down at his plate of supernoodles as if he didn't want to leave them, and Geoff joked that he could bring them along if he wished. Declining that part of the offer, Will gratefully accepted the invitation, and asked Geoff to give him five minutes to prepare. While he waited, Geoff turned to the TV and started watching the feature film *Willy Wonka and the Chocolate Factory*. Perched on top of the TV was one single Christmas card that was obviously sent from Stacey.

'So when is Stacey due back then?' Geoff asked.

'What's that, Geoff?'

Geoff turned around to repeat the question, and caught the gruesome sight of Will's naked back just before he pulled down a black sweatshirt over it. It was etched with legions of pink scars, and looked like it had been used as a chopping block in a butcher's shop. Geoff turned back quickly before Will had caught him looking.

'Oh, in about a day or so,' Will replied.

To hide the shock of what he'd seen, Geoff asked what Stacey had bought him for Christmas, and Will told him he was wearing it. Geoff looked over again to see him displaying the coal-black fleece jacket.

'Nice.' He remarked.

Will tapped his jeans pocket in readiness. 'All set then?'

At Geoff's home, Will was introduced to Jan for the first time, and was surprised at how petite she was. In return Jan appeared a touch unsure about Will's giant crab tattoo etched across his neck. However, after the customary pleasantries, Geoff took Will into the living room for a glass of wine, while Jan put the finishing touches to the buffet.

Soon all three of them were sitting at the table in the breakfast room tucking into paper plates of sausage rolls, spring rolls, vol-a-vents etc. As they ate, Jan was content to listen as Geoff and Will chatted about old times, and chuckled about all the scrapes they had gotten into in their youth. Jan even learned a few brow-raising revelations about her so-called squeaky-clean husband.

Then she asked Will all about Stacey, where she lived, and what plans they had for the future. Although one subject she did keep clear of (much to Geoff's relief) was about Will's recent spell in prison, and what crime he actually committed.

After they had eaten, Will insisted on helping to clear up, and once all that was done, he and Geoff chilled out in front of the box, while Jan finished off in the kitchen. On the TV there was a news report of another fatal stabbing late last night somewhere in Kent, and this started Geoff off.

'Even at Christmas time it doesn't make a difference to some of these low-lives does it? Do you know I was reading the North Wales Weekly news the other day and there was this story about some knob-head from Colwyn Bay who threw a kitten into a garden with two pit-bull terriers and enjoyed watching them tear it to pieces. I couldn't believe what I was reading. I mean what sort of scum has the mindset to do something like that?' He remarked, glancing across for Will's opinion, and saw the troubled expression on his face.

'You don't know those idiots do you?' He asked.

Will woke up. 'No, no, it just reminded me of something that's all.'

At that moment, Jan reappeared, and Geoff reminded her of the terrible kitten incident. Being a die-hard animal lover herself, she recalled how sickened she was by it. 'That was disgusting. He should be shot for that, I don't care what anybody says. Just what the hell is happening to our society when people can do such things, especially to poor innocent creatures like that?'

Will listened to their reactions, but kept his opinions to himself, and soon they drifted on to more pleasant subjects.

An hour or so later, Will decided it was time to leave, and suggested that the mile walk back to his flat would be a perfect chance to burn off some of his Christmas binge. But Geoff would have none of it. Despite having had consumed a few glasses of wine, he insisted on driving Will back home. Before leaving, Will thanked Jan for having him, and providing such a wonderful spread. Jan smiled back in appreciation and told him that next time he must bring Stacey along with him. Will promised that he would.

Arriving back at Will's flat, something was bothering Geoff, and he turned to his friend before he left him. 'You sure everything was alright before when I mentioned that kitten incident? For a moment you looked like you had taken it quite personal.'

Will took a very deep breath and uttered. 'Maybe it's time you knew the whole truth.'

Geoff immediately switched off the car's ignition, and was all ears.

'It reminded me of the incident that got me put away in prison. You see, deep down I've always been a big animal lover, cats, dogs, anything with fur and paws. And I've never been able to tolerate those who abuse these wonderful creatures. Back during my early courtship with Stacey, we had a black Labrador puppy called Georgie, and at that time we were still living in separate homes. But we decided that Georgie would stay at hers because he would be good company for her when she was alone. And when he grew up he would also be able to look after her and guard her house.' Will paused as if his hand was on the door handle to a room he really did not wish to enter.

'One day just before I arrived at Stacey's, Georgie escaped into her front garden without Stacey realising. Suddenly she heard this awful commotion coming from outside, and when she got there...' Will stalled again, his lip beginning to curl over his front teeth with anger.

'There was this pit-bull dog shaking Georgie around in his mouth like a rag-doll. And watching it, were these two nineteen-or twenty-year-old lads laughing and urging their dog on. Panicking, Stacey rushed over forgetting about the danger and tried to save our pup, and a neighbour, a big chap who saw what was going on, also came over to help. Frantically, Stacey tried to prise our dog from the pit-bull's jaws, and she remembers looking into Georgie's eyes and seeing him saying good bye to her with them.'

A lump stuck in Will's throat, cutting off his words.

'Jesus.'

'Finally, Stacey and the neighbour managed to get Georgie free despite getting bitten and cut themselves, and all those lads did was march off down the street with their dog back on the leash. Seconds later, I arrived and saw Stacey crying, holding poor Georgie in her arms with blood all over her hands. Then the neighbour told me what had just happened, and where the lads went, and I was off. About a hundred yards down the road, I spotted them, so I drove passed and stopped further down so they wouldn't know I was coming.'

'What did you do?'

Will, could only shake his head helplessly. 'Hell, absolute hell.'

Geoff waited for Will to find his words.

'First I broke the lads legs so they couldn't run away, then the dog tried to attack which turned out to be the best thing it could have done for me. As it went for me I grabbed it by putting my hand through its collar and twisting it around so I could strangle it to death. I made those two bastards watch me kill their dog right in front of them. And when I heard them plead for me to stop, I laughed. I laughed because I enjoyed seeing their pain, and I enjoyed seeing them fear what I was going to do to them next. When I dropped the dog's lifeless carcass in front of them, they knew what they did was wrong, but by then it was too late.'

Already shocked by what he'd heard, Geoff had to ask. 'You didn't kill them did you?'

Will turned to him with cold, blank eyes. 'No, but now they're going to spend the rest of their lives in wheelchairs. And some nights, when they remember what I did to them that day they're gonna piss their beds.'

'Did Stacey happen to witness any of it?'

Will turned back to look out of the windscreen. 'Only the last part of it, she appeared in the neighbour's car on the way to take Georgie to the vet. And it's because of what she saw me do that still haunts her to this very day.'

Geoff didn't know what to say, then asked about poor Georgie. 'What happened to your dog?'

'He had to be put down.'

Geoff sat there mourning for him, then added. 'Be that as it may, they deserved it, Will, don't beat yourself up about it.'

But Will wasn't satisfied. 'Thing is, Geoff, If I could turn back time I would do exactly the same thing, I wouldn't change anything, and that's what Stacey just can't seem to understand.'

Geoff sat there looking frustrated then Will reached over to shake his hand.

'Cheers for the invite today, and thank Jan again for me will you?'

Geoff took his hand. 'Yeah, of course I will, you're welcome anytime, you know that.'

Will smiled, and climbed out of the car. By the time he had reached the other side, Geoff called out. 'Hey, Will, at least you got the chance to catch those bastards yourself, you can be thankful for that.'

Will stopped, 'no, Geoff, I can be thankful that I didn't catch them killing my dog, otherwise I would be serving life right now.'

CHAPTER 21

His name was Gary Davies, and he was an eighteen-year-old youth who lived on one of the sink estates in Colwyn Bay. Always known for wearing a baseball cap, this tall, stringy waste of skin and bone just happened to be the culprit who was involved in the kitten throwing incident.

Boxing Day evening, Davies and two of his cronies were crammed into his customised sports car with the show-off tinted windows. Parked in pitch black darkness halfway around the Great Orme, they sat in wait for a rendezvous with some drug dealers who were going to supply them with that new controversial drug Meow, Meow. To Davies and co. this was the holy grail of a great mind blast which they had planned for their New Year's Eve rave next week. Davies seated in the back seat, like he was some sort of infamous gangster was the first to spot the approaching headlights in the rear-view mirror.

'Sorted,' he said, alerting the others

The car pulled up behind them and flashed its lights. Davies tapped his mate in the front.

'OK, let's do it.'

Both of them climbed out of the passenger's side and marched towards the car's headlights. Straight away, they could see it was an estate van, but as they got closer, Davies wondered what the hell this guy in the van was wearing over his head. As they reached the driver's door, Davies and his mate exchanged strange looks at this man sitting there in a balaclava. From the back of the van, two black figures leapt out on them, and slapped a cloth to their mouths containing chloroform. The two lads struggled frantically and Davies's cap was knocked off in the fight, then their bodies went limp. Seeing all this, the third guy waiting in Davies's car, fired up the ignition and skidded off, completely abandoning his chums.

Now that they were unconscious, the abductors lifted Davies into the back of the van. The other they left in the cold, wet grass to sleep off the drug, and then they drove off.

Slowly, Davies began to stir, his vision muddled and unsteady. He was sitting on the floor in a dark room, and he could feel cold tiles against his back. His hands were bound, and heavy tape covered his mouth. The whole place smelt of dried urine, and he began to puzzle what the hell was going on? Was this some rival gang getting vengeance? Well it definitely wasn't the drug squad. What the hell? He shook his head.

The entrance door opened and someone wandered in with a torch, the powerful beam making Davies's eyes squint. The figure squatted down beside him, and shone the beam right into his eyes, Davies tried to shy away from it, and muffled something abusive to his captor. The man said nothing in return, but held up a cut-out piece of newspaper, then trained the beam on it so Davies could read it. The headlines read:

CALLOUS YOB FEEDS KITTEN TO PIT-BULLS.

Davies's eyes registered alarm, and only then did he begin to realise that perhaps it hadn't been such a good idea after all. The man stood back up and trudged back out taking the sobering beam of light with him. For a few moments, Davies was left to sweat it out and reflect on what he had done, his heavy breathing raising his chest up and down.

Again the door opened and behind the intense cone of light, he saw the silhouette of the man and two sinister-looking shapes squatted down beside him. The two shorter shapes began to growl at the intruder sitting in the dark. Now Davies knew what was going to happen, and his heart began to thump in his chest. The two snarling Rottweiler's pulled heavily on their leashes, and the hand that was restraining them let them go. Davies screamed against his mouth tape as the dogs charged at him then the door was closed locking them all in.

*

'Have you seen the newspaper Geoff?' Jan marched through from the breakfast room.

Geoff's eyes were peeled to the TV screen. 'No, why?'

Jan breezed through still holding the newspaper. 'There's a report about a so-called vigilante attack on the young man who had thrown the kitten to the two pit-bull dogs. It says that a Mr Davies was found staggering around the North promenade covered in blood and suffering from severe flesh wounds. (reading from the paper) After he received hospital treatment, Mr Davies told police that he was kidnapped and taken to a secluded toilet in Happy Valley where he was locked inside and set upon by two Rottweilers. Mr Davies's injuries were so severe that he required an emergency operation to save one of his hands. The police are looking into the incident.

Suddenly, Geoff lifted his head from the newspaper. Meanwhile, Jan wandered off into the kitchen, her voice trailing behind her. 'Someone's beaten you lot to it. Unless it was one of your own who got him.'

Geoff reminded himself about the terrible story Will had told him about his pup Georgie. Then another terrible thought entered his head.

*

Stacey was now back from her Christmas break with relatives, and was enjoying an early evening stroll on the prom with Will. Will noticed that she looked a bit sullen.

'So did you miss me then?' he asked.

'A little bit,' she teased, and changed the subject. 'So when are you going to come over to my hotel for a change? Mum and Dad are beginning to think you're avoiding them.'

Will tapped a pebble away with the toe of his trainers. 'I will, I will, I just want us to establish ourselves a bit more first, you know. If we're relaxed together then they'll be able to see that, and it'll convince them, especially your mother that we're going in the right direction.'

'But we are relaxed,' She replied.

Will looked at her doubtingly, 'You sure everything went well at your relatives? You don't look very happy about it.'

Stacey lowered her head as if her troubled mind was weighing it down.

'Yeah, it went fine, but it's not that. Have you read the local newspaper today?'

'No,'

'Well, some chap threw a kitten into a garden with two pit-bulls...'

Will cut in, 'oh yeah, I heard about that in Geoff's.'

'Apparently, some vigilantes got him and locked him in the public toilets with a couple of Rottweilers and they nearly ripped him to pieces.'

'Good,' Will retorted, and Jan gazed at him sceptically.

'What?' he asked.

'Well, based on how you reacted with Georgie, sounds like your kind of retribution?'

Will gave her a tired look. 'I don't do things like that anymore, remember?'

Stacey eyed him closely, looking for any hint of guilt.

'Where the hell am I going to get two Rottweilers from?' he huffed.

Not wanting to start an argument, she let it go and walked on. 'OK, let's forget it then.'

Behind her back, Will sighed relieved then followed her.

Sunday evening, on Trinity Avenue, Tom and Charlie were sitting in the old banger waiting for someone to join them. Inside the car the mood was tense, both of them feeling the effects of pre-fight fear.

'So do you think this will sort it then?' Charlie asked.

Tom sighed. 'It better had. We need to get a message back to whomever they are that we want to sort it out. It's obvious that Merseyside outfit sent that team down to get us. We don't want to spend the rest of our lives looking over our shoulders.'

'Christ, I hope so. Sure we shouldn't tell Geoff? I mean we could still pretend it's the Wilkinsons.'

Tom shook his head. 'This is our problem remember? Wouldn't be fair to include the rest of the team. We started this, so we're going to sort it out once and for all.'

'What if this guy gets back to them and they want double their money back for the hassle of stealing their drugs?'

Tom felt like telling him to shut up then someone approached the car and got in. Nigel, the bouncer and ex rugby player straightened out his leather jacket as he settled in the back seat. Eyeing his two accomplices in the front, he sighed, OK, let's do it.

*

Having just showered, Geoff felt an itch in his groin, and thought about his chances of getting a jump with his wife later, after all, there was no work in the morning. Diving into the bedroom, he went to the wardrobe to secretly check on the supply of condoms to make sure. In the pocket of his tracksuit bottoms, his mobile phone vibrated against his thigh. Curious who that might be on a Sunday evening, he took it out. On the caller display window, it read. MIKE TEAM. Geoff thrust the phone to his ear.

'Hi Mike, what's up?'

'Geoff, we have a problem.'

Geoff plonked on the edge of his bed to listen. 'What is it?'

'It's Tom and Charlie, they've gone after the head of the Wilkinson's gang.'

Geoff stomach did a flip-flop. 'What?'

'They didn't want to get the team involved, and wanted to handle it themselves.'

'Bloody idiots,'

'Thing is they made me promise not to mention it to anyone else because it might endanger us all, but I couldn't just sit here and do nothing.'

'Shit, so where are they now?'

'They're on their way to the Ship Inn in Rhos.'

'OK, I'm on my way to pick you up, you can tell us the rest on the way there. And while you're waiting contact the others.'

'I will.'

Geoff ended the call, and adrenalin jetted into his stomach flushing out any previous thoughts of a roll in the sack with his missus. Not wasting a second, he threw on a tee-shirt and hoodie, and dashed through to the living room to see Jan.

'Was that you on the phone I could hear?' she asked as he burst in.

'Yeah, I've got to pop out... emergency... the team,' he blustered.

A look of foreboding came over Jan's face. 'Why what's happened?'

'Haven't got time, I'll explain later,' he said and kissed her on the forehead.

The feel of her soft warm skin made him want to stay at home with her safe and cosy, and it took every drop of courage he had to tear himself away. As he left, Jan tried to tell him to be careful, but Geoff didn't hear. Fearing for her husband's safety, she sealed her eyes and uttered a silent prayer.

At the boot of his car, Geoff checked that his nunchakus (two batons of teak wood joined by a chain, the weapon made famous in the Bruce Lee films) were safely inside, they were, and he was off. Moments later, he found Mike standing waiting by the Linx hotel roundabout on Conwy road, and Geoff flashed his lights to signal his arrival. Mike jumped in and Geoff shot off towards Rhos-on-Sea.

'Did you phone the others?' He asked.

'Yeah, Guy and Brad are going to meet us there.'

'So what's all this about then?'

Mike blew apprehensively. 'I don't know why they've decided to take it upon themselves, all I do know is that on Christmas Eve, Tom was talking to this guy Snoopy. He's the bouncers' local grass, he knows everything about everybody. After, Tom and Charlie were chatting amongst themselves and I just caught something about going to sort it out. So when I asked them innocently what that was about Tom told me they were planning to have a meet with the Wilkinson's gang, in the Ship Inn on Sunday night. So I suggested to him about mentioning it to the team, and he said no. As far as he was concerned, it was a matter for him and Charlie to sort out.'

'Why the hell didn't you tell us all this sooner?' Geoff flicked him a vexed glance.

Mike shrugged helplessly. 'I know, I know, I should have done, but they made me promise, shit,' he cussed himself.

Geoff shook his head. 'Why are they doing all this by themselves? That's what I don't understand.'

'I don't know.'

Geoff then asked Mike if he was tooled up, and Mike unzipped his Peter Storm jacket and showed him the tip of the baseball bat he used in the Wetherspoon's ambush. 'What about you?'

'Got the nunchakus in the boot.'

The air between them went silent, and the adrenalin began to flow; all Geoff could think about now was fight.

That sick, paralysing feeling as his body prepared to do battle. He was now lost in his own psychological hell. Will I be able to cope? Can I really handle this? What if we lose? What if we really get injured or worse? Christ, I wish I was back at home right now! Geoff was scared, Mike was scared, but neither would admit it to the other.

As they reached the small roundabout, the urge to dip down Glanwyddan Lane and head back home was overwhelming. Geoff swallowed courageously and proceeded onwards.

Passing the Llandrillo college, Geoff's mobile rang, and he flipped it out and tossed it over to Mike.

'Hello?' Mike answered for him. 'What, what?'

Geoff pulled in, mounting the edge of the kerb.

'It's Guy,' Mike told him.

Geoff waited on tenterhooks.

'OK, OK,' Mike obeyed, and ended the call.

'Well?' Geoff cried.

'They're not at the Ship Inn, Guy and Brad saw Tom and Charlie getting bundled into a VW transporter van. There were about a dozen men with them.'

'What the hell?' Geoff baffled.

'They must have been set up.' Mike explained. 'Guy said they're right behind them on the way back towards Penrhyn Bay.'

Geoff snarled with frustration, and pulled a quick U-turn in the road ready to double back. By the time they had reached the Penrhyn roundabout, the phone went again. Mike answered, and Geoff dipped his car in beside a row of shops.

'They've turned down Bryn-y-Bia road at the Llandudno-welcomes-you sign. They didn't follow because they saw the van stop further down, so they pulled in out of sight.'

'Tell Guy to get the van's registration number,' Geoff ordered him, and wheel-spun off to the top of Penrhyn hill.

Turning off at the brightly-lit Llandudno sign, they caught sight of Guy waving them down, and nearly slammed into the back of his grey car.

Guy and Brad dashed over as Geoff threw open his car door.

Guy puffed. 'We saw the van stop, and all of them got out and headed off into one of them fields.'

'How far down the lane are they?'

Brad cut-in. 'About a hundred yards or so.'

'Get yer tools,' Geoff ordered and darted to the boot of his car for his nunchakus.

As the others stood clutching their baseball bats, Geoff grabbed his sticks and slammed the boot shut. Noticing Guy holding a bottle with a dirty rag hanging out of the top, Geoff asked what the hell the petrol bomb was for?

Guy shrugged. 'Yer never know when it might come in handy.'

Geoff reminded him about the van's registration number, and Guy showed it scribbled on the palm of his hand. 'What do you want that for?'

'I'm going to give Phil a call, this is where we might need his help. If Tom and Charlie have walked into a trap, we don't want to do the same without a bit of back up, do we?'

*

Tom, Charlie, and Nigel were forced down on to their knees in the damp grass, their hands were bound behind their backs with insulation tape. They were in some dark woodland, and from their position they could see the illuminated bay beyond. Behind them, six balaclavared figures stood wielding hunting knives, and bats of their own. One of their captors spoke up in a thick scouse accent.

'So you came to try and sort it, did yer?' Bet you had a real shock when you found us waiting there for you.

Thought you get away with screwing us? Well don't you worry, we're going to take very good care of you all.'

The second he finished his sentence, what looked like a firework illuminated the black sky in a giant arc, and when it landed it exploded into a whoosh of flames. In alarm, everyone except the hostages scattered like chickens in a farmyard. Before anyone had the time to react, the team were on them. Mike clubbed one of the balaclavas out, Guy and Brad took out another three between them. And Geoff had already nunchuked one to the ground and was measuring up his second. In the flickering light of the petrol fire, the remaining balaclava member back-pedalled, knife in hand. Geoff, one nunchaka under his arm, the other held with his right hand, inched closer towards him, taunting him to either fight or flee. The tables were now turned and it looked like the team might just pull this off. They were wrong! Half a dozen more balaclavas rushed out of the darkness armed with .38 revolvers, and completely surrounded them. The team froze, and their hopes died along with the shrinking flames of the fire. The cold steel of a gun's barrel was pushed against the back of Geoff's head, and his nunchakas dropped to the ground. Now he wished he'd stayed home with Jan after all.

'Let's do em all now,' scouse balaclava snarled.

'I wouldn't do that if I were you?' Geoff warned, trying desperately to control the quiver in his voice. 'My mobile is due to go off any time now, and if I don't answer it, the police are going to be all over you.'

The scouser cackled. 'Ave yer erd this joker?'

'Bollocks,' sneered another.

'No, not bollocks, my mate's a copper, and he's ready on standby. I've even given him your van's registration number.'

'Oh yeah, what's his name then?'

'PC Philip Davies.' Geoff replied.

Someone, seemingly the leader of the gang and without a balaclava stepped forward. He had a shaved head and smiled, his gold tooth still managing to shine in the darkness. It was the Boss Man. 'So you are all in this together, are yer?'

Tom, still kneeling in the grass, shouted over. 'No, they're nothing to do with this.'

Geoff and the others frowned at him.

'Well, they are now.' The Boss Man swaggered over to Geoff. 'Think you're pretty hard, do yer?'

Not wanting to antagonise him, Geoff kept his mouth shut.

'Gozzo?' He called, and a walking Sherman tank of a man stepped up.

'Feel him out,' he ordered.

The rest of the balaclava gang shoved everyone else back except for Geoff, and Geoff looked around warily. The six foot five tank stomped up to Geoff and kneed him in the stomach knocking the wind right out of him. Geoff hit the ground feeling as though he'd just been shunted by a Juggernaut. Mike, Guy, and Brad made a move to help, but the pistol barrels pointing at them convinced them not to. Geoff coughed, winded and tried to get back to his feet, but a foot the size of a canoe thudded into his side, knocking him over again.

'Shit.' Geoff winced knowing that he wasn't going to able to take much more of this. He had to do something quick, so he played possum and stayed flat on his back. He waited for the man to stand over him ready to boot him again, then shot his foot up between his legs and kicked him full in the bollocks. The man staggered back like an old drunk, and clutched his sore balls. Geoff sprang back to his feet and delivered a crushing side kick to the man's lower abdomen. Over he went like a bag of wet linen and in a flash Geoff was all over him like a rash, raining kicks and punches from all angles.

Finally, two balaclavas hauled him off, leaving the man rolling around like a beached whale. Guy, and the team, punched the air jubilantly.

"OK, OK, that's enough,' Boss Man ordered. 'He'll do.'

'I'll do, I'll do for what?' Geoff said baffled.

The man, still nursing his swollen balls, was hoisted back on to his size fourteen trainers by his two comrades, and had to be supported for a while. The rest of the team sighed, relieved, not only had Geoff survived, but he had actually won the fight.

Boss Man spoke up. 'The thing is, you see, we already knew these dick-heads here' – pointing to Tom, Charlie, and Nigel – 'were going to Ship Inn tonight but we set a trap for them. They thought they were having a meet with one of my contacts. And then you lot turn up as well. Now that makes things even more interesting. The problem we're facing here is that these three prats are into us for fifteen grand.'

Geoff and the team didn't understand what the hell he was talking about.

'They owe us fifteen grand,' Boss Man underlined. 'They stole our drugs off one our mules and then the silly prats tried to sell it back to us.' He spat in disgust at the trio still on their knees. So here's how we're gonna sort it. As it happens, I also run illegal bare knuckle fights and have a very important event coming up for New Year's Eve, but I'm a man down. Now the only way I'm going to make my fifteen grand back that they owe me is to get one of the three stooges here to take the vacant place in the fight. And being that you're so concerned about fighting your mates battles for them, you can fight with them, or for them.'

'No,' Tom cried in protest and got clunked with the barrel of a pistol to shut him up.

'Wait a minute...?' Geoff interrupted, but was cut-off.

'It's your choice, if you fight, the debt is repaid and we'll let you off. If you don't fight, say goodbye to your mates.'

'What if we lose?' Mike piped up.

Boss Man drew a finger across his throat, then added. 'You've got a day to think it over.'

'Hang on a minute?' Geoff objected. 'What's all this about fifteen grand that they owe you? We didn't know anything about that.'

'Ask Snoopy,' Boss Man replied. 'He'll explain everything to you.'

'Snoopy, you bastard.' Tom snarled betrayed.

'He'll be the go-between, our messenger.'

'Where the hell's this Snoopy?' Geoff asked.

'Snoopy will be where he always is, he's not going anywhere. You tell Snoopy your answer tomorrow, and he'll tell us. You've got until six pm. Until then, we'll hold your three mates as collateral.' Boss Man gave the nod to his crew, and they began to haul Tom, Charlie, and Nigel off their knees.

'Don't worry, we'll take very good care of them,' The balaclavas sneered as they led them away, leaving Geoff and the team looking like lost survivors on a desert island.

But before he left them, Boss Man turned and said chillingly. 'Oh, by the way, the fight itself is to the death.'

Tom tried to pull away from his captors shouting, 'Geoff I'm so sorry.'

But Geoff and the team were too dumbstruck to say anything. All they could do was watch helplessly as their friends were being led away. Finally that all important call from Phil came through on Geoff's mobile.

CHAPTER 22

On their way back home, Geoff and Mike were still in complete shock. They certainly hadn't expected anything like this. What had started out as a tit-for-tat vendetta with a bunch of local thugs had now turned into a life-threatening money-debt with some big Merseyside drug gang. It was like something out of the movies. What the hell had they gotten themselves into? How the hell did Tom and Charlie end up owing fifteen grand to that lot? And how on earth did all this connect with the Wilkinson gang?

How could all this have started from one silly spat outside the Boulevards night club just over a month ago? Yet the worst part of it was now one of the team was going to have to fight a death match on New Year's Eve to sort the whole thing out. Who the hell was going to do that? Who the hell would sacrifice their life for a fifteen grand debt? How on earth were they going to get out of this mess? They needed answers and quick.

Geoff asked Mike about this Snoopy chap and where they could find him. Mike assured him that he knew where he lived, and so between them that was to become their first priority. Tomorrow early morning, they would all pay Snoopy a visit and if he didn't deliver, there was going to be another death match on the cards. In the meantime, Geoff prayed to God that this Snoopy guy hadn't done a runner.

When Geoff got back home to Jan, he tried his best to act as normal as possible and hide his cancerous worries. But Jan knew him only too well and kept pestering him what was wrong. Of course he couldn't tell her the whole truth, as she would fly into a raging panic, and want to phone the police straight away. To shut her up, he told her that all the trouble they had been having with that gang would soon be over, and when it was, he would quit the team for certain. It just wasn't worth the hassle anymore.

During the night, Geoff felt like he was lying on a bed of thistles, he couldn't sleep a wink. Even though Jan was lying beside him, she might as well have been a million miles away. How he wished he could confide in her and be comforted by her. And in return she would reassure him that there was an easy way out for him and the team. If only.

Geoff shook his head against the pillow, no. There was no easy way out of this mess, especially with the dreaded prospect of that death match? Deep down, he knew that when it came down to the crunch, he would be the one that would have to fight. After all, he was the leader of the team, he was the main instructor, and was the most experienced fighter in the squad. Therefore, the honour, the obligation, and the responsibility would naturally fall upon him. Great, he huffed quietly to himself.

And yet, if it did come down to the fight itself, Geoff began to question whether or not he could actually go through with it. Could he really risk losing everything, his life, his beloved Jan, and the thought of leaving her a widow? The answer to that was a resounding no.

Yet, could he also just drop everything and run away, and leave his friends to the mercy of these so called criminals? Could he walk away and let them die at the hands of these scum? Once again the answer was no.

*

The following morning, a day before New Year's Eve, all the team phoned in sick from their day-time jobs in order to try and sort out this complete mess.

Inside a run-down block of flat lets on the outskirts of town, the front door to one of the rooms was kicked open

224

with a reverberating crash. The team stood in the gaping doorway, and a whiff of God knows what instantly greeted them.

'Jes – sus,' Geoff scowled.

The room itself looked like the inside of a washing machine full of dirty laundry. On what appeared to be a bed, Snoopy, who hadn't even stirred with the racket, lay to one side of the bed curled up in a foetal position. Beside the bed on a small wooden cabinet, lay a used syringe, a tablespoon, and the powdery remnants of some narcotic drug. Mike rushed over and grabbed him by the scruff of his grubby Tee-shirt.

'Wake up, you double-crossing little bastard,' he snarled in his face.

'Shit, he hasn't overdosed has he?' Guy feared.

Snoopy began to stir like a patient coming round from a heavy dose of general anaesthetic.

'No, someone's drugged him so they could keep him here,' Mike said throwing him back down on the bed fruitlessly.

'How do you know that?' Geoff asked.

'Because otherwise he'd have done a runner after what he's done.'

'So how the hell are we going to get him to talk?'

Mike blew helplessly. 'We'll just have to wait for him to come round.'

Geoff turned away in defeat. 'Great. That could take hours, something we can't really afford right now.'

So for the next hour and a half, they slapped him, they tried dousing him in cold water, they even went out and fetched coffee to try and bring Snoopy back to his senses. At last, their efforts seemed to pay off, and Snoopy began to respond. Once they had his attention, Mike straddled him on the bed, while the others stood glowering down at him.

'Why did you do it, Snoopy? Why did you sell us out to that gang? Give us one good reason why we shouldn't finish you off right now?'

225

Snoopy rolled his head from side to side, trying to shake off the muddling effects of last night's drug. 'They've got my girlfriend as well,' he slurred. 'And they told me if I didn't set you up they would O.D. her.'

Mike glared down at him, just itching to pound him into the filthy mattress.

'So, what's all this about Tom, Charlie and Nigel owing them fifteen grand?'

Snoopy asked if he could sit up, and have a glass of water, and Mike reluctantly climbed off him while Brad saw to the drink. Snoopy proceeded.

'Apparently Tom, and Charlie stole a package containing about a half a kilo or so of cocaine from some lad in Llandudno who was a mule for the Wilkinsons. But the Wilkinsons themselves work for one of the top drug gangs in Liverpool, so it was actually their property.

Then thinking they were going to make a mint out of their little bundle, they, through a contact of mine, made the mistake of slinking off to Liverpool to try and sell it to this gang.

'Now the gang know who swiped it from them in the first place, and because they lost their connection, they want their fifteen grand's worth in money or blood.'

'So how did they know it was their drug?' Brad asked.

'They know because of the way they've mixed it, and tested it, the way it's packaged and all sorts.'

Guy interjected. 'Well, how did the guys know that the gang was after them then?'

'They sent a team down after them.'

'You mean the ones that met them outside the Wetherspoons?' Asked Mike.

'I thought *that was* the Wilkinsons.' Geoff frowned.

Snoopy shrugged ignorantly.

Geoff then raged. 'What the hell are Tom and Charlie doing stealing and selling drugs in the first place? Silly sods. Did you know anything about that, Mike?'

Mike spun around shocked at Geoff's insinuation. 'No, I had absolutely no idea.'

'So what does all this have to do with our war with the Wilkinsons?' Guy interrupted.

'What war?' Snoopy scratched his sweaty forehead.

'The war we have with the Wilknisons because of that night outside the boulevards.' Geoff explained.

'There is no war,' Snoopy said. 'This Merseyside gang are only after Tom, Charlie, and Nigel because of the drugs they stole from one of their mules. The fact that you had a problem with one of the Wilkinsons didn't even come into the equation. At first, yeah, there was the possibility that they might retaliate but it never happened. Then when word got to them that this drug gang from Liverpool might be after them instead they pretended to you it was the Wilkinsons to just cover themselves.'

Everybody was speechless, then Geoff found his voice.

'Wait a minute, are you trying to tell us that the Wilkinson gang were never after us in the first place, and all this tit-for-tat revenge was all for nothing?'

Snoopy nodded. 'That was until you involved yourselves last night.'

Mike jumped in. 'Well then how could you have known about last night then?'

'Because I got a visit straight after the incident last night telling me that the original plan had now been changed because of you lot. And now one of you would have to fight instead. And that you have until six pm tonight to decide. Then they stuck the syringe into me to keep me here.'

Geoff plonked himself down on the edge of the tatty mattress and thought of his two treacherous team mates. 'Well, thanks for that lads.'

'So that's why they didn't want to get us involved.' Mike spoke-up. 'That's why they made me promise not to tell any of you lot. They knew what they had gotten themselves into, and wanted to sort it out between them.'

'Yeah, but by helping them out we're now in it up to our necks,' Brad hit back.

'Yeah, OK, but if we hadn't tried to help they probably wouldn't be alive now would they?' Mike retorted.

Geoff shook his head. 'Still hasn't solved the problem though has it? One of us now has to fight a death match because of their stupidity.'

Guy stepped towards Snoopy. 'So what are these fights actually about?'

'SAC fights,' he replied.

Everyone gave him blank looks.

'Skull and crossbones – death matches. No weapons, just hand to hand combat.'

'Seriously?' Geoff questioned.

'Oh yeah. I know someone who went to one of them, and what he saw still haunts him to this day,' Snoopy told them.

Geoff began to feel nauseous, this was not what he needed to hear right now.

'How the hell can they get away with killing someone in a death match like that?' Guy asked.

'Oh, believe me, they have ways of disposing of bodies. Sometimes they're discovered in fatal car accidents, sometimes they're chopped up...'

Geoff cut him off, 'OK, we've heard enough.'

'So, who's going to be the opponent?' Mike asked.

Snoopy shrugged. 'Dunno, but I can find out if you want?'

'Do it!'

Snoopy nodded obediently. 'So what do I tell them about the fight, are you going to go through with it?'

Geoff turned to him. 'What happens if we don't?'

'They'll probably kill them, and then they might come after you for the money owed. Bloody glad it's not me.'

Mike gave him a snarl, then turned back to Geoff. 'So what do we say?'

'I don't know. I need to talk to someone first. For now, just get Snoopy's number,' he ordered just wanting to get out of this hell hole.

The others all followed except for Mike, who did as he was told and got the number. But before leaving he warned Snoopy that he better be ready to answer when they called him back or he would be next on their list.

Back inside Geoff's car, Phil the copper rang through on the mobile. As Geoff spoke to him, the rest of the team sat and waited with bated breaths.

'Right, we're on our way,' Geoff informed, and ended the call. 'Phil wants us to go straight over to his house now he's got something he needs to tell us.'

The team rolled their eyes as if to say, what now.

As Geoff started the car, Guy spoke up from the back seat, 'If this thing does go ahead, Geoff, how are we going to decide who's going to fight?'

Geoff glared back through the rear-view mirror and uttered ominously, 'I think we all know who that's going to be.'

Reaching Phil's home in the junction, the team filed straight into the living room, and a couple of extra chairs were laid out for them. Phil sat perched anxiously on the edge of the couch rubbing his clammy hands together.

'So what have you found out so far?'

Geoff leaned forward in his chair. 'As it happens, Tom, Charlie, and this guy Nigel have stolen some drugs from this big Liverpool firm, and now they owe them fifteen grand.'

Phil's head dropped into his hands.

'And to try and cover their tracks they pretended that the Wilkinsons gang were after *us*. Apparently we were never at war with them in the first place. But because we intervened with this other big Merseyside gangs plans last night trying to save these damn idiots, one of us has to save their skins by fighting a death match tomorrow night.'

Phil's sheet-white face emerged from his hands. 'Oh, the silly, naive greedy bastards. How the hell did they get hold of those drugs in the first place?'

Mike chipped in. 'They stole them off some lad in Llandudno who happens to be a mule for the Wilkinsons who in turn work for the Liverpool mob.'

Phil stiffened as if he was having a heart attack. 'Oh, shit, they never told me about that the stupid, greedy...' He clasped his nose between his fingers.

'What?' Geoff asked.

Phil stood up and paced about the room frantically.

'What, Phil? For God's sake spit it out.'

Phil tried to compose himself. 'I'm afraid I have a bit of a confession lads.'

Everyone braced themselves for another rollercoaster ride. Phil sat back down again.

'For the last month or two, Tom, Charlie and this chap Nigel have been operating a secret vigilante group service all of their own. And I've been supplying them with the necessary information to apprehend these criminals.'

'You, what.' Geoff roared.

Now that he'd dropped the bombshell, Phil proceeded to come clean with everything.

'After that merciless beating I took near the Boulevards that night, something snapped in me, and I decided then and there that things needed to change. Someone had to do something to teach all these degenerates out on the street some respect. Someone had to restore some law and order back into this town. Then Tom and Charlie paid me a visit one day not so long after you were all here to talk about starting a team. They told me they were forming their own vigilante group to provide a service to victims of crime. It was their way of making a bit of extra money on the side, after all, times are hard and we're all deep in a recession. At that time I had no problem with that.

'You had no problem with that?' Mike scoffed.

'Mike, let him finish,' Geoff hushed him.

'I didn't get any payment for that by the way, and I swear I had no idea about the drugs they stole, otherwise I would have pulled out of it straight away. Anyhow, this is how it worked. All the criminals who we targeted had either been charged or just reported, so I could access names and addresses on file with the computer at work.

And then I simply passed on the information to Tom and Charlie, and they did the rest. Tom even got his girlfriend Karen in on it. She acted as their representative to set up meetings with the victims and then collect payment off them once the service had been provided. It was as simple as that.'

'Christ, Phil, do you know what would happen if you got caught doing that?' Geoff said.

Phil eyed him coldly. 'I know, but I thought it was worth taking the risk at the time.'

Geoff and the team just sat there numbed, then Brad asked curiously, 'so how did they get away with dishing out this justice without getting caught themselves?'

'During the day, they wore beanie hats and sunglasses, and at night balaclavas! But getting back to the story, after their very last victim, remember the guy in the papers recently who got savaged by the Rottweilers for throwing the kitten to the pitbulls? The dogs belonged to Nigel by the way, after that I said that's it. No more, it's getting a bit too risky now.'

'Christ, Phil, I can't believe what I'm hearing, not from you, a respectable copper,' Geoff said.

'I am still a respectable copper, Geoff, that's why I wanted to give these low-lives a taste of their own medicine, and issue others with a warning that their yobbish behaviour won't be tolerated anymore. I wanted to put a stop to these mindless crimes and make this town safe enough for people to be able to walk down the streets again.'

'But, Phil, that's what we all thought at the very beginning, remember? But look where it's got us.'

'Yeah, but this has only happened because of Tom and Charlie's greed, without that nobody ever would have known,' Phil replied.

Geoff just sat there staring at him, trying to come to terms with it all. Brad on the other hand wanted answers. 'So what do we do now?'

Geoff took a deep breath. 'Well, we have two choices, fight or flight. We can fight and end this thing once and for all, or we go our separate ways today, cut our loss and hope for the best. We sacrifice our mates' and spend the rest of our days looking over our shoulders. What do you think?'

Guy sneered. 'Why don't we let one of them fight, it was them who got us into this mess?'

Mike glowered at him. 'So you suggest that we turn our backs on them and forget about it. Bury our heads in the sand and hope it will go away?'

Geoff took over. 'Thing is we could have done that last night when you phoned us about what was happening. We all could have said forget it, let them sort it out themselves, after all that is what they wanted. But we didn't do that, did we? No, we jumped straight into our cars and came to our team mates' aid, we were all willing to risk our lives to help them just as they would have done for us. No, the time to turn our backs was last night. I believe we have already made our choice.'

Everyone listened, but no one seemed to agree just yet.

'That's the pact we made when we formed the team. That's the sacrifice we've made and now we have to see it through.'

Suddenly Mike had an idea, and cut in. 'What if we pay back the fifteen grand between us, then there would be no fight?'

Geoff was dubious, but it was worth a try. 'Can we raise that sort of cash between us all?'

The rest of the team gave manageable shrugs, so Geoff ordered Mike to get on his mobile to call Snoopy and find out. And while they waited they discussed the dreaded possibility of who was going to have to fight.

'It's got to be me, hasn't it?' Geoff snorted.

'No way, Geoff you're not doing it. None of you are.' Phil put his foot down. 'Sod the job, let me get the Serious Crime Squad on it?'

Geoff shook his head. 'There's not enough time, Phil, and besides, if it all goes pear-shaped, they might come after us and our families, and that's something I just couldn't live with. If we can pay them off great, if not then what?'

Geoff cut-off as Mike reappeared. The look on his face wasn't very encouraging.

'If we want to buy our way out, it'll be fifty grand.'

'*Fifty grand*,' everybody cried. 'Why fifty grand?'

'Because that's how much they are expecting to make out of this fight. Even if we paid back the money they're still a man short for the fight, and they can't let all their punters down.'

Geoff threw up his arms in defeat. 'Well, that's it then, we're screwed.'

'Geoff, don't do it, there's got to be another way,' Phil pleaded.

'Like what? If I don't do it, they'll make one of the others fight so nothing's going to stop it, is it?'

Phil began to panic. 'Just give me the chance to handle it with the police, it's worth a try, don't you think?'

But Geoff didn't agree. 'Listen, Phil, if one of them got killed in this fight, I would spend the rest of my life knowing that I had a better chance of winning than they did, and I let them down. I'm the most experienced fighter, I'm supposed to be the instructor. Deep down I would feel like a traitor and a coward, and I don't think I could ever respect myself after that, no matter what they've done. Every time I go to sleep at night, I would see their faces. Every time I looked in the bathroom mirror first thing in the morning, I would see them staring right back at me.'

Everyone fell silent thinking about what Geoff had said, everyone except Phil who could only shake his head at this utter lunacy. Mike dared to break the silence.

'So do you want me to call and tell them yes?'

Geoff looked across at him. 'We've still got a few more hours before the deadline. Let me talk to Will first.'

Geoff arrived at Will's and pressed the bell to his flat. Right now, Will was probably his last hope of finding a solution to this lethal situation. Standing there outside he felt like a patient with terminal cancer waiting to see a specialist, and praying that he would hear some good news. He pressed the door bell again, and tapped his foot on the step impatiently – still no answer.

'Shit,' he raged. 'Will, don't be out now for God's sake. Why is it whenever you need someone in an emergency, that'll be the only time you can't get hold of them?'

Desperately, he tried to reach him on the mobile and discovered to his disbelief that Will's phone had been switched off.

'I don't believe this,' he shrieked, looking skyward for some divine assistance. Busily, he tapped in a text message for Will to contact him ASAP.

Jumping back in his car, he sat there for a second, his hands gripping the steering wheel with such force that he felt it would snap off. The pre-fight nerves had already begun, and the adrenalin had started to flow. Sitting there all alone, Geoff felt scared, and he tried to remember what Will had taught him about fear and what it actually meant. To combat it, he breathed in and out through his nostrils, and that seemed to help. But what he really needed right now was Jan his wife. He needed her company, and he needed her reassurance.

'I've got to tell her,' he said. 'I can't keep this to myself anymore. It's not fair on me, and it's not fair on her. But what if she blows everything to the police? Maybe if I don't mention the death match to her. Shit,' he cried, and started up the car.

CHAPTER 23

Back at home in his kitchen, Geoff told Jan everything except for the drugs, and the death fight. In response Jan just stood there mouth agape.

'Are you crazy? Geoff, you're acting like an immature yob.'

Geoff got ready to batten down the hatches and ride out the storm of the century.

'A fight, you're going to take part in an illegal bare knuckle brawl just to sort out this mess you've all gotten yourselves into? Well, that certainly doesn't sound like the great, honourable, law-abiding neighbourhood watch scheme you've been telling me about, does it?'

'No it doesn't,' He replied sheepishly.

'No, Geoff, this whole thing has got out of hand and it has to stop right now. You're a respectable forty-year-old dispensing optician with a wife, and it's time you started acting like it.'

'But I'm going to stop it, Jan,' Geoff pleaded. 'As soon as this is all over that's it, I'm done. But I can't pull out of this one, I just can't.'

'Why can't you? Why don't you just say no, and if you get any hassle, then report them to the police.'

If only it was that simple, Geoff thought. 'No, Jan, please just bear with me for this one, I can't back out of it.'

'Well, then there's got to be more to it, hasn't there?'

Geoff didn't know what else to say, other than he had to protect her from the real truth.

'Jan, just listen to me....'

'No, Geoff, you listen to me? This is not happening,

why the hell do you have to fight? Why does it have to be you?'

'Because it's my responsibility.' Geoff threw up his arms helplessly. 'I'm the head of the team.'

'And when is this fight supposed to take place?'

'Tomorrow night.'

'*New Year's Eve*, are you kidding me?'

Geoff didn't answer her.

'Oh, that's great! Just great, not only are you going to risk getting seriously hurt in a stupid unlicensed fight, you're doing it on one of the most celebrated nights of the year. This gets better and better.'

'Jan, I swear to you after tomorrow night, that'll be it, just please help me out until then?'

Jan dived for her leather handbag. 'No, Geoff, I'm going to my mum's, and if you want your wife back you better do some serious thinking. It's me or the fight, you can't have both. And don't worry I won't take your precious car, I'll get Mandy from work to drive me there.'

Geoff followed her through to the front door. 'Jan, for God's sake, don't be like this.'

Jan swung the front door open. 'No, Geoff, the choice is yours – my mind is made up.' Then she slammed it shut behind her.

Geoff snatched the door open, and called after her, but she ignored him.

Five minutes later, Geoff drove up beside her as she walked down Bryn Gosgol road.

Slowing the car to her walking pace, he tried desperately to make her see sense, but she ignored him.

'Come on, Jan, you can't walk all the way into town, at least let me drive you?'

'Forget it, Mandy's meeting me at the bottom of the road, so go back home and worry about your big fight.'

But Geoff stayed with his wife until Mandy arrived in her own raven-black motor. Without so much as a word to her husband Jan climbed straight in, and Geoff watched them drive off. Finally, he gave in to defeat. He sat there with the engine still running, his mind so cabbaged that he almost didn't hear the bleeping text message received on his phone. For a second, he thought it might be Jan, but the message was from Will asking what was up?

'Will, where the hell have you been?' he cried with relief, and immediately sent a text back to let him know he was on his way over.

When he arrived at Will's flat, Will, looking in high spirits, told Geoff that he and Stacey had been to the afternoon matinee at the junction cinema, which explained why his mobile was switched off. However, as soon as he heard the entire story of what had happened to Geoff and the team, Will's face turned ashen.

'A death match, are you serious?' he cried.

'I don't have any choice, Will. If I don't fight, they'll probably kill Tom, and Charlie, and this other guy, or they'll make one of them fight, and I have a better chance of winning than they do.'

'A death match, Geoff, means to the death. Are you willing to risk you life, Jan, everything all because of these guy's mistakes? Their mistakes, Geoff, not yours.'

Desolated, Geoff slumped on to Will's couch and sank his head into his hands. 'Will, what the hell do I do?'

Seeing that hounding him wasn't going to help matters, Will elected to be a bit more tactful. 'When is this fight supposed to take place?'

'Tomorrow night, New Year's Eve.'

Will sat on the window chair facing him. 'Geoff, these guys are trained killers, they train like professionals, they have to because they know they can't afford to lose. You're nowhere near ready for a fight like that. For God's sake don't do it, I beg you?'

Geoff just sat there with his head moving from side to side.

'How much do they owe?' Will asked.

'Tom and Charlie owe this gang fifteen grand, but they want fifty to buy our way out of the fight.'

'Fifty, can't get hold of that sort of money in twenty four hours.'

'Where is the fight being held?'

Geoff shrugged. 'Don't know that yet.'

'They're probably keeping the location a secret for security reasons. ' Will then erupted with frustration. 'Shit, I knew something like this was going to happen. When have you got to let them know by?'

Geoff emerged from behind his hands. 'Six o'clock tonight.'

Will glanced at his faulty Seiko, and banged it with the tip of his fingers.

'Shit, Geoff, what time is it now?'

Geoff had a peek at his mobile. 'Five-thirty-one.'

'Talk about short notice. Listen, Geoff, you can't do this, tell them you'll pay the fifteen grand and that's it. I can get the cash for you, and then tell them to piss off.'

'But what about Tom and Charlie?'

'They got themselves into this scrape, they'll have to get themselves out. It's not your problem. You weren't the one who stole the drugs, they did; you shouldn't have to pay the price for that. Say no, and then go and pick up your wife.'

'Is that really the right thing to do though, Will?'

'No, Geoff, but in a life-threatening situation like this, it's the sensible thing to do. Remember, Geoff, ego? When someone pulls a knife on you and you have a clear path in front of you... RUN.'

Geoff flipped back in the couch, his face puffy and flushed.

'It's a lot easier said than done, Will.'

'No, it isn't, Geoff. It's not your fight. Do you want to give everything up for a couple of idiots who were out just make a quick buck on the side? Isn't your wife Jan more important to you? Do you really want to give all that up for them?'

Right now, Jan was the key word, the key meaning that made any sense amid this absolute madness. And the more

Will drilled it into him, the more his resolve began to crumble until finally he could see that Will was right. So while he still possessed the courage, and the right frame of mind, Geoff called Mike to tell them that the fight was off.

When the call was done, it felt like a massive weight had been lifted off him. But then there was the guilt, and that began to chip away at his conscience almost immediately.

'The lads will never forgive me for letting Tom, and Charlie down like that,' Geoff groaned.

'Yeah, but are any of them volunteering to fight?'

Geoff began dialling his mobile, 'Just going to let Jan know she can come home, now I've cancelled the fight.'

Will gave him a bit of privacy.

Geoff growled irritably. 'Can't get hold of her, or she's just being stubborn.'

'Send her a text?' Will suggested.

'Naw, I want to tell her personally. I'll give her a little longer to fume, then I'll try again when I get home.'

Then it hit him once more. 'Will, are you sure I'm doing the right thing?'

'Why should an innocent man risk his life, and take the rap for a couple of greedy drug dealers caught up in a web of corruption? If they wanted to play the game, then they have to take the blame.'

Will was right, but Geoff knew that he was the one who was going to have to live with the guilt, and he was the one who would have to pay that price. Nevertheless, he stood up, and thanked Will for probably saving his life as well as his marriage.

'Any problems, you know where I am,' Will told him.

Tapping his shoulder, Geoff thanked him again, and left.

Just as Will flopped back on to his couch to try and absorb everything, his mobile rang – it was Stacey. In an irate tone, she told him that she had just had an extremely concerned Jan on her doorstep, with a very disturbing story about Geoff becoming involved with illegal bare- knuckle fighting. And if it wasn't too much trouble could I get Will try to talk some sense into her incredibly stupid husband?

A bit miffed that this had reached Stacey's ears, Will explained that he had already convinced Geoff not to fight, and that was as far as he intended to get involved. Yet just to be sure, Stacey held him to his word, by making him swear on it. Reluctantly, Will made the promise.

*

Early evening, Geoff kept on trying to get hold of his wife, but she wouldn't answer her phone. He cussed at her obstinacy.

'Come on, Jan, for God's sake. You can be a right stubborn cow sometimes.'

He even sent her a text to let her know that the fight was off, yet still no reply.

Becoming concerned by this unyielding silence, he decided to ring her parents just to make sure she was there. But before he had the chance to dial, his mobile rang. Relief flushed through his body, but it was short lived, as it turned out to be Mike.

'Geoff mate, we've got a new problem.'

Geoff's stomach churned in anticipation – shit, what now, he thought?

There was a momentary silence. 'They've got Jan.'

Geoff's whole body went numb.

'Geoff, they're using her as insurance to make sure that you turn up for the fight. I'm sorry mate, this is all so messed up.'

For a second, Geoff couldn't even speak.

'They said you need to be ready for eleven o' clock tomorrow night, and an hour before they'll tell us where to meet them for the pick up. They said they'll release everyone after the fight is over. We'll all be there for you, Geoff.'

The call ended, but Geoff kept the phone pinned to his ear, nothing but silence pouring down his eardrum. Eventually, he peeled the mobile from his ear and somehow found a way through the fogginess in his head to call Will.

Will answered him straight away.

Geoff wheezed barely able to hold his voice together. 'Will, they've got Jan. I don't know how but they've got her, my wife. What the hell am I going to do?'

'Shit, no,' Will replied.

'They're holding her for insurance so I show up for the fight. Now I've got her involved in all this.' Completely losing it now, Geoff began to take it out on his old pal. 'Thanks for that, Will, why the hell did I listen to you? If I'd have just agreed to fight, at least she would have been safe. Cheers.' He hung up on him.

Immediately, Will tried to ring back, but Geoff ignored him, slung his phone on to the couch, and sulked off to another room.

Ten minutes later, Will arrived at Stacey's hotel, and when she answered the door she immediately saw the look on his face.

'They've kidnapped Geoff's wife to make sure that he fights.'

Stacey's head dropped in anguish. 'Right, Will, I think it's time to call the police, don't you?'

'No, I don't Stace, it's too risky now. These guys are not just petty criminals, they're an organised racket, they're the big boys.'

'So what do you suggest?'

Will took a deep breath. 'There's only one way out of this and that's to do what they want and fight.'

'No, Will, you can't let Geoff go ahead with this madness and fight.'

'No, I'm not going to. I'm going to have to fight for him.'

'What?' Stacey shrieked.

Will was careful not to let on that it was actually a fight to the death and that it all revolved around drugs.

'Stacey I have to. I'm the only one sufficiently trained to deal with a fight like this. I can't sit back and let my old mate get seriously hurt' – or killed, which he purposely left out – 'and besides, it's my fault they've got Jan because it was me who told Geoff not to fight, so I'm responsible.'

Stacey's alarm quickly turned into anger. 'No way, Will, you promised me no more trouble, you swore to me that you wouldn't get involved in this anymore. You promised me that you've changed. You promised.'

'Stacey, I have to do this, I have to.'

'No, you don't, Will. Look I'm sorry for Jan and Geoff for the danger they're in, but this is nothing to do with us. The only way we can help them is to contact the police and let them deal with it.'

But Will was adamant. 'No, Stacey, police involvement could be disastrous now. I'm afraid I underestimated them. In taking Geoff's wife, they've let us know that they're willing to go to any lengths to get what they want, and you don't mess with people like that.'

'Listen, Will, you're still on probation you know. If you get caught up in this mess you could go back to prison and do your full term. That's another two years. And if that happens that's it between us, no more chances. You messed up our lives over Georgie, and I'm not going to let you do it again.' She stood square on to him. 'Now I'm going to give you a choice. At eight o'clock tomorrow night, I want you here all dressed up ready to celebrate the New Year. We're going out remember? And if you're not here by eight, then don't ever bother coming here again, you will have lost me for the last time.' Her ultimatum delivered, she slammed the door in his face.

Will stood there looking at the thick double glazed window in the door, the frustration and volcanic anger swirling around inside him like a terrible beast trying to escape. But Will wouldn't let it, nowadays it was he who was in control.

That night, Geoff lay awake in his bed and looked across at the empty space where his wife Jan should have been. He ran his hand over the cold linen under the duvet, and called out to her in his grief. Jan, I'm so sorry for what has happened. The last thing in the world I would ever do is put you in any kind of danger. The thought of losing you is tearing me apart. I really need you right now, I can't handle all this alone. I'm scared of losing you, and I'm afraid to die.

I'm not fighting for my life anymore, I'm fighting for ours. I'm going to fight with everything I've got because now someone has threatened to take you away from me. And for that I'm willing to die. I hope you can forgive me for all of this, try and sleep for now and I'll be there to pick you up tomorrow night I promise.

Geoff closed his eyes and sobbed quietly in the dark, the loneliest place in the world.

Likewise, Will, his old pal, was also lying awake in his flat facing an incredible dilemma of his own. Should he take on the fight for Geoff now that Stacey had given him this ultimatum? Paradoxically, he was now in a similar position as Geoff – how on earth did that happen? One minute he was enjoying a lovely afternoon at the cinema with his re-united girlfriend, and suddenly everything changed. Just as he was wet cementing the foundations to his brand new life, back with Stacey, someone had come along and sloshed right through it again. Will clasped his hands behind his head and cursed this unbelievable turn of events. What was he supposed to do? It was a no-win situation.

If he doesn't fight, he loses Geoff. If he fights, he loses Stacey for ever. And If he loses the fight itself, then he loses everything. Why did Stacey have to do this to him?

For the past four years, all Will had thought about was getting back with Stacey. The years he spent in prison, the pain, the waiting, the sacrifices he had to make in order to win her back. And now it looks as though all that effort might have been for nothing.

The following day, Geoff seemed to drift around in a daze like a condemned man hours before his execution. In case the worst should happen tonight, he checked that his will, stowed away in the attic was up to date. Also, he wrote a very poignant and loving letter to his wife, and left it on her pillow.

During the rest of the day, Will continued to try and contact him, but didn't get an answer. Geoff didn't even read his text messages. In Geoff's mind, Will had only made matters worse by trying to help. And without wishing to complicate the situation anymore, he thought it best to keep himself to himself. However, in the afternoon, Geoff had to pop out just clear his head a bit, and ironically that was when Will arrived in a taxi, to find him gone. Thwarted again, he thrust a short note through his letterbox basically telling him, sorry for sticking his nose in, and to contact him ASAP.

Seven thirty that evening, Will lay on his bed, hands clasped behind his head still musing over the toughest decision of his life. Stacey or help Geoff? Stacey or help Geoff? Live or risk death? Live or risk death? Beside his bed, stood his backpack stuffed full of all his belongings.

Seven-fifty-five, Stacey was dressed all ready for her New Year's night out with Will. She sat in the lounge of her hotel gazing out over the illuminated North promenade. Her face was all made up, a thin layer of foundation, a lick of eye liner, and a smearing of glossy lipstick she looked like one of two brides waiting to find out who the groom was going to marry.

Seven-fifty-eight, the front doorbell rang, and her heart leapt in anticipation. Standing up, and composing herself, she walked calmly to the front door. When she opened it, she found Will standing outside dressed in his heavy duffel coat, with his hair gelled back, and his face clean shaven. Stacey's face softened and as her eyes met Will's she waited for him to say it.

Nine-fifty-five, Geoff sat in the living room wearing his grey hooded tracksuit. The TV was turned off, the house was tidied from top to bottom, and he was ready to go. On the easy chair beside him lay his seventies-retro leather bomber jacket, kept only for special occasions. A minute later, his mobile rang, it was Mike.

'Geoff, we're to meet them on Glanwyddan Lane on the turn off to the Queen's Head in twenty minutes. Me, Brad, Guy and Phil are coming to pick you up. See you in about five minutes.'

'OK,' was all Geoff said, and he ended the call.

Tentatively, he scrolled down to Will's number and just looked at it. All things considered, Geoff would have given anything to have had Will in his corner, but by his own choice, he knew this wasn't going to happen. Maybe I should have called him back? He thought. I suppose I can't blame all this on him. Geoff's head tottered with regret, a whole life-time of regret. Through the thin material of the polyester blinds, he saw two headlights pull up. Geoff's dead eyes came back to life and he uttered to himself time to get my wife back.

CHAPTER 24

THE FIGHT

On route to Glanwyddan lane, the remaining team, Geoff, Mike, Phil, Guy and Brad were all piled into Guy's grey motor. The mood between them was extremely sombre. Even more so after Mike had informed everyone (prior to picking up Geoff) that Geoff's opponent was indeed a very dangerous fighter by the name of 'Razor' who had already won two other death matches. Yet despite their hidden fears, the lads all had faith in their highly respected teacher.

However, Phil, sitting next to Geoff in the back of the car couldn't contain his anxiousness about this fight any longer. 'Geoff mate, please reconsider this, give me and my colleagues a chance to sort all this out, don't go through with it. All it takes is one phone call to stop it, that's all?'

But Geoff knew it was too late for any reprieve. 'I appreciate that, Phil, but I won't take any chances when it comes to Jan. I would rather die fighting for her than face a life living without her.'

Guy looked up through the rear view mirror and with a bit of a nervous quake in his voice, said, 'you can do this, Geoff! You can win this; you have to believe that.'

Mike chipped in. 'Geoff, remember you are not going there to die, this is not a death sentence, you're going there to win. Do whatever you have to do, to survive, anything. The first chance you get, end it, then get your arse out of there.'

Geoff was moved by their encouragement, but their words were only candle-lights in a dark grand canyon.

Down Glanwyddan lane, the car's headlights scythed through the pitch blackness, and soon they found the turn off to the Queen's Head. There at the side of the road, parked in the dark was a transit van waiting for them. Everything from there on seemed to happen in fast forward motion. The team were told to pile into the back of the van and leave the car with the keys inside.

Inside the van, they were all blindfolded and driven around for about quarter of an hour to try make them lose their bearings. Finally, the van stopped, and with their hearts thundering in their chests, they were led up some stone steps and along a flat gravelled footpath. When they reached the destination, their blindfolds were removed and they found themselves at the bottom of what looked like a disused quarry. Standing in front of them were about a dozen people forming a kind of human ring and they were surrounded by larger circle of fire torches. In the light breeze the fire torches' flickering flames cast ghostly shadows against the jagged limestone cliffs above. From the air, the whole place must have looked like a lighted helipad.

All the ring people stared back at the team with great anticipation. They were the betting folk, the businessmen, the crime lords, people in the know. Just as the team exchanged strange looks between them, they were greeted by the Boss Man, the chap with a single gold tooth and the leader of the Merseyside gang.

'Glad you could make it. Right then, we'll begin in a few minutes. Remember this is a skull and crossbones contest, hands must be taped.' He thrust a roll of boxing hand wraps into Geoff's chest. 'No weapons, no referee, you get your mates back after the fight.'

'What about my wife?' Geoff cried.

Boss Man stuck his face in Geoff's. 'After the fight!'

'Can I see her before the fight?' He pleaded.

Boss Man didn't answer, and swaggered off leaving them to it. Guy tapped Geoff's arm.

247

'Come on, Geoff, let's get on with it.'

Geoff slid off his leather jacket revealing his grey tracksuit underneath his whole body trembled with a mixture of fear and the cold. Immediately, Guy got on with wrapping Geoff's hands, and talked quietly to him like a dutiful trainer. 'Geoff, if I see you in serious trouble I'm not going to just stand there and watch.'

'I know, I know,' Geoff nodded, trying hard to keep his hands steady for Guy to bind them.

Meanwhile, the rest of the team could do nothing else but stand there and watch. Phil, himself, was so wound up he looked like he was going to faint at any second. When his hands were done, Geoff began to limber up, stretching and pulling on his limbs. Suddenly Mike tapped his arm urgently, and Geoff stopped. Breezing past them was a squat, block-looking shape making its way towards the human ring. The man was Geoff's opponent 'Razor' who was about five-ten with a tanned bald head, and draped over his boulder- like shoulders was a large black reefer jacket. Behind him, like a long tail, were his vocal entourage, about ten of them, all tanked up, gum-chewing cronies who gave Geoff and his team daggers as they passed by. One of them even drew his finger across his throat to signify Geoff's fate.

Geoff's legs almost turned to liquid, and another spurt of adrenalin shot into his system. Right there and then, he felt like running for his life. However, the team were quick to stick up for their man by staring them out and rubbing Geoff's back to show their support. Razor then entered the ring to a chorus of reverberating claps and whistles. Seemingly unmoved by the praise that was heaped upon him, he turned in the centre of the ring and shrugged off the heavy jacket and tossed it over to one of his men. Geoff was surprised not to see a steroid-pumped up freak, but instead his opponent was a flabby mass of flesh painted all over in tattoos. Time to start, Boss Man reappeared ready to usher Geoff over to the ring. Geoff stripped down to his white sports vest, and let the tracksuit top fall to the ground.

'God bless you, Geoff.' The team patted him, and Geoff attempted a weak, appreciative smile.

As they made their way, Geoff could feel the cold bite into his bare arms.

His mouth was like an ashtray and his legs felt wobbly, but he made it to the centre of the ring to face his foe. The rest of the team gathered ringside, and Guy shuddered. 'This is crazy.'

Mike, Brad and Phil just stood there in a paralysed daze.

Geoff stood in the centre of the ring accompanied by Boss Man, both of them only a few feet away from Razor. The two combatants eyed each other. Geoff was perhaps a couple of inches taller, but was out weighted by about thirty pounds. Razor with evident scar tissue over his forehead and a boxer's classic flattened nose stared back at Geoff with the calm confidence of a marksman who had his prey ready in his sights. Geoff, however, almost telepathically asked this man in front of him if he was really prepared to kill another man. He got nothing back in return.

Boss Man stood between them like a referee giving them the last minute instructions.

'OK, you both know the score, this is a not a straightener, it's all in, no weapons, no submissions, give em a good show, best of luck to the both of you – touch hands.'

Razor almost thumped Geoff's wrapped knuckles, giving him a taste of his power and aggression. Both opponents stepped back ready to begin, and for a second Geoff thought he might have just pissed himself. Boss Man held up his hand ready to start, but before he had the chance, a balaclava member rushed up to him and uttered something in his ear. Razor growled in frustration, and limbered around to ease the delay. Geoff however, his chest pumping in and out with nervous tension wondered what was going on.

Meanwhile the spectators began a low inpatient booing. After some clandestine discussions, Boss Man approached one of the spectators, a tall man with brilliantine shining hair and donning a long black woollen jacket. By now the booing had almost become a chant. The tall man gave the Boss a nod, and the word was quickly passed down.

Like a ghost, he glided past by the team they didn't even hear his footsteps on the short grass. Mike, Guy, Brad and Phil watched slack-jawed as he entered the ring. The crowd went into a confused silence. Geoff turned and saw Will approach him wearing a black hooded tracksuit. He stopped beside him.

Geoff was speechless, but the sight of his old pal coming towards him was like spotting a life boat on the horizon coming to rescue him from the sea.

'Will, what's going on?' he asked him.

Will flicked a look at him then turned to the tall man with the slick-back hair.

'So you want a bit of a wager?' asked the tall man

'I want to buy my way into this fight. I've got fifteen grand, if I win I get my money back, if I lose then it's all yours?'

Geoff glared back at him, and then over to his staggered team's faces. Razor, not having experienced anything like this before, smirked at the cheek of this minnow standing in front of him. The tall man, however, sucked on this mouth-watering proposition with balls attached to it and found it all too tempting to refuse. He smiled back. 'OK.'

Will slipped his hand inside his tracksuit pocket and handed over a thick wad of notes to Boss Man.

'Wait, Will, you don't have to do this,' Geoff cried, but Will calmly waved him aside as if he was merely in the way.

Boss Man and the balaclava quickly escorted Geoff back out of the ring to stand with his stunned team. Will eyed his opponent closely, he watched how he stood, which leg he preferred to lean on, his expression, his eyes, everything. Next he glanced down at the watch Stacey had bought him. He unbuckled it, and tossed it over to Geoff who just about caught it. Then he slipped out of his tracksuit top and lobbed that over as well, leaving only a well muscled torso in a black sports vest.

Razor looked over to the tall man as if to say do we go or what? He got back a nod in return. The fight was on.

Geoff and the team watched wide-eyed and with hearts ready to burst. Razor lumbered forward in a crouch while Will circled to his right, keeping his distance. Razor looking like a bloated Mike Tyson tried to inch his way nearer to Will and cut him down ready to pounce. But Will wasn't going to have any of it and continued shifting about. For now at least Will intended to see exactly what artillery his opponent had. Razor made a feint, and Will darted out of the way causing the crowd to boo him.

'Don't listen to them, Will,' Geoff shouted. 'You do what you have to.'

Becoming a tad frustrated, Razor straightened himself and re-set his stance as if to say to Will that he was completely relaxed, and hopefully lure Will into an attack. But cunningly Will stuck to his game plan.

They continued moving about with Razor trying to hunt him down, then Will decided it was time to go up a gear. Will cut his distance down and allowed Razor to get in a bit closer. Razor's eyed twinkled with delight as he saw that Will was falling into his trap. He lurched forward with a big right followed by a winging hook – both missed. The blows were hard but sloppy, Will thought.

He gave Razor another chance and he responded again with some wild punches. Will retreated but only enough so as not to take the full brunt of the blows, and he caught one in the right rib. The team winced, and Razor's mates cheered with encouragement.

Will felt winded, but he had only done this so he could taste his opponent's power. Again he dabbled in danger, and Razor launched another attack. He threw a few low jabs, and tried to come over with a big right haymaker which Will took on the arms. Will felt the weight of the punch alright, but he wasn't fazed by it. Razor tried to finish off the attack with a thumping low kick to Will's thigh which knocked Will off balance. The crows ooh'd and ahh'd.

'Come on, Will,' Geoff shouted.

Will had now seen enough of what Razor could do and it was time to go to work, he moved safely out of range, then stopped dead like a bull ready to charge. Razor lifted his head to say 'come on then', and Will gave him a sarcastic grin. Razor went after him but this time Will didn't run. As Razor came into range firing a power-house right, Will ducked to his left, and came under with a sickening left hook to the ribs. It sounded like someone hitting a bag of cement with a golf club.

'Yes,' the team cried.

Will stayed within range and as Razor followed him, he pumped out jolting left jabs in his face which rocked his fat head back. Geoff and the team clenched their fists jubilantly.

Instead of back-pedalling, Will moved side to side so he could remain in range and fire off his own power shots. Razor continued after him throwing wild desperate blows, just looking for that one big punch, but Will kept that ram-rod jab in his face. Soon red welts and tiny swellings started appearing on Razor's face, but still he continued to come forward. Yet as he did, Will would jab, even double jab, and move his head to the side so Razor didn't get to counter punch. Will even threw the old right punch, left punch combination just for good measure.

The expression in Razor's face had now changed he looked like someone who had been given the wrong answer sheet to an exam. Seeing this Will was ready to step up another gear and started trading with him to get off his own power shots. Call it sod's law, or whatever, whenever things seem to going to plan something always goes wrong. And this happened in the form of Will stepping into a divot or small burrow in the ground and he toppled over. The team held their breaths, and Razor's men screamed for him to get him.

Way ahead of them, Razor threw himself down on Will, who just managed to jam his legs out to stop him from getting on top. Frantically, Razor tried knocking Will's legs out of the way to get to him for a ground and pound. His large blubbery arms flailed away at Will's head but none of the blows got through as they were blocked. To get himself out of this dangerous situation, Will only needed to catch an arm so he purposely drew his legs in a bit so Razor could lean over him more. This seemed to work as Razor threw his whole body weight into a poleaxe blow aimed at Will's head. Expecting this, Will shifted off his right shoulder and using Razor's momentum, rolled him off to the side and straight into an arm bar. In total panic, Razor bit down hard into Will's calf muscle, and Will had to release the grip.

Both of them scrambled back to their feet, but Will was quicker and thundered into Razor's lower stomach with a deep side kick. Razor staggered back for the first time – clearly he was hurt by this. The pair of them now started to blow a bit, Razor a tad more than Will.

Sensing a weakness, Will switched his game plan and began goading Razor into attacking him. Moving perilously close so he could even smell his body odour, Will dared him to try and pound him. Razor roared like a wounded lion and threw himself head first into Will, his arms swinging wildly. Will closed his guard and held on as best as he could.

'Will, get the hell out of there,' Geoff cried, but what Geoff didn't realise was that Will was trying to get Razor to burn himself out.

Catching most of the blows on his arms and shoulders, he bravely or stupidly continued to wave Razor in. With spit and slaver running down his chin, Razor charged in again but this time Will came out of his guard and turned his hips and shoulders into a tremendous right punch. The blow smashed into Razor's forehead stopping him dead in his tracks, his feet seemingly, wanting to carry on without the rest of his body. Will switched to his left for a cracking left hook to Razor's temple breaking his equilibrium. Geoff and the team were going crazy.

Razor staggered sideways and tried to turn his face away from a crashing roundhouse kick which connected with his head. Down he went, but as Will lined him up for the kill, Razor's mates fearing for his downfall, rushed the ring to try and protect him. Geoff and the team were ready to pile in too but the balaclava security immediately leapt into the fray with their .38 revolvers, and began herding them all back out of the ring.

However, unbeknownst to everyone, this rush into the ring was just a crafty subterfuge for one of Razor's mates to slip him a pocket sized blade. A kobun knife to be precise. Finally order was restored and the fight could continue.

Geoff shouted over in protest. 'Oh yeah, now he's had a good time to recover. That's not fair.'

Will keeping his cool turned back to Razor and let his head drop back as if to say here we go again. Razor a bit unsteady on his feet, and blood trickling out of his nose was careful to conceal his weapon so that only the short serrated blade poked out in between his fingers like a claw. With renewed confidence, he began to pursue Will again. Will wanted to see what Razor had left, and made the mistake of allowing him get in close again. That's when Razor slashed his forearm. Will leapt back clutching his arm in shock.

Geoff reacted straight away. 'Hey, he's got a knife, what's going on? I thought it was no weapons.'

But Geoff's protests were ignored, even Mr tall man looked on impassively as if he had money on Razor and didn't want to rock the boat. Geoff tried to rush into the ring, but Mike and Guy restrained him. Will looked around, vulnerable. What the hell was he supposed to do now he couldn't even use his tracksuit top as a shield. Quick thinking, Geoff tried to toss it over to him, but one of the balaclavas snatched it away. Despondently, Will gazed down at the deep flesh wound and set himself ready to fight for his life. Razor smiled hungrily and began the chase. Will did his best to keep as much distance as possible and use his legs to try and block the strikes. But all Razor had to do was slash his way through, catching Will across the thigh twice, and then the knee cap.

Geoff and the team winced in horror. Will limped back and realised that he had to change his tactic quick or his legs were going to get cut to pieces and he would be a sitting duck. But a sitting duck Will was becoming, as his movement was now hampered by his injuries, and Razor found it easier to hunt him down.

Switching to Will's upper body, he caught him across the shoulder, the chest and the stomach causing serious damage to the muscles and tendons. Will scowled in agony, it was like being gouged with searing hot needles, but he continued.

'Shit, shit.' Geoff panicked.

With blood streaming down his arms, and seeping through the jagged slits of his black vest, a soporific shock began to take its hold on Will, slowing him down even more. He missed dodging another slash which tore down the side of his cheek bone, crying tears of blood instantly. The wound was deep and glistening. Will staggered back, eyes blinking, losing their focus a little, the loss of blood causing more shock and confusion. Desperately, he glanced towards Geoff and the others signalling that he was in trouble now.

Geoff made a move, but the balaclavas stopped him with their revolvers. Razor exhausted from all the knife gashing glanced over to the tall man for the order to finish Will. He received a curt nod.

'No,' Geoff cried, and the balaclavas had to restrain him.

Razor envisioning the New Year with yet another reprieve, another victory, lurched in for the killer stab. Will sensed him coming and held out his hands to try and save his life, but Razor came underneath and thrust into Will's abdomen as if he wanted to gut him like a fish.

Standing there helpless in the clutches of the balaclavas, Geoff went limp with horror as he saw Will hunched over the knife, motionless. Above him, Razor's whole body quivered under the strain as he held on to the knife with all his strength. But the look of satisfaction on his face soon began to dissolve into alarm as he could feel his hand slowly pulling away from Will's body. The blade hadn't even struck, the lethal stab had been blocked in a double wrist-lock. Will had set his own trap and fooled him. Turning his head towards Razor, he eyed him like a demon who had just snared an unsuspecting soul. Razor knew his time was up, and he almost smirked at the irony. In a nano-second, Will turned his wrist over, spinning Razor's arm, and with the palm of his hand, snapped the joint at the elbow. Razor cried open-mouthed, and his dead arm dropped the weapon. Will fired a battering roundhouse kick to Razor's chest knocking him to his knees. Will, soaked in blood, dived over him, pulling on the broken arm for leverage, and stretched him out into a crucifix hold.

Locking him within a cage of bone and muscle, Will pulled on Razor's head with all his might until the atlas, the critical juncture of the skull and spinal cord snapped. Razor was killed instantly, and would not see that New Year after all. Will collapsed exhausted

Geoff, the team and the whole crowd froze with disbelief.

Feeling Razor's almost severed head rolling on his chest like a football on a piece of cord soon made Will want to move. Straining with fatigue, he wriggled out from under Razor's cumbersome body, and scrambled back to his feet.

With only the mellifluous sound of the torch flames flickering in the breeze, Will limped back out of the human ring. Everybody stood aside and let him through. Geoff and the team watched reverently, and were uncertain whether or not to approach him. Then Geoff remembered Will's watch and his tracksuit top, and that gave him the excuse he needed.

'Guys, wait here a minute,' he told them, and marched towards Will.

But it was the tall man who first blocked Will's path. He handed back Will's fifteen grand, and in a cut-glass English brogue, he said. 'Astonishing, fight my friend.'

Will looked up at him. 'Where are the hostages?'

'Don't worry, we always keep our word, my chaps have just gone to fetch them.'

Will nodded wearily and pushed passed him, hearing the man say that if he ever wanted a career out of fighting, just let him know.

'Will?' Geoff called out to him.

Will stopped, and half-turned his body to him. For a second Geoff struggled to get his words out. 'Thanks, Will.'

Will's head moved with acknowledgement, and Geoff winced silently at the gory sight of his pal's lacerated cheek bone. Fortunately, the bone itself had taken the brunt of the force so it had avoided the important facial muscles and tendons.

'Should get those wounds seen to Will?'

'Don't worry, I've already got that sorted.'

Still trying to come to terms with what had happened, Geoff stuttered. 'Shit, Will, I thought you were a gonner there.'

Will shrugged. 'Well, I wasn't quite as bad as I let on, he was a fly caught in my web.'

Geoff smiled weakly, 'How did you know where we were tonight? How did you manage to find us?'

Will huffed. 'I've still got low friends in high places.'

'Well you were right about one thing,' Geoff confessed. Will lifted his head in question.

'You were right about there's nothing like the sight of a battlefield after war to inspire peace between kings and generals. I know what you mean now.'

Will was glad to hear but too tired and bloody to show it at the moment.

'Listen, Geoff, I don't want to appear rude, but I've got to get these wounds patched up.'

'Let us drive you to A and E?' Geoff pleaded.

Will shook his head. 'Can't go to the hospital, edged weapons have to be reported to the police.'

'So where will you go then?'

'I know some people, they're already waiting.'

Geoff didn't need to ask who these people were he was simply content in knowing that Will would be taken care of.

Will turned around to leave. 'Got to go, Geoff, see you around sometime.'

Geoff remembered the watch and the top. 'Will, I almost forgot, here s' your top and your watch that Stacey bought you?'

Will stiffened as if the mention of her name slashed him deeper than any weapon. He looked down at his empty, trembling wrist, and sealed his eyes against the agony of a broken heart. Holding his voice together, and hiding his face from Geoff, he said, 'the watch is broken now, Geoff. I can't fix that anymore.'

Geoff knew exactly what he meant, and it sickened him to the stomach at how cruel Fate had been for him. 'Will I'm so sorry I...'

'Geoff, Geoff?' someone called out to him.

Geoff turned to find Jan standing with the team, plus Tom, Charlie and Nigel. There she was, alive, and completely unhurt. His heart soared and forgetting his old pal for a moment, he rushed over and they fell into an embrace. Will nodded with contentment, they were safe, all of them safe, then he limped silently out of their lives.

Geoff wrapped himself up in his wife, smelling her sweet aroma once more, and he thanked God. He lifted his head from her shoulder and saw Tom, Charlie and Nigel being comforted by the rest of the team. They, too, looked drained, but relieved. Tom caught Geoff's eye, and they both just stared at one another. But Geoff was too relieved to be resentful, instead, he just shook his head at him – at least they were all alive. Sparing a thought for Will, he looked over to where he had been, but there was only darkness. Will had gone. Would they ever see him again?

Jan turned Geoff's face back to hers, and he could see in her eyes what I bloody fool she thought he had been. He pressed his face against hers and forgot everything else for now. High above them, the black sky crackled with the sound of fireworks, beautiful florid colours exploded all around. And as the country began the nationwide celebrations, Jan lifted her husband's chin and said to him, 'Happy New Year, Geoff.'